TO SWOON
AND
TO SPAR

Also by Martha Waters

To Marry and to Meddle

To Love and to Loathe

To Have and to Hoax

TO SWOON AND TO SPAR

A Novel

MARTHA WATERS

ATRIA PAPERBACK

New York   London   Toronto   Sydney   New Delhi

ATRIA
PAPERBACK

An Imprint of Simon & Schuster, Inc.
1230 Avenue of the Americas
New York, NY 10020

First Atria Paperback edition April 2023

ATRIA PAPERBACK and colophon are trademarks of Simon & Schuster, Inc.

For information about special discounts for bulk purchases, please contact Simon & Schuster Special Sales at 1-866-506-1949 or business@simonandschuster.com.

The Simon & Schuster Speakers Bureau can bring authors to your live event. For more information or to book an event, contact the Simon & Schuster Speakers Bureau at 1-866-248-3049 or visit our website at www.simonspeakers.com.

Manufactured in the United States of America

1   3   5   7   9   10   8   6   4   2

Library of Congress Cataloging-in-Publication Data

Names: Waters, Martha, 1988- author.
Title: To swoon and to spar : a novel / Martha Waters.
Description: First Atria Paperback edition. | New York : Atria Paperback, 2023. | Series: The Regency vows ; 4
Identifiers: LCCN 2022037396 (print) | LCCN 2022037397 (ebook) | ISBN 9781668007907 (paperback) | ISBN 9781668007914 (ebook)
Subjects: LCGFT: Novels.
Classification: LCC PS3623.A8689 T617 2023 (print) | LCC PS3623.A8689 (ebook) | DDC 813/.6—dc23/eng/20220812
LC record available at https://lccn.loc.gov/2022037396
LC ebook record available at https://lccn.loc.gov/2022037397

ISBN 978-1-6680-0790-7
ISBN 978-1-6680-0791-4 (ebook)

For Lisa and BriHo,
who are the reason I write about friends who are like family.

And for Jane,
who will someday be old enough to read this.

Prologue

It was a dark and stormy night—or, rather, it should have been.

In reality, it was a sunny, breezy afternoon—one of those mild April days that truly felt as though summer were properly on its way. It had been a wet, cold winter, and Penvale had more than once wondered why, precisely, he'd thought it wise to leave London to return to Cornwall in *January*, of all months.

Today, however, he could not help thinking that the atmosphere would be well served by some of the bleak, stormy weather for which his ancestral home was so famed. Because he—Peter Bourne, seventh Viscount Penvale, owner of one of the oldest stately homes in all of England—was ghost-hunting.

Penvale didn't really believe in ghosts, of course. He was a practical man, not given to flights of fancy. There was simply no chance that a house—and certainly not *his* house—could be haunted.

And yet here he was.

"Did you hear that?" his wife asked.

Penvale turned slowly, surveying their surroundings. "I did," he said, squinting into the gloom. It might have been a sunny afternoon, but they were in one of the unused bedrooms on the third floor, the curtains drawn to prevent any light from entering, the furniture still covered to ward off dust, and this all lent an eerie, lonely mood to their activities.

The household staff was in the process of airing out these rooms in preparation for a house party they would be hosting in a couple of weeks' time. Penvale's sister and brother-in-law and closest friends would be staying with them for a fortnight, taking in the sea air, enjoying long walks along the scenic cliffs atop which Trethwick Abbey was perched, and generally savoring all the comforts the estate had to offer.

Penvale thought a haunting might cast a bit of a pallor on the proceedings.

"I think it came from the wardrobe," his wife continued uncertainly, her large blue-violet eyes mirroring some of his own unease.

A moment of silence.

"The wardrobe," Penvale repeated, casting a wary glance at the piece of furniture in question, a hulking presence in one corner. "Well, I suppose I should check inside."

"Yes," his wife agreed.

Neither one moved.

"Penvale?" she prompted.

"Yes, of course," he said, taking a few steps toward the wardrobe; no sooner had he made it halfway across the room, however, than there was another ominous *thump*, this one coming from the opposite wall.

Penvale paused. "That," he pronounced with great certainty, "did not come from the wardrobe." He turned back to his wife, noticing that she'd gone paler.

"No?" she ventured, her voice more hesitant than he'd ever heard it.

"No," he said more firmly, advancing on her slowly. Her eyes were fixed on his face as he approached, close enough that he could detect the fresh citrus scent that always clung to her skin.

Then, without warning, the silence between them was shattered by an earsplitting, unearthly scream.

And the candle in his wife's hand flickered out.

Chapter One

Penvale had known nothing good could possibly come from his butler's appearance at the study door before the man even opened his mouth.

To begin with, it was not yet noon, and Penvale's friends weren't the sort to call on him this early. Some—his sister, for one—had adopted the fashionable practice of sleeping late, and the others were so smugly, happily married that there was little temptation to stray far from home until considerably later in the day. Penvale was in the habit of morning exercise—a swim in the warmer months, a walk or a ride in the winter—and then a couple of hours spent in his study, with a general understanding between him and his staff that he was not to be disturbed. But the wary look on his butler's face informed him that whatever was about to come out of Smithers's mouth was not likely to improve his morning.

"My lord, your uncle is here to see you."

Penvale swore. His uncle was his father's younger—and only— brother, but the two men had been estranged for years prior to

5

Penvale's father's death, and every interaction Penvale had ever had with his uncle had led him to believe the man an utter ass.

"Thank you, Smithers," he said wearily, resisting the temptation to allow his head to drop to his desk. "You may show him in."

In actuality, where he would have *liked* to have Smithers show his uncle was to the nearest pigsty, but he somehow thought that even the most obedient of butlers would balk at this request. Mud was terribly difficult to scrub out of fabric, after all.

A moment later, his uncle walked into the room. It had been a few years since Penvale had last seen John Bourne in the flesh, but he still looked largely the same: brown hair liberally streaked with gray, hazel eyes that matched Penvale's own, and a rather diminutive frame that did nothing to lessen the cunning, canny look in his eyes.

"Uncle," Penvale said calmly, determinedly not rising. "How unexpected."

"Peter," his uncle replied, nodding in acknowledgment, and Penvale immediately stiffened. No one—not his friends, not even his own sister—called him by his given name. He'd inherited the viscountcy at such a young age that he'd grown used to being addressed as Penvale, the title becoming as worn and comfortable as an old pair of shoes. He had memories of his parents calling him Peter, and of Diana doing so in the squeaky voice of a young child, but no one else had done so since then, and to hear the name now, on his uncle's lips, caused a visceral thrill of distaste.

"Penvale will do fine," he said shortly. "Please, sit." He didn't think he'd allowed his hostility to come through in his voice, and he had an excellent poker face.

His uncle took a seat opposite him, surveying his surroundings as he did so. Penvale could practically see him calculating the probable worth of every object in the room. Not that Penvale was in a position to judge, considering he'd done the same as soon as he'd moved into the house, which had been the London residence of the viscounts Penvale for generations.

Penvale leaned back in his chair, refusing to be the first to speak; he wasn't the one who'd shown up unannounced and uninvited. The role of haughty nobleman was not one that came naturally to him—possessing a title without its accompanying estate did tend to keep a man humble—but his desire to make his uncle uncomfortable proved to be excellent motivation.

He took a sip of tea from the blue-and-white china teacup sitting to the left of his elbow. It had gone lukewarm, but he bravely carried on, pointedly declining any display of hospitality toward his uncle. As an Englishman, Penvale didn't ordinarily like to suffer the horrors of lukewarm tea, but sacrifices must be made for the sake of rather pettily sending a message, et cetera.

"I'll not beat around the bush," his uncle said after a moment, and Penvale mentally awarded himself the first point. "I'm prepared to sell Trethwick Abbey to you at last."

Penvale froze for a moment before leaning back in his seat. Trethwick Abbey had been the country seat of the viscountcy and was also the rare estate that was unentailed from the title, meaning that when Penvale's father had died and there were steep death duties to be paid, with the estate already in debt, there had been little choice but to sell it. And his uncle, who had made a fortune with the East India Company, had immediately presented himself as a willing buyer.

Penvale himself had been only ten years old at the time, and even if he'd attempted to raise some sort of objection, there'd been no chance that his father's solicitors would have listened to him. Instead, he'd watched as the idyllic home of his childhood was sold to a man he'd never met—a man he knew his father had despised. He and Diana had been sent to live with their mother's sister, and that had been the end of it.

Until, that is, Penvale had left Oxford, taken up his seat in Parliament, made his presence in London known, and begun making discreet inquiries about what price his uncle would be willing to sell Trethwick Abbey for.

The answer: none that Penvale could afford. Not yet, at least. And for the better part of the past decade, that answer had remained the same.

Which was why he met his uncle's sudden pronouncement with nothing more than a careful "Oh?" He refused to let himself get his hopes up—not about this.

"The last time my solicitor heard from yours, you made an offer that I rejected," his uncle said calmly, leaning back in his seat, lacing his hands over his stomach, and looking for all the world as though he were quite at home and not the slightest bit uncomfortable. "I still won't accept *that* price, mind you—but if you were prepared to increase it by ten percent, I'd be amenable."

Penvale's mind was racing; he hadn't really thought his uncle would accept his most recent offer—he'd merely been trying to find out if he was interested in negotiating, which had not been the case at the time.

So what had changed?

"I'd be amenable on one condition," his uncle added, and Penvale's heart sank as he waited to learn what unreasonable demand would be forthcoming.

"I have a ward who's in need of a husband, and I'd like you to marry her."

"You're doing *what?*" Diana asked, and then proceeded to drop an entire glass of brandy on the floor.

"Diana," Jeremy said in pained tones, "I do not understand why you treat drinks with such reckless abandon."

"For heaven's sake," she said, recovering from her shock and bending to collect the glass, casting an exasperated glance at the wet spot on the Axminster carpet in her library. "I threw a drink at you *one time*, Jeremy—"

At this, Penvale looked inquiringly at his friend.

"And I probably deserved it," Jeremy confirmed with an inexplicably fond look at his wife. "But now, to continue flinging about perfectly good brandy—!"

"I shall make it up to you later," Diana said, batting her eyelashes, and Penvale wondered whether it would be too dramatic if he jumped out a window.

"None of that, please," he said, covering his ears. "My delicate constitution can't handle lewd banter involving my sister."

"*Involving*," Jeremy repeated. "She was the only one *doing* any lewd bantering." He adopted an expression of angelic innocence. "I have been on my very best behavior."

"Is that what you call it?" Diana asked thoughtfully. "Because if my memories of this afternoon in the drawing room are accurate—"

Penvale was a man of nearly thirty, the holder of an ancient title, a member of the House of Lords, for Christ's sake. But he did not hesitate for a single second before walking over to his sister and firmly clapping his hand over her mouth.

9

"You're a brave man, Penvale," Jeremy said, reclining in his arm-chair before the fireplace. It was a wet, dreary evening in mid-January, but it was warm and cozy indoors, a fire crackling merrily in the grate. "I think she'd bite my hand off if I tried that."

"You," Penvale said with all the smugness of an elder brother, "do not currently possess information she is desperate to be privy to." He glanced down at Diana. "Will you behave now?"

Diana narrowed her eyes at him but made no move to physically assault him, which he took as a good sign, and he slowly removed his hand.

"You were saying," she said in tones of exaggerated sweetness, "that you are going to be *married?*"

Penvale, sensing that the situation was under control, busied himself at the sideboard pouring a glass of brandy to replace the one Diana had dropped. Diana, for her part, flounced back to the fireplace and—in what Penvale was convinced was a move designed purely to spite him—sank down upon her husband's lap.

"Oof," said Jeremy.

"Be quiet," Diana told him affectionately.

"Uncle John paid me a visit today," Penvale said, stoppering the bottle of brandy and crossing the room to resume his seat before the fire, fresh glass in hand. "It seems he is ready to sell Trethwick Abbey at last."

As he'd expected, Jeremy and Diana both sat up straighter at this news.

"Why do I sense there's some sort of catch?" Diana asked suspiciously.

"Because there is, naturally," Penvale said gloomily, staring down into his glass. "Apparently, he acquired a ward at some point in the past few years—the daughter of an old friend from his years in the navy, I believe."

Diana frowned. "I don't recall ever hearing of her," she said, sounding rather put out. Diana's ear for gossip was excellent, and she seemed to consider any she did not know as a personal affront.

"Her father was a gentleman but did not possess a title, so the family might not be familiar to you. Evidently, she is not fond of town, so our uncle has allowed her to rusticate in Cornwall until now," Penvale explained. "It seems to have belatedly occurred to him, however, that he could relieve himself of this burden by simply marrying her off—and how efficient it would be to pawn her off on *me* and save himself the bother of trying to find someone to sponsor her for a Season." He strove to keep any note of bitterness out of his voice as he spoke; he was nearly certain what he was going to do, so there was no use moping about it.

"Penvale," Diana said, rising to her feet and beginning to pace—a sure sign that she was deeply perturbed—"you cannot seriously be considering going through with this."

"I assure you, I can," Penvale said, watching her walk back and forth before the fire. "Sit down. The sight of you pacing is disturbing."

"The notion of you marrying some infant country bumpkin that you've never even *met* is disturbing!" Diana retorted, flopping onto the armchair next to Jeremy's. Without looking at her, Jeremy reached out and took her hand.

"She's not an infant, she's one-and-twenty," Penvale said coolly. He had specifically asked, as he didn't trust his uncle not to marry off a girl still in the schoolroom. "And I haven't agreed to anything yet—I've asked to meet her before anything is decided, to make sure she's not being forced into this against her will."

"But if she's agreeable, you plan to go through with it?" Jeremy asked. He was regarding Penvale quite seriously; it was not a look Penvale was accustomed to seeing on the face of the Marquess of Willingham, infamous rake and seducer, always ready to laugh at a bawdy joke or open another bottle of spirits. Jeremy's marriage to Diana the previous autumn had been a love match, though, and Penvale had never seen his friend take anything as seriously as he took his wedding vows.

That did not, however, mean that Penvale was in any mood to be lectured about the sanctity of marriage by a man who, not six months earlier, had sustained minor injuries climbing down a trellis to escape a lover's irate husband.

"I do," Penvale said shortly, in a way that he hoped would forestall further argument. "To begin with, I'm fairly sure that if I reject this offer now, my uncle will never sell Trethwick Abbey to me, just to be a bastard." Every interaction he'd ever had with the man supported this supposition, after all. "Furthermore, what do I care? I've a title—I was going to have to marry at some point, if only to have an heir, so who am I to complain when a bride has practically been dropped into my lap?"

"How romantic," Diana said with an eye roll.

"Oh, yes, and your marrying Templeton in your very first Season was itself the height of romance," he shot back, referring to Diana's first husband, whom she'd wed for entirely mercenary reasons and who had left her a very young, very rich widow.

"Penvale," Jeremy said pleasantly, "don't be an ass."

Penvale opened his mouth to retort, then shut it again, scrubbing a hand wearily across his face. It had been a long day, and he did not feel like ending it by quarreling with his favorite people. "The point is," he said, "I'm not holding out for a love match, so I don't see why I shouldn't take this opportunity." He looked directly at his sister.

"Diana . . . we could go back to Trethwick Abbey at last. We could go *home*."

Something in her expression softened. Penvale was often told how strong the physical resemblance was between him and his sister, with their honey-colored hair and hazel eyes—they even shared a few mannerisms. But Penvale could never quite see it; when he looked at Diana, he simply saw his little sister, who had been his most steadfast companion since childhood, even as she sometimes drove him mad.

"I barely remember it," she said, more gently than he'd heard her speak in quite some time. "I was so young . . ."

In that moment, their five-year age gap—which normally felt slight, especially now that she'd married Jeremy—seemed to stretch between them like a gulf. Trethwick Abbey loomed large in his memories: the imposing gray stone house, of course, but also the land that surrounded it, the cliffs and rolling green hills and wild, tumultuous ocean offering the constant sound of crashing waves.

He hadn't seen it in twenty years, yet it had lived clearly in his mind all this time—and he finally had his chance to reclaim it. He damned well wasn't going to let it slip through his fingers. "All the more reason for me to see this through, then—so you can come visit." He drained the remainder of his drink in one long gulp, relishing the slight burn in his throat. He cast a glance out the window, where a cold rain beat against the glass, and was glad he'd brought his carriage this evening.

The clock chimed eleven, startling Penvale; he hadn't realized it had grown so late. "I should be off," he announced, rising.

"You needn't go yet," Jeremy said, but Penvale waved him off—he'd never once felt unwelcome here, but he was also sure that, mildly horrifying as the prospect was, Diana and Jeremy would have little difficulty occupying themselves once he was gone.

He paused, surprised by the slight pang he felt at the thought of them tucked up cozily here together while he retreated to Bourne House alone. But, he reminded himself as he said his farewells and waited for his carriage to be brought around, if tomorrow went well, his days of living alone were numbered.

Chapter Two

Jane Spencer hated London.

It was January, so she didn't imagine anywhere in England was particularly warm and cheerful at the moment, but she couldn't think of a less pleasant place to spend a gray, cold afternoon than this bleak, dirty city.

Her guardian's London house was on a quiet street in Mayfair. Although he owned the house rather than renting, there was nothing inviting or personal about the empty rooms she found herself wandering through listlessly.

"Don't sulk," he'd told her at breakfast that morning with an amount of good cheer that had set her on edge instantly. "You're meeting the viscount today."

The viscount. It seemed like an awful way to refer to one's own nephew—no name, just a reference to his title—but what did she know? She was not in possession of any uncles, or nephews, or any family at all. That was the reason she was here, in Mr. Bourne's keeping. He and her father had served together in the navy long ago, before Jane was born, and had evidently been close; what she had learned of Mr. Bourne's character in the past three years had done little to endear her father's memory to her.

And so here she was, in London, preparing to meet a man who might marry her—another man into whose possession she might be traded. This time, at least, she did not plan to meekly accept her fate.

Jane stood in the drawing room, staring down at the street below. What would the viscount be like? she wondered. Not that she'd be bothered by him for too long; she'd worked out well enough how to rid herself of her guardian and was fairly certain she could repeat the trick.

"Jane." Mr. Bourne's voice came from behind her, curt and impatient. "The carriage is ready—it's time to go." She turned to face him, and she saw surprise register on his face. "Oh. You look . . . quite nice, actually."

She knew she did. She was not accustomed to dressing in the height of fashion—there was little occasion for it in the wilds of Cornwall—but Mr. Bourne had sent her to the modiste immediately upon her arrival in town a fortnight earlier, and she wore the results of that visit now, a high-necked gown of green wool, cut to hug her curves just so. Her heavy mass of dark hair was pulled back from her face in an elaborate coiffure that Hastey—a former housemaid recently elevated to the position of lady's maid for the purpose of this visit—had seen in some fashion plate or other. Jane would never be beautiful—her features were a bit too stern and angular for that—but she knew without looking in a mirror that she looked her very best.

Because that was the point.

She had a husband to acquire.

Penvale was less surprised than he should have been when Diana and Jeremy appeared on his doorstep not ten minutes before his uncle and Miss Spencer were due to arrive.

"Of course you are here," he said in resignation as Smithers showed them into the drawing room.

"Of course we are here," Diana agreed, sailing into the room as though she owned the place, then settling herself in her favorite yellow brocade armchair. "You cannot possibly think that I would allow you to betroth yourself to a stranger without my guidance."

"Did it ever occur to you, Diana," Penvale said, leaning against the mantel, "that I might not be *interested* in your opinion?"

Diana paused for a moment to consider. "No. Don't be absurd. Jeremy, sit," she added, patting the chair next to hers.

Jeremy rolled his eyes. "I'm not a dog, Diana," he said, before turning to Penvale and adding, "I did try to talk her out of this, you know."

"I'm sure you did," Penvale said darkly; a lifetime as Diana's brother had taught him how well any attempt went to dissuade her from a course she was already set upon, and he usually didn't bother with any such efforts. He wasn't ashamed to admit that her will was much stronger than his own—the only thing he'd ever truly been single-minded in his pursuit of was Trethwick Abbey.

"However," Jeremy added, throwing a sharp look at his wife, "we have agreed that she will not be doing any talking. *Right*, Diana?"

Diana offered what she seemed to think was an appropriately meek smile, which Penvale found unnerving. "Indeed."

Jeremy appeared to be suppressing a smile. "There's no need to lay it on quite so thick."

"I don't know what you're talking about," Diana said innocently. "Ladies are meant to be seen and not heard—the motto by which I live my life."

Jeremy and Penvale snorted in unison, and Diana grinned.

"Mr. John Bourne and Miss Jane Spencer, my lord," Smithers

intoned gloomily from the doorway. Smithers had come with the house, a relic from Penvale's grandfather's days as the viscount, and while Penvale at times found the man's rather funereal air to be a bit mood-dampening, he could not help but think it was well suited to his feelings about this meeting. No matter what he had told Diana and Jeremy the evening before, Penvale was not exactly leaping with enthusiasm at the prospect of marriage to a woman he didn't know.

"Jane Spencer," Diana repeated in an undertone, her vow to be seen and not heard apparently forgotten. "Can you think of a more forgettable name? I expect she'll be mousy and plain to match."

Penvale, while feeling a bit bad for the unfortunate Miss Spencer, could not help but privately agree. Which was why it was something of a surprise when the woman who walked into the room was utterly . . . striking.

"Yes, Diana," Jeremy murmured as he rose to his feet, clearly amused. "I see precisely what you mean."

Diana, for once, had no reply, which Penvale would have found deeply satisfying had he not been so distracted.

Miss Spencer was not beautiful; that fact was immediately obvious to Penvale. Her features were not harsh, precisely, but stern in a way that had none of the soft loveliness of so many of the ladies whom the *ton* considered great beauties. Her skin was fair, her cheekbones pronounced, her hair dark and thick. She was not tall, but what he could see of her figure hinted at appealing curves, in contrast to the sharpness of her face. It was her eyes, however, that made her so difficult to tear his gaze from. At first glance, they appeared violet, standing out vividly in her pale face, framed by sooty lashes; after a moment's consideration, however, he concluded that they were merely the deepest, most unearthly shade of blue he'd ever seen.

She was not *restful* to look at, he thought; she was not like Diana's friend Emily, who'd been widely considered the greatest beauty of her debut Season, golden and lovely and soothing to regard, like a particularly beautiful painting. Miss Spencer was too vivid, too strange, for that. Nonetheless, he found it impossible to look away from her for a long moment, and his first thought was to wonder why his uncle was so desperate to marry her off—this was not at all the mousy, plain creature Diana (and, truthfully, he) had envisioned. He couldn't imagine it would be too difficult to find her a husband.

At that precise moment, however, Miss Spencer's gaze landed on him, and her face broke into a fierce scowl.

Ah, Penvale thought. That might have something to do with it.

"Peter," his uncle said jovially, instantly setting Penvale's teeth on edge. "And little Diana, is it?"

Penvale darted a glance at his sister, privately thinking that his uncle must have remarkably little concern for his own safety to address her as such.

"You may call me Lady Willingham, Uncle," she said in her frostiest tone; beside her, Jeremy looked to be thoroughly enjoying himself. "Would you care to make introductions?"

"May I present my ward, Miss Spencer?" Penvale's uncle said, just barely on the polite side of mockery as he sketched an elegant bow. "Jane, may I introduce my nephew, Viscount Penvale, my niece, the Marchioness of Willingham, and her husband, the Marquess of Willingham?" He added this last bit rather as an afterthought, but Jeremy didn't look remotely offended. He offered an entirely correct bow as he murmured Miss Spencer's name, employing the charm that had made him so famously—or perhaps infamously—popular with the ladies before he'd married Diana. Penvale watched this grumpily, before belatedly recalling that *he* was the prospective husband here and that it wouldn't do to be upstaged by his own brother-in-law. He stepped forward, taking Miss Spencer's proffered hand and bowing over it.

"Miss Spencer," he said, straightening. "It is a pleasure to meet you."

"Is it?" she asked skeptically, and Penvale blinked; her scowl had eased as quickly as it had appeared, but she was regarding him with what could only charitably be called extreme suspicion.

"Excuse me?" he ventured, releasing her hand and stepping back slightly so that he was not towering over her.

"I believe she said the pleasure is all hers," his uncle said, too loudly, and Miss Spencer attempted something that approached a smile.

"Precisely," she said, glancing down at her hands, which were now clasped tightly before her.

"Shall we sit?" Penvale suggested. Miss Spencer's manners did not seem to be terribly polished, and he watched while she took a seat next to his uncle, her spine stiff as she looked around the room. He noticed that she avoided the eyes of everyone present, and he felt a deep sense of misgiving. She did not give the impression of a lady eager to be wed—and damn it, he wasn't going to force her. The prospect of finally regaining Trethwick Abbey after all this time—of realizing the goal that had remained tantalizingly out of reach for his entire adult life—was more appealing than he could put into words, and the thought of giving it up now, when it finally seemed possible, made him feel a bit ill. But still, he could not force a woman to marry him against her will.

He *would* not.

Dimly, he realized that the others were conversing and that he'd completely neglected to follow the discussion. Fortunately for him, the *ton* was so dull and predictable that it was not really necessary to pay attention to what was being said—he could have chimed in with one of half a dozen or so rejoinders and would have stood a decent chance of saying exactly the right thing.

Or so he could *usually* have done. He'd neglected to account for Diana.

"... so I, naturally, told Penvale that if he ever wanted to be able to show his face in our aunt and uncle's home again, I would require a hefty payment. Fortunately, he received more pocket money than I did, and had enough to buy my silence."

"But what was he planning to *do* with the pig?" Miss Spencer asked with a frown, helpfully enlightening Penvale on which precise childhood anecdote Diana had felt it necessary to share in the two minutes he'd allowed his attention to wander. He briefly wondered how their conversation had possibly arrived at this point so quickly, but decided it might be best not to know.

"I think he just wanted to get it settled in the barn more comfortably—it was about to have piglets, and he wished to observe the process. But he thought it easiest to pay me off, after I threatened to tell our aunt he intended to bring it into the house."

A rather shocked silence fell—at least on the part of Miss Spencer and her guardian; Penvale and Jeremy were accustomed to Diana.

"Diana," Jeremy said after a moment, "this sounds a bit like extortion."

"Oh, it was," she replied serenely.

"I used to wish for a sister," Miss Spencer said, still frowning. "But if this is what they're like, I think I might have been better off without one."

This, naturally, caused Diana to frown as well, though Penvale did not really see what cause she had to be unhappy—the story she had just chosen to share hardly painted her in a flattering light.

"Miss Spencer, I feel I should assure you that my sister and I are actually quite close," he said, feeling that the conversation was not presently going as well as he might have hoped.

"Despite her attempts to see you accused of crimes you did not commit?" Miss Spencer asked dubiously. "Is she threatening you now as well? Is that why you are eager to marry me and return to Cornwall—to escape her clutches?"

There was a rather loud cough from Jeremy that Penvale recognized as a hastily suppressed laugh.

"I promise you, I am not being extorted by my sister," Penvale assured her.

"Anymore," Miss Spencer added. "Is this normal sibling behavior?"

Penvale, perversely, began to feel a bit defensive on Diana's behalf. "I don't think she ever intended to get me in trouble—she was really after the money."

"Interesting," Miss Spencer said, still sounding very doubtful.

"You've mentioned that you do not have siblings, Miss Spencer," Penvale said, trying to redirect them toward more polite—or at least less openly combative—territory. "Were you and your parents close? I'm sorry to hear of your father's death." He paused, realizing that he wasn't entirely certain when her father had died—it couldn't have been that recently, since she was clearly out of mourning. "Er, belatedly sorry, I mean."

"We were not close," she said, ignoring his somewhat floundering attempts at offering condolences. "My mother died when I was a baby, and my father was in the navy and often away. I was more or less raised by servants."

"Ah," Penvale said. "And where was this?"

"Essex. A small village you wouldn't have heard of."

"Essex is lovely," he said, trying to summon something, anything, to say that might make conversation with her feel less like pulling teeth. He paused, trying to conjure a memory of anything noteworthy about the county from his brief visits. "Very nice ... cows," he offered feebly.

"I hated Essex," she said, lifting those striking violet eyes to meet his gaze directly. "I was more than happy to leave for Cornwall—it's beautiful there. Unlike London," she added sharply, a note of distinct distaste evident in her voice.

"Miss Spencer," Diana interjected, "is something wrong? Have you been brought here today against your will? Should I summon the authorities?"

Miss Spencer regarded Diana coolly. "Is this your usual strategy when meeting potential wives for your brother? To speak to them so bluntly that they are shocked and scamper off like frightened little mice?"

Penvale bit his lip, suddenly possessed of the strangest desire to laugh. It wasn't often that Diana encountered a woman who seemed utterly unintimidated by her, and it was even rarer to find this trait in a lady who was several steps down from Diana on the social ladder.

Diana, for her part, did not seem remotely cowed. "Miss Spencer, I can assure you that nothing about this entire conversation has been ordinary—up to and including the fact that, as far as I am aware, this is the first time my brother has seriously considered marriage."

Miss Spencer returned that unsettling gaze to Penvale. "You must really want that house."

And, because he did indeed really want that house, Penvale decided that he'd had quite enough of this unproductive line of conversation, and he rose. "Miss Spencer," he said, "there is a lovely garden behind the house—would you care to take a turn about it with me?" He cast a dark look at the other occupants of the room. "Alone?"

She eyed him for a moment. "All right," she said, rising and completely ignoring his proffered arm. "Ring for that butler of yours and have him fetch my pelisse." She paused. "Please." She added this last word as though bestowing some sort of boon upon him.

Penvale was already exhausted, and they hadn't even left the room yet. He glanced over his shoulder, and his mood was not improved by the sight of Diana and Jeremy offering him silent mocking salutes.

This was not going well.

Jane gave herself a stern mental shake as she walked through Bourne House with the viscount, he walking slightly ahead of her, his shoulders stiff with what she guessed was irritation. Not that she could blame him, she supposed—that drawing room conversation had been something approaching a farce.

She had been so determined, before arriving, to present her most charming side to him. She was not eager to be married, but she'd wagered that the viscount would at least be somewhat more enjoyable company than his uncle, and she'd decided she would do whatever was necessary to ensure that this marriage took place. Despite the fact that they'd exchanged barely three sentences, all of which could be politely described as testy, she thought she'd guessed correctly. Marriage to the viscount would be preferable to being controlled by his uncle, and so lure him into marriage she must. It seemed, frankly, a somewhat daunting task—he was an aristocrat and moved among the most elevated ranks of society. Jane's father had been a gentleman, and her years at finishing school had been spent among a set of well-connected girls of some means, but Lord Penvale was undoubtedly far more impressive a match than she ever would have dreamed of for herself. It was therefore time to make use of every ounce of charm and every feminine wile she possessed. However, when concocting this plan, she had neglected to consider one important fact: Jane had never been charming in her life. It had not helped that she had entered the room to discover that Lord Penvale was not alone—she hated being surprised by unexpected people.

Furthermore, even if she *had* been prepared to meet them, she suspected that the marchioness would have caught her off guard. Lady Willingham was nothing at all like the polite, simpering society wife Jane would have expected. Ordinarily, she might have appreciated the marchioness's bluntness, but today she hadn't found it terribly enjoyable, since she was fairly certain that Lady Willingham was simply trying to make her as uncomfortable as possible.

Furthermore, Jane's temper had not improved when she had heard the marchioness speculating about her appearance as she walked in— it had, in fact, given her some satisfaction to see Lady Willingham's dumbfounded expression when she caught sight of her. Jane might not be a great beauty, but no one could ever accurately describe her as mousy. If only she had not followed up that small moment of triumph with a complete inability to make polite conversation.

Speaking of which . . .

"This is a lovely house," she offered, and Lord Penvale glanced over his shoulder at her, slowing his pace slightly so that they were walking abreast.

"Thank you," he said. "I'm pleased to hear there's at least one thing about London that meets with your approval." There was something in his voice that made her think he might be almost . . . amused. This was unexpected, but it did nothing to improve her temper. "That is related to why I asked you to speak with me."

"Because . . . I dislike London?" she asked, perplexed. They entered a room that, from a quick perusal, she realized was the library, and he immediately made for a set of French doors along one wall.

"Yes," he said simply, opening the doors and stepping back to allow her to pass through. "You seemed so displeased to be here today that I wanted to ensure that my uncle wasn't forcing you to marry me against your will."

"Oh," she said, feeling perversely irritated that he would be even remotely considerate when she had certainly done nothing so far to endear herself to him. Then she paused on the terrace, surveying the garden before her. "*Oh.*"

"My mother loved it out here," Lord Penvale said, coming to a halt at her side and rubbing his hands together against the January chill. It was a gray, damp day—the sort of day when the cold seemed to seep into her bones and linger there. But even in the dead of winter, the gardens were beautiful. A tall hedge surrounded the perimeter, creating the feeling of a peaceful retreat from the world, and a formal garden with flower beds was set behind a wall in the center of the outer garden. Jane imagined it would be a riot of color in the spring and summer. She knew they were in the middle of London, but she felt suddenly at ease in a way she had not experienced once in the entire duration of her stay in town.

It wasn't Cornwall, but it was still lovely.

"I can see why she adored it," Jane said, turning to him with the closest thing to a natural smile she had managed all afternoon. "I feel as though I can take a deep breath at last, away from all the noise and bustle."

"London has some very nice parks, you know," he said as he led her to a bench and waited for her to take a seat before sinking down beside her. "Perhaps a visit to one of them would improve your opinion of town."

"I doubt it."

He inclined his head to the side, studying her. "You don't stand upon niceties, do you, Miss Spencer?"

At these words, she stiffened. Everything seemed less easy between them now that they were seated—when they were walking, with their gazes focused ahead, she had not felt the weight of his attention like a burden on her shoulders. Sitting on this bench beside him was something else entirely. She kept her eyes downcast, but that only served to draw her attention to the fact of his leg so close to her on the stone bench that it was brushing against the edge of her skirts.

"I do not believe in niceties, my lord."

He barked out a surprised laugh, and she cast a quick glance sideways. He was even more handsome when he laughed.

She had not been prepared, upon entering that drawing room, to find him appealing. She had supposed, of course, that he was not terribly elderly—her guardian was hardly in his dotage, so the viscount must be somewhat young. But for a man to be willing to agree to—or at least consider—marriage to a woman he'd never met? She'd naturally assumed there was something horribly wrong with him.

Perhaps, she imagined, he'd been disfigured in a tragic accident? Or, even better, during the war? If she allowed her imagination to run wild with romantic possibilities, she went so far as to envision a handsome face with a horrible scar on one half, perfectly invisible when viewed in profile from the other side, so that the viewer would gasp in horror when he turned to reveal his true countenance.

(Jane was very fond of novels.)

She had not been prepared to find herself face-to-face with a young, fit viscount—one who would surely have little difficulty convincing other, prettier, more eligible ladies to wed: ladies of rank and fortune. Which had led Jane to her previous conclusion: He was desperate to get his house back.

This, with regard to her long-term aims, was unfortunate. But it did mean that her utter inability to make any semblance of polite conversation shouldn't be too much of a hindrance to matrimony.

"Well, Miss Spencer, if you do not *believe* in niceties, then I'll spare you any attempts at bland observations regarding the weather and get to the point: I'd like to marry you but will do so only if you are willing." Despite his laughter a moment ago, there was no trace of amusement in his voice; he merely sounded . . . determined.

"I've been working to build my personal fortune for years in the hope that my uncle would one day sell Trethwick Abbey to me," he continued, "and if I must marry you to convince him, I'm more than prepared to do so." He stated this matter-of-factly, his voice emotionless; in that instant, Jane wondered if he'd ever entertained visions of a more romantic proposal of marriage. But then he did not seem the sort of man to harbor romantic fantasies. "But I won't go through with it if you're not amenable to it—my desire for a house and a parcel of land shouldn't come at the expense of the happiness of a lady I do not even know."

This, Jane had to grudgingly admit, was surprisingly decent—more decent than anything she'd expected to hear from a man who, if his uncle were to be believed, spent most of his time at the card tables. Was that the *work* he alluded to? she wondered. If he considered playing a game of vingt-et-un to be work, then she somehow thought he wouldn't last long on a wet Cornish hillside with tenants and sheep and actual problems to manage.

"I will marry you, my lord," she said. "As I find living with your uncle to be rather . . ." She trailed off, searching for the correct adjective. "Unpleasant."

This was nothing more or less than the truth. Mr. Bourne had never been unkind to her, exactly, but after a childhood spent without the constant presence of a parent, she'd been surprised by how much she disliked living in a house with a male authority figure swooping about, prone to dropping into a room at a moment's notice to make some sort of demand. She had imagination enough to suppose that there were certain people with whom it might be entirely tolerable— enjoyable, even—to share a home (although, in truth, her experience so far with the male sex did not make her overly optimistic about the odds of enjoying living with a husband).

But Mr. Bourne, with his constant, small intrusions—acting surprised and annoyed to find Jane in a room he had entered; relaying messages to her for the staff, rather than deigning to speak to them himself; demanding to know why she had not yet befriended any of the girls in the village, as though this were some sort of crime (and having made no effort to offer any introduction that might have eased her way)—well. It—*he*—rapidly became bothersome. Indeed, he became all the more bothersome the longer Jane spent at Trethwick Abbey, because with each day that passed, an undeniable truth had become clear: She loved it there. But living there with Mr. Bourne was hardly how she wanted to spend the rest of her life.

And the moment she had come to realize the truth of these two facts, entirely in opposition to each other, was the moment the first threads of her plan had begun to form.

She raised her eyes from her lap, still avoiding Lord Penvale's gaze, which she could feel on her face. "I do not have an expectation of romance," she said stiffly. "All I would ask of you is that I don't have to spend any more time in town than is necessary."

"You truly do hate it here," he said mildly. It was an observation rather than a question, but she nodded nonetheless.

"I do."

"Have you ever been here other than on this visit?"

"Well," she said slowly, "no."

"I see. And has it occurred to you that you might like it more some other time of the year? When it's a little less . . . gray?"

"It has not," she said, more fiercely than she intended. If there was one thing she despised, it was when someone tried to tell her that her opinion was wrong. "Because an improvement in the weather would mean that London was overrun with a passel of aristocrats, and I'd be forced to make polite conversation endlessly, and—"

"And I've already witnessed how much you enjoy polite conversation, yes." There was a smile in his voice; despite his seemingly genuine concern for her consent to their marriage, she could not otherwise find much to admire in a man whose every statement seemed laced with some faint amusement—amusement which she strongly suspected was at her expense. At that moment, she felt particularly keenly the gap—not just in age but in experience and social standing as well— that stretched between them. He went on, "All right. Your demands seem reasonable enough. There may be one factor that will complicate things a bit, however."

"Oh?"

"I'm a viscount."

She rolled her eyes, turning to look fully at him. "I noticed," she said waspishly. "Did you somehow miss the fact that I have referred to you as 'my lord'?"

"No," he said, exasperation creeping into his voice at last. "And you can stop with the 'my lord,' by the way—just call me Penvale. It's what everyone else does."

"All right, *Penvale*," she said with exaggerated patience. "What is your complication?"

"The fact that, as mentioned, I'm a viscount means that I'm going to need an heir. Eventually."

"I'm aware," she said with a dismissive wave of her hand. "And I am willing enough to be your broodmare, I suppose, if that's what is required of me." She spoke as bluntly as she could, attempting to shock him in order to stave off the embarrassment that was causing warmth to prickle at the back of her neck. The physical aspects of marriage had been something of a mystery to her for years, until she had finally lost patience with her own ignorance the year before and bribed Hastey— who had three married sisters and had apparently been entertaining the competing affections of two of the stable hands herself—to explain matters to her. She had also discovered an exceptionally educational, highly inappropriate collection of books hidden away in the library at Trethwick Abbey that had filled in many of the blanks left from her conversation with Hastey.

"I—you—" He appeared to be at a loss for words, and Jane mentally congratulated herself on having managed to fluster a man whose experience presumably far outstripped her own. "I intended to tell you that I wouldn't press my advances on you," he said after a moment, apparently recovering enough to speak in complete sentences. "In light of the fact that this marriage is more or less being forced upon us both." For the first time, there was the faintest note of bitterness in his voice, a reminder that, deep down, he didn't want to marry her, either. "And I don't see any need for you to immediately become my *broodmare*, as you so charmingly put it. I've no interest in hearing the pitter-patter of small feet around the house anytime soon, which means we needn't trouble each other in that way until such a time as we decide we're ready."

This was unexpected—Jane had been given to understand that men were exceedingly eager to get beneath a woman's skirts, regardless of how the woman in question might feel about the matter—but naturally, it suited her.

"Should we agree on it?" she asked briskly. "When we intend to consummate the marriage, I mean, if it is not to be immediate?"

Penvale regarded her for a moment, a hint of a smile twitching at his mouth. "I don't suppose 'whenever the mood strikes us' would be an acceptable response, given the circumstances."

Jane cast a fleeting glare in his direction before redirecting her gaze to her lap. "Not if you ever wish to produce that heir, since I'm not certain *that* particular circumstance will ever arise."

"Shall we revisit the matter on a quarterly basis, then?" he asked, his manner businesslike, though an edge of amusement lurking in his voice made Jane wonder uncomfortably if he was making fun of her.

"That seems reasonable," she said cautiously.

"All right, then." A pause. "If we've nothing else to discuss—" He broke off. "Would you just—just look at me for a moment?"

She lifted her head and met his eyes. They were a clear hazel, the flecks of green more visible in this light than they had been indoors, and the look in them was . . . steady, somehow. Serious.

"If you're certain about this, then I'm prepared to go back indoors and tell my uncle that we've come to an agreement. But if you are uncertain, speak up now, because once we are betrothed, I mean to see us married in efficient fashion." Determination was written in every word he uttered, and Jane had a suspicion that he would be quite annoyed if she got cold feet the night before the wedding. He had the air of a man who had resigned himself to a task and was ready to see it through.

"I'm certain." She thrust out her hand abruptly. "Shall we shake on it?"

He looked at her hand, appearing a bit startled. "I must confess, I've never had a young lady offer to shake my hand before."

"I assure you, I'm nothing like the young ladies you have experience with," Jane said, and Penvale offered a crooked grin as he reached out to shake her hand.

"Of that, Miss Spencer, I am already well aware."

Chapter Three

"*I do believe, Penvale, that you're about to claim the honor of un-*dertaking the most ill-advised marriage of the year."

The words were mild, pleasant, even, but the green gaze that pierced Penvale from the other side of the table was sharp.

It was the night before his wedding; the banns had been called for the third and final time at church that morning, and Penvale and Miss Spencer were to marry the following day.

Penvale had invited his friends to dinner: Jeremy and Diana, as well as Lord James Audley and his wife, Violet; and Violet and Diana's friend Emily and her new husband, Lord Julian Belfry. Once the meal had been cleared away, the ladies had retreated to the library, leaving the gentlemen to their port and conversation. This was a practice that Penvale and his close friends did not often observe—the ladies tended to remain with the gentlemen for their after-dinner drinks, and the fact that they had not done so tonight left Penvale with a feeling of dark foreboding regarding whatever his sister was so eager to discuss with her friends out of their husbands' hearing.

"Audley, bugger off," Penvale said without heat. "Besides, it's only January—I've no doubt someone will make a much more disastrous match by March or so."

"I wouldn't bet on it." Audley's tone lost a bit of its easiness. "You're marrying a girl you've spent all of five minutes with, just so you can get your hands on a crumbling pile of stones in bloody Cornwall."

Audley, Penvale knew, was being deliberately provoking; he was perfectly well aware that, to Penvale, Trethwick Abbey was a good deal more than a crumbling pile on the coast. To Penvale, it was everything. Which meant he would do anything to get it back, even marry.

"Audley does have a point, old chap," Jeremy said from where he was reclining in his chair halfway down the table. He and Diana had been seated directly opposite each other at dinner, and Penvale was almost certain there had been something inappropriate occurring underneath the table during the soup course.

"Though I should note," Jeremy added, "that I've met the lady in question, and whilst she can't carry on a polite conversation to save her life, she is certainly not lacking in a strictly aesthetic sense."

"Jeremy, are you feeling well?" Penvale asked a bit peevishly. "'Aesthetic' seems advanced for your vocabulary."

"Willingham, your wife has to be one of the bluntest women I've ever met," Belfry added lazily, taking a sip of port. "I hardly think you're in a position to judge a lady for not being polite." Although he had just criticized Diana to both her husband and her brother, Belfry did not look remotely concerned as he leaned back in his chair, cravat loosened—perhaps because this was less of an insult and more of an honest statement of fact.

"Fair, Belfry," Jeremy said. "But that is largely a matter of choice on her part. She can be nice when she wishes to be." He gave a wide, satisfied smile. "*Very* nice."

"I would give you every penny I possess to never hear you speak of my sister in such a way ever again," Penvale said in pained tones.

He hadn't kicked up too much of a fuss when Jeremy and Diana had decided to wed—the role of domineering elder brother was never one that had interested him, and his general philosophy was to avoid butting into the affairs of those around him as much as possible (as the rest of the group did that all too well), but he was approximately three bits of innuendo away from demanding that Jeremy meet him with pistols at dawn. (Which would be rather unfortunate, considering Penvale was a terrible shot.)

"My point is," Jeremy said, dismissing Penvale's trauma with a wave of his hand, "she can turn on the charm when it suits her. Miss Spencer seems fundamentally unable to do so."

"Well, that won't be much of an issue, since she hates London," Penvale said. "I don't expect she'll wish to come to town very often."

A short, appalled silence followed this declaration.

"So you're going to rusticate in Cornwall for the rest of your life?" Audley asked, sounding disturbed.

"Have any of you ever *been* to Cornwall?" Penvale asked, irritation creeping into his voice. "You make it sound as though I'll be on a remote desert island."

"I'd think that would be a great deal more pleasant," Belfry said.

"Certainly warmer," Audley muttered.

"In any case," Penvale said, growing a bit exasperated, "whether or not Miss Spencer enjoys town is entirely irrelevant, since there is nothing at all stopping me from coming to town whenever I wish, regardless of how she feels about it. She's welcome to remain in the countryside; there's no need for my plans to affect hers."

"Spoken like a man who's never been married," Audley said, sounding cheerful. Penvale sensed that they were about to embark upon the portion of the evening in which his friends, all happily married, began to smugly dispense sage advice, and he frantically attempted to head it off.

"My marriage is not a love match, Audley," he said shortly. "I am perfectly aware that you and Violet are nauseatingly attached to each other—lately," he added, which was a bit unsporting; Violet and Audley's marriage, while a love match, had suffered a lengthy estrangement that had been repaired only the previous summer. "But I don't care about any of that."

"As a man who recently married for convenience, Penvale," Belfry interjected, "I regret to inform you that it does not always go quite according to plan." Belfry and Emily had married the previous autumn for purely practical reasons, but it had not taken long for stronger feelings to develop between them.

Penvale's situation, however, was entirely different. Belfry and Emily had known each other before they'd wed, and no one had been terribly surprised when they'd fallen in love, given the obvious interest between them. Penvale, however, was marrying a woman with whom he'd had precisely one conversation—a woman he'd met less than three weeks before. He didn't think he needed to worry about inconvenient feelings cropping up in *his* marriage. And this was just the way he liked things: orderly. Uncomplicated. He had conducted the entirety of his adult life in such a way as to ensure that he remained far removed from messy emotional entanglements, and he saw no reason for this to change just because he was going to stand up in a church and speak some vows that he didn't feel particularly beholden to.

He said as much to his friends and was met—predictably—with a set of eyebrows raised in unison.

"Did you rehearse that ahead of time?" he asked grumpily.

"I do not think this is going to be as simple as you think it will,"

Audley informed him. "You're getting married; you're tying your life to someone else's. You can't simply go about your days as though she doesn't exist—that sounds like a bloody miserable existence. I spent four years attempting to do just that, and it was hell. I wouldn't wish that on you."

Penvale regarded his friend for a long moment, knowing, despite the irritation he felt at the meddling, that Audley meant well—and that, furthermore, he believed everything he was saying. What Audley didn't understand—*couldn't* understand, as besotted as he was with Violet—was that Penvale did not want the same thing from marriage as his friends did. He'd watched them all, over the past summer and autumn, fall in love with their wives, and it had all been terribly . . . messy. Distracting.

Penvale had never thought seriously about marriage—wives were expensive, and he had other plans for his fortune. There had been no room for a wife in said plans, and he didn't feel the loss, never lacking for friends and, on occasion, female companionship. And so, now, finding that his long-held plans and marriage were inextricably linked was causing him to reconsider what his life would look like. But he already knew that his marriage would be nothing like those of his friends.

"I intend to be a decent husband to Miss Spencer," he said, leaning back in his chair and glancing from Audley to Jeremy to Belfry in turn. "She won't want for anything. But I've no intention of allowing my marriage to affect anything else about my day-to-day existence. I've a perfectly good life here in London; once I've settled in at Trethwick Abbey and seen that all is running smoothly, I expect I'll be in town frequently, regardless of whether Miss Spencer wishes to come with me."

"Penvale, old chap," Jeremy said with a wide grin, "I truly cannot *wait* to see how this works out for you."

Being married, Penvale was pleased to discover, was so far little different from bachelor life.

It was the morning after his wedding—which had been a suitably quiet affair, for all that his friends attempted to turn the wedding breakfast into something considerably more raucous, given the amount of champagne on offer—and he was in his study, looking over a few last pieces of correspondence from the piles on his desk (Penvale had never been terribly tidy) before he departed for Cornwall the following day.

His wife, Smithers had informed him, had risen late and taken breakfast in bed. Penvale had no idea how she'd occupied herself after that point, which seemed like an ideal state of affairs to him.

Penvale returned his attention to the letter before him, which summarized the state of his accounts now that he'd paid his uncle's asking price for Trethwick Abbey. He hadn't spent his entire fortune, but it was undeniable that he'd want to ensure the estate was turning a tidy profit fairly soon so that he wouldn't have to economize. He had a number of ideas about potential improvements—he'd made it a habit to read plenty of books on land management and agricultural reform over the past decade, all in preparation for this day—but he wouldn't have a clear idea of what changes were necessary until he saw the estate and took a good look at the account books. Which was why they were leaving town tomorrow.

Penvale rubbed the bridge of his nose, squinting at the words before him, his vision blurring a bit. He needed to step away from his desk for a while, he thought; part of the reason he was so fond of morning exercise was that he tended to get a bit twitchy if he sat still for too long. Swimming in the warmer months, and riding or walking in the winter, cleared his head. He rose, heading for his study door with half-formed thoughts of a ride in Hyde Park, perhaps stopping on Curzon Street to see if Audley wished to join him. He was just reaching for the doorknob when the door was opened by Smithers. "Your uncle is here, my lord," he intoned.

"For God's sake, *why?*" Penvale muttered, the faint headache forming at his temples threatening to worsen.

"I could not say, my lord," Smithers replied somberly. "Shall I show him in?"

"No," Penvale said shortly, moving past his butler. "I'm going for a walk. If he wishes to talk, he can accompany me."

His uncle did indeed wish to talk, as evidenced by the fact that he fell into step beside Penvale without complaint. Bourne House was on St. James's Square; given that it was a bleak gray day in the last week of January, the square was largely deserted, other than a few harried-looking nannies trying to shepherd their bundled-up charges on a healthful walk in the biting wind. Penvale, who had never minded the cold, turned up his collar against the wind and took a deep breath, inhaling London's winter scent of smoke and rain.

"What's this about, then?" he asked without preamble; now that the wedding was over and all the paperwork had been signed, he had been hoping to see as little of his uncle as was possible for the foreseeable future. Even if Penvale did not find the man smug and tiresome, the fact was that his father had despised his younger brother, and for Penvale—who still clung to a small boy's worshipful memories of his father—this was reason enough for his dislike.

"I just thought, now that the deed has been done . . ." his uncle began, leering a bit; Penvale, naturally, had no intention of informing him that he'd spent an entirely uneventful, celibate night in his own bed, Jane asleep in the viscountess's bedroom through the connecting door. "The time has come to warn you."

"Warn me of what?" Penvale asked, keeping his voice carefully neutral; he could tell that his uncle was trying to get some sort of reaction out of him.

"The fact that the house you just paid me so handsomely for"— here, his uncle paused dramatically; Penvale kept his eyes resolutely fixed ahead, refusing to humor this fit of theatrics—"is *haunted*."

Penvale snorted. "You cannot be serious," he said. "What did you actually want to speak to me about?"

"You may laugh now," his uncle said dramatically, "but you'll change your tune soon enough, once you arrive. I thought you should be prepared."

"Uncle," Penvale said, with what he felt was admirable patience, "I know that you do not truly believe that the spirit of the fourth viscount is lurking in the wine cellar, so why don't you tell me what this is actually about?"

"There have been . . . problems," his uncle said. "Missing objects that turn up in an entirely different place than where they belong. Strange noises at night. A figure in white seen rounding a corner in a darkened hallway but never coming close enough to touch. I found something that looked like a bloodstain on my bedspread one night, and—" Here he broke off with a shudder; Penvale, certain that this was for dramatic effect, refused to ask him to finish the sentence.

"I shall be on my guard," he said dryly, wondering if this was his uncle's idea of an elaborate joke.

"I can see that you think this is my final trick—convincing you that there is something unnatural afoot. But," his uncle said, taking a step closer, "my trick was convincing you to marry Jane and take this house off my hands. I'm well aware that you could have paid a higher price for it, but I consider myself well rid of it. It's your problem now—and so is Jane."

Penvale's irritation was simmering beneath the surface, but he refused to allow his uncle to see it; he'd never been one for unnecessary displays of emotion, and he was generally slow to anger, difficult to provoke. He wouldn't let his uncle be the one to cause him to act otherwise. "Describe the viscountess that way again," he said, his voice mild, "and I'll ensure you're not admitted to a single drawing room in London."

This was not an idle threat—his own title would do a lot of the work for him if he truly wished to see his uncle cast out of polite society, and he was certain that Diana could do the rest. His uncle seemed to recognize this truth, because his eyes narrowed, but he said nothing more.

"Good day, Uncle," Penvale said, offering a curt nod as he turned to head back in the direction of Bourne House. "Let's try to avoid meeting any time in the remotely near future, shall we?"

He walked away before his uncle had the chance to reply.

❧

Penvale and Jane's leave-taking the following morning was achieved with significantly more fanfare than either one of them might have desired.

"I wish I were an only child," Penvale said gloomily as soon as he walked out the front door of Bourne House to find his sister and friends assembled at the bottom of the steps.

"That's the spirit, brother dearest!" Diana said cheerfully. It was a sunny day at last, and Diana—who did not believe in bonnets but made an exception for elaborate hats—was smiling at him from where she was tucked under Jeremy's arm. She was wearing a wool gown of a vibrant blue, complete with a matching fur-lined pelisse and hat.

"We couldn't let you vanish into the Cornish wilderness without saying our proper farewells," Audley said darkly, but there was a twinkle in his eye, and Violet was dimpling beside him.

Penvale turned, realizing that he'd been so busy projecting an air of weary resignation at his friends that he'd forgotten about Jane. He found her hovering in the doorway, frowning at the scene below. Penvale took quick steps toward her and offered her his arm. "Are you ready?" he asked her in an undertone.

Those vivid eyes of hers were fixed first on his friends assembled in the street and then, apparently, on his cravat. "Why are they here?"

He heaved a sigh. "Because it's what they do." He leaned closer. "It's their way of showing affection, but I can't let on that I know that, or it will only encourage them."

She glanced up at him, their eyes locking for a second. "They're displeased you're leaving." It was a statement, not a question.

"No," he said, then paused. "Well, yes," he allowed. "But they're pleased that Trethwick Abbey is mine again, even if it means not having me at their beck and call at all times."

He'd said it jokingly, in an attempt to lighten her strangely heavy mood, but her expression remained somber. "You needn't make excuses for them—it's not a bad thing, having friends who care for you." She reached out and took his proffered arm. "Shall we?"

The next few minutes were a flurry of well-wishes and promises to visit: "As soon as the roads clear of mud this spring, we'll be there, whether you want us or not!" was Diana's way of saying farewell, which sounded more like a threat than a promise. By the time they were safely in Penvale's carriage, tucked under blankets with warm bricks to ward off the chill, he was feeling slightly weary from the whirlwind. He loved his friends, but they could be a bit much at times—one of the reasons he'd always been perfectly content to trail along in their wake rather than leading the charge into whatever their latest adventure might be. He glanced across the carriage at Jane, who was seated opposite him, and he froze; if he'd been a bit drained by his friends' exuberant farewell, she looked positively exhausted. Her face was drawn, and she leaned her head against the seat back, her eyes shut.

Penvale relished the opportunity to study her for a moment, unobserved. With her eyes closed, she looked younger. She *was* young, he thought—one-and-twenty was not young to be married, but the fact that she'd never had a proper Season and was freshly arrived from the country without ever having mingled in fashionable society made her seem younger than Diana and her friends had at the same age. By the time Diana was twenty-one, she'd already been wed and widowed and was mistress of her own home, subject to no one's whims but her own. Jane, however, had been handed from one man to the next like a cow bartered between farmers.

Her eyes fluttered open, catching him once more in that vivid gaze—for approximately half a second before her face creased into a frown. He wondered if he should begin taking offense to the fact that she seemed to frown whenever she saw him.

"Why are you staring at me?" she asked, her eyes skittering off him to focus on something outside the window. The carriage had begun moving, jostling slightly as it rolled along, and through the window, Penvale could see a series of Mayfair mansions flashing by. "You look like a deer."

"A *deer*?" Penvale asked, indignant.

"You are familiar with them, I assume?" she asked. "Despite the fact that you've spent so much time in town? Long of leg, brown of hair, round of eye?"

"I know what a bloody deer is, thank you. I've simply never been compared to one."

"There's a first time for everything, I suppose," she said, watching London pass by out the window, but she turned away after a moment, rummaging in the valise she'd insisted on bringing with her into the carriage, separate from the rest of her luggage. After a few seconds of searching, she triumphantly extracted a well-used copy of a book whose title Penvale couldn't make out; he noted numerous dog-eared pages and worn lettering on the spine and concluded that this was not Jane's first time reading this particular volume.

Without so much as another glance at him, she opened the book upon her lap, bent her head, and began to read.

Penvale watched for a moment in silence before clearing his throat. She turned a page.

He cleared his throat again, a bit louder this time.

"If you are trying to get my attention," she said without looking up, "you could simply say my name."

"Do you enjoy reading, then?" he asked, striving for a blandly pleasant tone.

"Since we have been in this carriage for approximately five minutes and I've already opened a book, I should think the answer to that would be obvious."

"Perhaps you merely find my company tiresome and would be willing to take any means of escape offered," he suggested, waiting for her to correct him.

"Both can be true," she said, turning another page.

Penvale sputtered, and her mouth curved up at the corners.

"What are you reading?" he asked, curious in spite of himself.

"'Reading' seems rather an optimistic verb to use at the moment," she said waspishly, resting a finger at a particular spot on the page to mark her place as she spoke. "But if you must know, it is *The Romance of the Forest* by Mrs. Radcliffe."

He raised his eyebrows. "You do not strike me as a lady given to romantic fantasies," he said, and her eyes met his at these words, the expression in them scornful.

"And why is that?" she asked sharply. "Because I do not simper and sigh and act like an utter fool? Is that the only sort of woman who could possibly have any dreams of romance? Or who could enjoy a romantic novel?"

"Well," he said, realizing he had no good response to this question.

"What do *you* like to read, my lord?" she asked, and he could not help thinking that he'd never heard someone address him in a way that was so scrupulously correct and also so disdainful.

"I've spent quite a bit of time reading books on agriculture," he said carefully, feeling as though any word he uttered at the moment had the potential to be weaponized. "Sheep farming, drainage improvements—that sort of thing."

Something flashed across her face at these words, gone before Penvale could properly process what he'd seen, but all she said, with an eloquent lift of the brow, was: "Strange, since you do not strike me as a gentleman given to farm labor."

Penvale leaned forward, feeling oddly defensive, considering that she was, of course, correct. "The truth is, Jane, you don't know anything about me."

"That is precisely my point."

Without another word, she returned her attention to her book.

This time Penvale did not interrupt.

Chapter Four

"That," Jane said darkly, "is only one bed."

"It is," Penvale agreed gloomily beside her.

"This may be the thing that breaks me at last," she said, hands on her hips. "I need *space*. I need room to *move*. I need *privacy*."

He leveled a baleful look at her. "You're nearly a foot shorter than me and you think *you're* the one who is going to suffer under this arrangement?"

"I have never shared a bed before," she said evenly. "Are you really going to try to tell me that you can say the same?"

To this, obviously, he had no reply.

Point to Jane, she thought triumphantly. Her triumph was short-lived, however, given the fact that nothing about their immediate situation had changed: They were somewhere in rural Cornwall, on a rainy evening in early February, at the only inn for miles around, on the final night of a journey stretching well past a week—and there was only one room available.

And that room had only one bed.

"Fine," she said, throwing her hands up in the air. "There's nothing to be done about it, I suppose."

"Thank you, Penvale, for finding us accommodation in the midst of extreme difficulty," he murmured as he shrugged out of his coat. "Despite everything that has gone wrong today, you have managed to secure us lodging and a warm dinner."

"If you're waiting for me to fall at your feet in gratitude, you'll be waiting a long time," she warned, removing her cape and laying it neatly on the back of a chair. "If you hadn't been so certain that we could reach Trethwick Abbey by nightfall—"

"An assumption that made considerably more sense this morning, as we were departing under sunny skies, than it does at the moment, yes," he shot back, plainly irritated. He rubbed the bridge of his nose, which she had noticed he tended to do when he was tired or frustrated. Or, as was the case at the moment, both.

It had been a bad-luck sort of day; they had departed their last inn just outside Plymouth under promising conditions—the roads were unusually dry for February, and Penvale, eager to hasten their arrival at Trethwick Abbey, had insisted they push on even after dark fell in the late afternoon.

And then it had started raining. The road had quickly turned into a muddy mess, slowing their progress until they had little choice but to stop for the night—and they'd been in the middle of bloody nowhere, as Penvale had phrased it, when this decision was finally made.

Which was how they found themselves here, at a tiny, tucked-away inn, staring at the bed that was to accommodate both of them this evening.

Further contemplation was forestalled by the arrival of dinner and a small copper tub, and by the time Penvale and Jane had dined in testy silence and then bathed in less testy silence, since they'd taken turns stepping into the hall while the other took a bath, Jane wanted nothing more than to curl up in a warm bed and see this day finished. She tucked herself into bed while Penvale went about the room extinguishing the candles, and she burrowed deep beneath the sheets, even pulling a pillow over her head for good measure. She was nestled down in her warm little cocoon, eyes shut, ready to sink into a well-earned slumber . . .

When what felt like a block of ice was suddenly in direct contact with her skin.

"Good God, did you stick your feet in a cold stream before climbing into bed?" she cried, sitting bolt upright the moment his foot brushed her ankle. She was wearing her warmest and least seductive nightgown, a high-necked flannel monstrosity that was supremely cozy and supremely unattractive. (Those attributes often, she had found, went hand in hand.)

"My feet are always cold in the winter!" he said defensively, sitting up as well.

"Then why aren't you wearing more *clothes?*" she hissed, gesturing at his general person. He'd put on a shirt after his bath, which had—if she was completely honest with herself—prompted her quick retreat to the bed, because the sight of him in nothing more than a shirt and his smalls was disturbingly distracting. Oh, it was decent enough—all the interesting bits of him were demurely covered—but there was more of his legs visible than she felt was entirely proper, and where the shirt was loose at his chest, she could see golden skin and hair.

It had made her appreciate the vital role that cravats played in keeping society functioning, and now, thanks to his unnaturally cold feet, she was sitting up next to him, and her eyes kept snagging on the skin visible at his throat and chest, and it was . . .

Well, it was very difficult to focus.

"What is wrong with you?" he asked, sounding halfway between concerned and annoyed. "Do you have a fever? You look flushed."

"A fever?" she exclaimed, lowering her head and allowing her heavy curtain of hair to partially shield her face from his gaze. "I don't feel feverish—I feel half frozen!"

"I promise you, I did not kick you on purpose," he said stiffly, and then there was a fair amount of rustling as he made rather a production of scooting to the side of the bed, putting as much space between them as was possible under the circumstances. "Is that better?"

"I suppose," she grumbled, aware on some level that her degree of indignation was out of proportion to the offense. However, she was doing exactly what she always did when she felt shy or embarrassed or uncertain: She was excessively bad-humored to make up for it.

"Good night, then," he said, and she glanced over in time to see him roll away to extinguish the final candle on the bedside table, his back to her, allowing her to gaze appreciatively at the broad expanse of his shoulders, covered by the fine linen of his shirt. She settled back down to sleep as well. She wondered idly as she shut her eyes what he did to gain those muscles—it wasn't as though the life of a dissolute aristocrat would lend itself to much labor.

To be entirely fair, she wasn't certain that he *was* dissolute—at least not by the standard of other men of his class. His uncle had mentioned that he had a taste for gambling, but she'd never seen him drink more than a couple of glasses of wine or spirits at once.

He was a bit of a puzzle. And they were going to live together, so she'd have plenty of time to figure him out. If she wanted to. She wasn't sure she *did* want to—particularly not when he was tugging on the bedspread so hard that she was pulled toward him against her will.

"Were you raised in a barn?" she asked, cracking open one eye to glare at him, realizing as she did so that she was considerably closer to him in the bed than she'd been a few moments before.

"Were *you?*" he demanded. "You've stolen all of the bed linens."

She lifted her head, peering down first at her side of the bed, then his, and realized that he wasn't entirely incorrect. "And you couldn't have just politely asked for some rather than rolling me around like a fat sausage in a pan?"

"I apologize, little sausage," he said with exaggerated gallantry. "But perhaps you would like to share a bit of your warmth?" Jane pressed her lips together to suppress a sudden, slightly hysterical urge to laugh; for his part, Penvale looked almost embarrassed, a somewhat remarkable state for a man who did not, so far as Jane had observed, seem to be remotely self-conscious. "I could have phrased that better," he added sheepishly.

"Quite," she said in her frostiest tones. She flung a handful of blankets in his direction, deliberately *not* considering what other ways she could offer to warm him here, in a bed, on a cold winter night.

Her last words to him, as she rolled over once more and prepared to drift off, were: "If you call me a sausage again, I will murder you in your sleep."

His only reply was a low chuckle.

Penvale came awake slowly the next morning. At some point during the night, he'd burrowed deep under the bedspread, where he lay facedown, the sheets pulled up to his neck. He could feel the cold air of the room on his head and was reluctant to leave the coziness of the bed—or, for that matter, to open his eyes. Perhaps Jane was still asleep as well, and they could simply lie here peacefully, dozing on a chilly February morning, the picture of comfort and domesticity.

These thoughts were rudely interrupted when a damp, freezing-cold cloth was flung onto his head.

"What the hell," he demanded, engaging in a fair bit of undignified limb-flailing as he struggled to extricate himself from the bedspread. He blinked blearily, taking in the sight of his wife, wrapped in a dressing gown of similar age and aesthetic appeal to that of her nightgown, sitting in an armchair before the fire, watching him with some satisfaction.

"Was that cold?" she inquired innocently. "I suppose I could have heated the water in the basin first, but it seemed like an awful lot of trouble."

"What is *wrong* with you?"

"If I had to suffer your cold feet, then it seemed as though some degree of revenge was in order." She examined her fingernails idly as she spoke.

"You know, annulling this marriage seems more appealing with each day that passes," he said, flinging the damp cloth onto the floor and shoving back the sheets, shivering as the cool air of the room hit more of his skin.

"No, it doesn't," she said serenely. "You want that house."

Penvale could not argue, so he contented himself with pulling his shirt over his head before she had a chance to look away, hoping to embarrass her. She didn't blush, but she did avert her gaze in a hurry. Penvale decided that, on the whole, he'd take it.

"Get dressed," he said, reaching for a pair of trousers. "I'm going to go check on the state of the roads. As you so kindly pointed out, there's a house waiting for us."

For once, she seemed content not to argue, and within an hour they had breakfasted and were back on the road. It was slow progress, given the previous day's rain, so it was nearly dark when they found themselves rattling down a long gravel lane, through a pair of imposing wrought iron gates, and up a steady incline before coming to a halt in front of Trethwick Abbey.

Penvale peered out the window at his ancestral home in the dim light of dusk—a place so terribly alive in his memories but which he had not actually seen with his own eyes since he was a boy of ten.

Trethwick Abbey was a uniform weathered gray stone, featuring large mullioned windows and matching turrets on either end of the building. Perched on a hilltop, lawns sloping away from its walls in three directions, it was situated at the edge of a dramatic sea cliff. From the back of the house, Penvale recalled, one could walk along the narrow path that clung to the cliff's edge and peer down to the rocks and crashing waves below. Diana had never been afraid of much as a girl, but she'd clung to his hand when they'd walked that path. It was one of the rare times in his life when he'd felt like her protective elder brother.

He sensed Jane's eyes on him, but he did not look at her as the carriage door was opened and he leaped down. He turned back to offer his arm, which she took somewhat reluctantly as she stepped down beside him. Her head came up only to his shoulder, but she was wearing a bonnet that matched her green woolen cape, and she looked . . .

He struggled for the right adjective. "Pretty" wasn't the word to describe Jane at all; her features were too stern, the lines of her face too sharp. "Handsome," perhaps, was closer, with those vivid eyes and glossy dark hair; as she stood there next to him, she looked every inch the wife of a viscount. A wife any man might be proud to parade around on his arm.

So long as she remained silent.

"Are you going to keep gaping, or can we possibly go inside, where it's warm?" she asked impatiently, tugging on his arm. It was strange, he thought, to be bringing his bride home, only to realize that she knew this place better than he did. She had been living here for the past three years, after all; he hadn't so much as laid eyes upon it in nearly twenty.

The heavy oak front door opened as they climbed the steps, lit by flickering torchlight, and a careworn face that Penvale recalled from his childhood awaited them as they walked inside.

"Crowe," he said, nodding at the butler; he remembered thinking even as a boy that Crowe was old, but the figure before him was truly elderly, his face heavily creased with wrinkles. There was pride in the way Crowe held himself at stiff attention, however, and in the entirely correct bow he offered.

"Lord Penvale," Crowe said. His gaze moved to Jane, something flickering there. "Miss Spencer."

"It's Lady Penvale now, actually," Penvale said, even as Jane opened her mouth to reply, and he watched something soften slightly in his butler's austere appearance.

Crowe glanced between them. "Mr. Bourne's letter informing us that you would be assuming ownership of the house left out a few details, it would seem."

"Why does that not surprise me?" Penvale murmured, then added in a louder voice, "I believe my uncle has already arranged for his things to be sent to him in London. Is the viscount's bedroom ready?"

"It is, my lord," Crowe confirmed. "Mr. Bourne did not sleep in the viscount's bedchamber."

Penvale, who was turning to walk up the stairs, paused at this. "He didn't?"

"No, my lord," Crowe said. "He slept in a suite of rooms in the southern wing of the house. I believe he found the view superior."

This seemed unlikely to Penvale, since the viscount's suite of rooms had the best views in the entire house, featuring enormous windows looking out over the tumultuous sea far below. Something within him eased at the knowledge that his uncle had not been able to bring himself to sleep in the room that once belonged to Penvale's father.

"See that Lady Penvale's things are moved into the viscountess's bedroom," he said.

"Oh," she said, faltering. "I'm perfectly happy to remain—"

"But I am not," he said shortly, turning to her and lowering his voice. "I know that this is an unusual marriage in some respects, but I do not think it unreasonable to at least expect my wife to sleep in the adjoining room."

He was fairly certain that none of his friends slept in adjoining rooms; he'd never made inquiries in this regard, but he'd stake a sizable portion of his remaining fortune on Audley, Jeremy, and Belfry sharing a bed each night with their wife.

"Did you wish to go to your room to rest this afternoon?" he asked Jane.

"Because sitting in a carriage is so exhausting."

"Ah, Jane, you do sweeten any conversation," he said amiably; he might have the world's most ill-tempered wife, but he wasn't going to allow her to sour his mood this evening. He was *here*, at Trethwick Abbey, realizing a dream that had been years in the making.

Today was a glorious day.

"My lady," came a sharp voice, and Penvale turned to see Jane looking inquiringly at a woman of middling years who was wearing a perfectly pressed apron and demure lace cap. Her brown skin was faintly lined, and there were streaks of gray evident in her dark hair, but her gaze was alert and wary. Penvale surmised that this was the housekeeper—a different woman than the one who had held the position in his boyhood.

"Yes, Mrs. Ash?" Jane asked, her voice gentler than it normally was.

"The . . . mysterious events," Mrs. Ash said ominously. "They have resumed once more."

"What do you mean?" Jane asked, frowning; she cast a quick half-glance over her shoulder, as if hoping Penvale hadn't heard.

"Several members of staff have reported hearing odd sounds," Mrs. Ash said, a hint of ghoulish pleasure evident in her voice. "Strange moans—one could almost mistake them for the howling of the wind, except we've heard them on perfectly still nights. One of the maids heard a baby crying. There were footsteps overhead, coming from a room that's been closed up for years, no signs of footprints in the dust when we went to investigate."

Penvale's brow furrowed as he listened; this, undoubtedly, was what his uncle had meant by his rather peculiar warning back in London. Apparently, he hadn't been fabricating it entirely.

"Mrs. Ash, is it?" he asked, stepping forward, feeling that he should take this situation in hand. She nodded, unblinking, her expression cool. She offered the shallowest of curtseys. "I couldn't help over-hearing," Penvale continued, offering her a bland smile, "and my uncle mentioned something similar to me before I left London. I hope you and the other servants have not been too distressed."

"One of the housemaids has threatened to quit, my lord," Mrs. Ash said, any hint of warmth that had been present in her manner toward Jane now entirely absent. Penvale supposed the household staff must be somewhat uncertain about his arrival, having no notion of what sort of employer he would prove to be. "And," she added, "the lads don't like to let on that they're frightened, but everyone is on edge." She spoke the words almost as a challenge.

"I'm sure they are," he said slowly, his mind working. Privately, he thought it likely that one of the "lads" was behind this series of events—though for what purpose beyond frightening the housemaids, he couldn't guess. "Now that Lady Penvale and I are home, I would be more than happy to investigate. We can't have any housemaids quit-ting, after all."

"Indeed, my lord," Mrs. Ash murmured, not sounding convinced that he would be able to solve this puzzle. "Shall I show you the house?" she asked more briskly. "We weren't certain when you'd be arriving, or I'd have had the staff waiting to meet you out front."

"There's no cause for that," Penvale said, following the housekeeper as she set off through the high-ceilinged entrance hall, Jane at his side. "It's a freezing day, I wouldn't want them to all line up in this weather to greet us." He felt Jane's eyes on his face for a fleeting second, but when he glanced down at her, she was looking away.

As they went from room to room, Penvale spotted a familiar piece of furniture here, a portrait there. He could fault his uncle for many things, but he appeared to have been a fairly scrupulous caretaker of the house, and he had employed a competent staff—there were no worn cushions or faded wall hangings or dusty shelves to be seen. Casting a sideways glance at Jane, listening intently to Mrs. Ash, he wondered how much of her own touch could be seen here. Had she taken a hand in the running of the house?

". . . and through here we have the library," Mrs. Ash said as they approached the end of a hallway on the second floor.

Penvale sensed a change in Jane as soon as they walked through the doors—she straightened a bit, and when he looked at her, he saw a certain brightness in her eye and eagerness in her expression that he had never witnessed when she was looking at *him*.

He surveyed the room before him: Floor-to-ceiling shelves lined the walls, and large windows offered dramatic views of the crashing sea. A set of French doors led out onto a narrow terrace; Penvale had a sudden recollection of his mother watching the sun set over the ocean from that spot. He swallowed at the thought.

Even on a bleak day, there was plenty of natural light, and a fire burned in the large stone fireplace dominating one wall, an emerald green chaise occupying pride of place before the fire.

Another flash of memory: Penvale's father seated on that chaise, Penvale tucked up close beside him, his father's soothing voice reading to him from one of the countless leather-bound tomes that filled the shelves.

Penvale shook his head, brushing the memory aside like cobwebs.

". . . Miss Spencer—Lady Penvale, I mean—has ordered some novels of her own for the collection," Mrs. Ash was saying. "She spends the most time here, so if you are looking for a specific book, she is the one to ask."

Penvale cast a considering glance at his wife, who, as ever, did not seem terribly delighted by the prospect of any prolonged conversation with him. It was fortunate that Penvale had never spent too much time worrying over what people thought of him—he had his friends, who tolerated him with good humor; he had his sister, who had threatened to physically harm him on numerous occasions but who, deep down, was quite loyal; and, when he wanted it, he had female companionship. All these connections allowed him to proceed in the course of his life without finding himself taxed by undue emotions or worries. But had he been a man more given to such concerns, he suspected that Jane's blatant disinclination to be in the same room with him would have begun to sting a bit.

These thoughts were prevented from becoming too morose, however, because at that moment there was a *thump* against the windows.

Penvale, Jane, and Mrs. Ash turned in unison, just in time to see something dark and feathered drop like a stone.

"Just a bird blown into the glass," Penvale assured the housekeeper, who had a hand pressed to her chest.

"It's not terribly windy," Jane said, frowning at the window.

"And Cornish birds are accustomed to wind," Mrs. Ash said solemnly, her gaze fixed on the window as if she'd just seen a harbinger of her own death.

"It likely didn't see the glass, then," Penvale said. Privately, he could not help but wonder whether Jane's affection for Gothic novels had spread like a disease among the household staff, if this was how they reacted to a stunned bird.

"I'm sure you're right," Jane said, her tone indicating quite the opposite. "Let's continue, shall we?"

Later that evening, Penvale was in his suite of rooms, listening to the storm outside. He'd forgotten what winters in Cornwall were like—not as cold as those in London but with fierce storms that rolled in off the sea. How many winter nights had he spent in Bourne House, listening to the drizzle tapping against the windows, longing for the sound of a Cornish storm? He'd never feared them, not even as a boy—he'd loved the howling wind, the noise of the waves crashing below.

And here he was, amid a storm at Trethwick Abbey once more, warm and snug in an armchair before the fire in the sitting room attached to his bedchamber, a glass of brandy in hand.

This was it, he reflected. Everything he'd spent the past decade of his life working toward. He'd carefully hoarded his fortune; rather than spending money on drink or women, as seemed the habit among gentlemen, he'd invested the money he'd earned at the gaming tables in funds and dabbled in the stock exchange. And it had paid off in the end, for here he was, drinking brandy in a room that had belonged to his father and his father's father and generations of viscounts before him. His single-minded focus had led to this moment.

So why, then, did he feel oddly . . . hollow?

He was acutely conscious, all at once, of the many miles that separated him from his friends. He had a sudden vision of them all settled cozily before a blazing fire at Audley's house, warm drinks in hand, perhaps playing a raucous game of charades. The thought made him feel rather melancholy, and he grimaced in disgust at himself. It had been a long day, to cap a long, uncomfortable journey, and his exhaustion was clearly making him maudlin.

TO SWOON AND TO SPAR

The sole thought that comforted him as he made his preparations for bed was that, with the noise of the storm, any unnatural sounds that might pipe up during the night would be lost to the howling wind. Anyone wishing to haunt his house would need to wait until tomorrow.

Chapter Five

A disturbing sight greeted Jane at the breakfast table the next morning: her husband, in apparent good humor, glowing with health, already seated and waiting for her.

This was not at all what she'd been expecting—Penvale was an aristocrat. A viscount! He'd lived a life of idle luxury. He was supposed to be late to bed and late to rise, greeting the day with a bleary eye, courtesy of the previous evening's excesses.

Instead, here he was, appearing entirely alert, clean-shaven and immaculately attired, calmly slicing a sausage into small pieces, his eyes on the newspaper before him. She cast a surreptitious glance as she passed behind him to take a seat, expecting it to be one of the London papers—days old, given their remote location—but, to her surprise, she realized the one he'd selected was the *Royal Cornwall Gazette*. She sank down into a chair opposite him and reached for the teapot, slightly nettled that he hadn't so much as acknowledged her presence. While she had always thought the dictum that a gentleman should stand whenever a lady did was silly, she nonetheless found his failure to do so a bit jarring.

She filled her teacup, taking care to ensure the china teapot made a particularly heavy *clunk* when she set it back down on the table.

Penvale's eyes didn't budge from the newspaper.

She stirred a lump of sugar into her tea, making sure her spoon clattered loudly against the cup.

Penvale turned the page.

Just as she was beginning to wonder whether he'd notice if she stripped naked and danced atop the table, he glanced in her direction as he reached for a piece of toast—

And visibly started.

Unbelievable. Had he not even known she was here?

"When did *you* get here?" he asked, making her feel vaguely like she'd committed a crime by daring to sit down at her own breakfast table.

She supposed it was his breakfast table now. It had never really been hers.

The injustice of this fact burned at the back of her throat. It wasn't that she was unaware of all the ways the world was unfair—she had only to look at the small whitewashed cottages inhabited by the estate's tenant farmers to understand how an accident of birth could lead to vastly differing fates in life. And while she'd had the good fortune to be born the daughter of a gentleman, with a mother whose dowry had kept the family quite comfortable and ensured that Jane's education— with a governess and, later, at finishing school—was provided for, her upbringing had been nothing compared to the luxury that Penvale and his friends were accustomed to.

Despite that understanding, it pained Jane all the same, the knowledge that this house and land that she had come to love so much would never be hers, would instead be transferred from the hands of one man to another. Into the hands of a man who had not even visited the estate in two decades.

She was coming to understand how badly he'd wanted his home

returned to him, how much of his life had been centered on this goal. But did he love Trethwick Abbey the way she did? Was it freedom to him the way it was to her?

Somehow she thought not.

"I've been sitting here for a couple of minutes now," she informed him, ignoring the jug of milk to take a sip of hot, sweet tea. "Should you have your ears checked, in addition to your eyes?"

"All of my senses are in perfect working order," he said, which Jane did not think was entirely true; after nearly a fortnight observing the way he squinted down at every newspaper he picked up on the occasions when he was able to acquire one at their lodgings, she was nearly certain he needed spectacles, but if he was content to stubbornly persist (as men, she understood, were generally fond of doing), then who was she to waste her breath suggesting otherwise?

"I suppose I'm not yet used to having someone to breakfast with," he said a bit sheepishly. There was an odd note in his voice, and for a fleeting moment she had the strangest thought that he might be as lonely as she had always been.

Surely not, she thought, dismissing the idea as soon as it had occurred to her. She'd seen his easy rapport with his sister, his friends—what could this man know of loneliness?

"I did not expect you to be up so early," she said, rising from her seat and crossing to the sideboard, where an array of breakfast dishes was laid out; apparently wishing to compensate for his earlier lapse in manners, he immediately sprang to his feet.

"Ah," he said, watching her survey the food options before her. "You were expecting me to remain abed until early afternoon, then roll into the breakfast room still half-foxed and reeking of spirits, and prepare to begin the entire cycle of indulgence anew?"

This was so close to what Jane had been envisioning that she felt her cheeks heat. She kept her back to him as she filled her plate.

"Something along those lines," she hedged, finally mustering sufficient sangfroid to return to her seat with her plate and face him. "Why *are* you up so early?"

"I am not as dissolute as you imagine me to be," he said, taking a sip from his own cup; she sniffed, registering that it was coffee, not tea, and then wondered at herself for wishing to know such a small detail about him. "I'm in the habit of morning exercise, and I've already gone for a ride." He set his cup down, his gaze never wavering from her face as he spoke, and Jane's eyes dropped to her teacup. "You are correct, though, that this is earlier than I usually rise in London. I know that my tenants keep different hours than I do, and I intend to begin visiting them today, so I thought I ought to make an early start."

"You . . . you mean to visit the tenants?" Jane asked, frowning as she glanced up at him again.

Penvale's frown matched hers. "I do," he said slowly. "If there are roofs to be mended or empty larders that need to be filled, these things will need to be addressed immediately."

Jane watched him carefully as he spoke—there was none of the posturing she might have expected, the air of a man who was pleased to let her know how competent he was. Instead, he spoke simply and matter-of-factly of what he clearly viewed as nothing more and nothing less than his duty.

"And," he added, "I'll want to ensure the estate's finances are in good order. I've a meeting with the steward—Cresswick, is it?— scheduled for tomorrow, but I'd like to make my own observations beforehand about how things are being run."

Jane found it strangely reassuring to hear him discussing matters so practically. She felt much more at ease with the notion of him approaching the estate as a business, something to be handled with cold pragmatism, than she did with any of the glimpses of him that conflicted with her assumptions about what sort of man he was. She could not afford to soften toward him, not when doing so would endanger all the plans she had so carefully put into motion.

"Well, I hope that you enjoy yourself," she said, casting a doubtful eye at the window. It wasn't raining, but it was a blustery sort of day, one that she could already tell would involve a sharp wind that would cut through however many layers of clothing one wore to shield against it.

"Will you be remaining at home?" Penvale asked, the question clearly coming from a sense of obligation rather than from any genuine curiosity; even as he spoke, he was busy folding his newspaper, his attention elsewhere.

"Yes," Jane said distractedly, her mind already on her own plans for the day.

"I'll leave you to it, then," he said, and rose from the table, leaving Jane to finish her rapidly cooling breakfast in silence.

Ahh, she thought happily.

Just the way she liked it.

❧

Penvale's absence that day certainly made one thing easier to manage: a much-needed discussion with Mrs. Ash, the housekeeper. This meeting did not take place until well into the afternoon; Jane spent most of the morning in conversation with Mrs. Robin, the cook, followed by a leisurely tour of the house, taking note of the various improvements she wished to make—ideas that she'd had for years but which had never been within her power to enact. It was quite liberating, being a wife instead of a ward.

She had a solitary luncheon on a tray in the library, an arrangement that suited her perfectly, as it allowed her the chance to read a few chapters of the novel that currently occupied her attention. (*Persuasion*, which she had acquired a copy of in London—town was good for a few things, she would admit.)

Around midafternoon, however, she made a point of seeking out Mrs. Ash, who was engaged in reviewing the week's shopping list that Mrs. Robin had provided.

"Lady Penvale," Mrs. Ash said, her stern face brightening as she looked up, her demeanor a far cry from that which she'd presented to Penvale upon their arrival the day before. "I was hoping you'd stop by to see me."

"I thought we had some matters to discuss," Jane said, settling herself in a chair opposite Mrs. Ash in the small room that Mrs. Ash and Crowe used as a butler's pantry, and where they reviewed the household accounts. "Ginger biscuit?" she asked, unfolding the napkin she held in one hand to reveal a few of Mrs. Robin's treats, fresh from the oven. Seeing Mrs. Ash hesitate, doubtless over the perceived impropriety of eating with Jane given the newfound difference in their stations, she added wheedlingly, "Go on—I do feel self-conscious if I'm the only one eating when I'm in company."

This was true, though it was also true that Jane was often self-conscious when she was in company, regardless of whether food was involved. She felt more relaxed around Mrs. Ash than she did around many people, given their long acquaintance—she had been the housekeeper at her father's house in Essex, and when Jane had come to live at

Trethwick Abbey, Mrs. Ash had accompanied her, since the previous housekeeper had departed recently. Mrs. Ash had been uncertain, given that she had never managed anything nearly so grand as a country estate, but Jane, for one, had been thoroughly grateful to have a familiar face in her new home.

"I thought your performance yesterday afternoon was quite convincing," Jane said after a moment of quiet, contented consumption of biscuits.

Mrs. Ash beamed. "Did you? I worried I was laying it on a bit thick."

"Not at all," Jane assured her. "The point is to unsettle him."

"He didn't seem terribly convinced," Mrs. Ash said, doubt evident in her voice.

"He fancies himself a practical sort of man," Jane said dismissively. "But give him a few weeks of this, and his mind will start playing tricks on him." She paused to take another bite of biscuit. "The bird at the window was an inspired touch."

"That bird flew into the glass two days ago, and I wouldn't let the gardeners dispose of it—I thought it might come in handy. Never let a good corpse go to waste, that's what I always say," Mrs. Ash added.

"How sensible," Jane agreed, deciding not to inquire as to precisely how many corpses Mrs. Ash kept on the premises.

"I think so," Mrs. Ash said cheerfully. "What's next, then?"

"We need to proceed cautiously," Jane warned. "He is inclined to be skeptical, so we must build our campaign slowly. And we don't wish to make a mistake like we did with Mr. Bourne and cause him to want to sell the house altogether."

The campaign in question was one Jane had commenced several months earlier, when she'd decided that she could no longer allow her future to be decided by her guardian. What better way to rid herself of his company than to convince him that his house was haunted? Initially, she had thought merely to spook him sufficiently to ensure that he spent all his time in town, leaving her more or less to her own devices at Trethwick Abbey. Apparently, however, Jane's notion of what was mildly unsettling as opposed to nightmarishly horrifying was different from the average person's, and soon enough she realized that Mr. Bourne was not content merely to absent himself from Trethwick Abbey, but that he intended to sell it altogether.

Jane had panicked and come perilously close to confessing all to him in an attempt to ward off the sale—she envisioned a future in which she was forced to live with Mr. Bourne in London, attending all sorts of horrid society events and eventually being married off to the highest bidder. Before she could completely lose her head, Mr. Bourne's plan became clear: to marry her to the nephew interested in purchasing the estate, thereby killing two birds with one stone. At this point, Jane's panic had abated slightly—and another possibility began to present itself to her.

After all, if she could frighten off one Bourne man, why couldn't she scare away a second?

To be sure, if this mysterious nephew wished to regain his estate badly enough to marry a woman he'd never met, he might prove to be a bit stubborn, but Jane was confident that the reality of life on a remote Cornish cliffside (and some well-timed supernatural occurrences) would be sufficient to break the will of an indolent London gentleman.

And so, now that the marriage had taken place and she found herself back home, all that remained was the next part of her plan: chasing away her unwanted husband.

"No christening gowns drenched in blood appearing in his

bedroom in the middle of the night only to vanish later?" Mrs. Ash asked a bit regretfully.

Jane sighed. She was rather proud of that innovation—it was remarkable what an antique christening gown (rescued from a trunk in the attic), a bit of pig's blood from the butcher, and a sneaky servant hidden in a dark room could accomplish—but since this had proved to be the final straw, and Mr. Bourne had announced the following day that he intended to sell the house, Jane supposed she had better rein in her more ghoulish impulses. "I think not. We'll want to start with something more subtle."

"It's the dead of winter, in any case," Mrs. Ash said. "He's not likely to want to make that journey back to London, no matter what happens here. May as well start slowly to begin."

"It's not just the weather keeping him here," Jane said, her mind full of what she'd observed of her new husband thus far. "He seems to truly care for the house." This undoubtedly complicated things, but there was no cause for alarm—it might even be fortunate, as it meant there was little chance he would be frightened into selling the estate, as his uncle had done. All she had to do was convince him that Trethwick Abbey wasn't a terribly pleasant place to live, compared to the luxurious, ghost-free environment of town.

"Mr. Crowe remembers him from his boyhood," Mrs. Ash said hesitantly. "He seems to regard Lord Penvale with some affection." Or as much affection as a stoic English butler was capable of.

"Never mind that," Jane said briskly, trying to drive away the memory of Penvale's serious expression as he'd discussed his tenant visits, and the niggling concern that he wouldn't be as easy to frighten away as his uncle. "He's a London gentleman—he hasn't lived in Cornwall since he was a boy. Soon enough he'll realize that lonely moors and cliffs aren't as exciting as balls and card games, and he'll be racing back to town as quickly as he can. All we'll do is encourage him to make that realization a bit sooner than he might have done otherwise."

"But what of you, love?" Mrs. Ash asked, her face creasing with concern. "I know you want this house to yourself, but once he leaves, you'll be all alone—and since you'll be wed, it's not as though you can ever marry someone who could live here with you."

"I don't mind being alone," Jane said, which both was and wasn't true. She didn't *mind* it, in the sense that it was how she had spent much of her life. She was accustomed to it. And she certainly preferred it to the feeling of being in a room full of strangers, unable to think of a single interesting thing to say. And, for that matter, to living under the thumb of a domineering man who cared nothing for her thoughts or preferences.

Therefore, Jane had a plan, and she intended to follow it.

And that meant she had a house to haunt.

Chapter Six

Little more than a week into his tenure as lord and master of his ancestral home, Penvale was beginning to think that this business wasn't all it was cracked up to be.

It had been a long day—his tenant visits the previous week had revealed a few leaking roofs that could not wait until spring to be repaired, and Penvale had made immediate arrangements for them to be mended. This afternoon, however, while he'd been holed up in his study with his steward, trying to make sense of the previous year's accounts, he'd been interrupted by the arrival of one of the possessors of a previously leaking roof, now eager to complain that it had been mended improperly. (This had devolved into a lengthy explanation on the wrong sort of straw that Penvale, frankly, did not understand.) After listening to this grievance vociferously aired for over a quarter of an hour, Penvale finally lost patience and—with a bit less tact than he might have wished to display—flatly informed the man that, if he and his family were warm and dry, then it would suffice until April, at which point Penvale promised he would take another look at the roof.

No sooner was the first tenant gone than the roofer from the village appeared, complaining bitterly that if the tenant farmer did not stop griping about the repair, it would ruin his reputation and scare off future business. Only once Penvale had managed to reassure him otherwise did he finally beat a retreat, still bearing an expression of dark foreboding.

Penvale rested his elbows upon the papers scattered across his desk, head in his hands.

"Shall we leave it here for today, my lord?" Cresswick, his steward, asked diplomatically.

"Yes," Penvale said wearily. "Is it always like this around here?"

"More or less," Cresswick said. He hesitated, then added, "Your uncle was not a sympathetic listener, my lord, and I handled most of the matters myself. I expect the farmers do not know what to expect, having a viscount in residence who is willing to hear their complaints himself. They might be . . . testing you. A bit."

"Lovely," Penvale muttered, a wave of exhaustion washing over him. He'd never considered himself to be idle—certainly not compared to many of the men he knew. When he was not at the card tables earning his living, such as it was, he was carefully reading every book he could find on estate management and recent innovations in agriculture, or meeting with his solicitor or his man of business about the status of his investments. He went on long rides or swam until his arms ached, and he was a good friend and brother, always nearby whenever Diana or Jeremy or Audley had some need of him. He made time for the occasional dalliance when his schedule permitted and a particularly pretty widow caught his eye, slotting those liaisons into his calendar like he would any other meeting.

His days, in short, had been full. It was only now, facing the litany of issues that faced any titled man with an estate to manage, that he began to see the difference between keeping himself busy and truly being so.

"Give it a bit of time, my lord," Cresswick added, and when Penvale nodded his thanks, he offered a short bow and departed.

Penvale sighed, the noise loud in the sudden silence. His head was pounding, as he'd noticed happening with greater frequency when he'd spent hours squinting at figures or correspondence. Perhaps he should have seen his doctor before leaving London.

London seemed very far away at the moment. He'd been in Cornwall not even a fortnight, but his life in town was beginning to feel like a distant memory. He wondered what his friends were doing without him—no doubt they were all cozied up together, enjoying their wedded bliss.

What was Jane doing now, he wondered idly, drumming his fingers on his desk. It was a gray, dreary day, as so many English February days tended to be, and given the drizzle he could see through the window behind his desk, he doubted she was outdoors.

All at once, he decided to go in search of her, for no particular reason other than the fact that it was a rainy day and they were both indoors and, well . . . she was his wife.

Before he could rise from his desk, however, he became aware of a sudden prickling at the back of his neck and had the oddest sensation that he was being watched.

He looked around the room, knowing perfectly well what he would find: a few empty chairs and a set of bookshelves full of tomes on estate management and old account books. There was no one to be seen—where would they even hide?

The uneasy feeling did not abate; if anything, it intensified, and he took a few steps forward, walking around his desk to approach the bookshelves, examine them more carefully. Nothing looked amiss, but he could not shake his lingering unease.

Shaking his head at his own foolishness, he turned back to his desk—

And froze.

Because at that precise moment, he heard someone whisper his name.

He whirled around, his heart pounding in his chest, but nothing had changed. It was still an empty room.

An empty room in which someone had just whispered to him.

Penvale was so deep in thought that at first he didn't even notice Jane in the library.

He entered the room slowly, almost without realizing where he was. He'd wandered the halls, his head a mire of thoughts and half-formed questions, and his feet seemed to have brought him here of their own accord. He glanced up only once he was well into the room, moving in the direction of the fireplace, and he saw her.

She was tucked into an armchair before the fire, her knees drawn up toward her chest, her slippers discarded on the floor before her. There was a book open on her lap. She hadn't dressed her hair properly that day, merely plaiting it into a heavy braid which fell over one shoulder, tendrils of loose hair framing her face. She was wearing an old gown several years out of fashion, and she had a woolly gray shawl wrapped around her shoulders. Her fair cheeks were flushed from the warmth of the room, and there was a tea tray on a nearby ottoman, a chipped china teacup still half-full.

It was a thoroughly domestic, cozy scene—or at least it would have been, had it not been spoiled by one small detail: Jane's violet eyes were currently fixed on him with an expression that could only be described as exasperated.

"What are you doing here?" she asked.

All at once, the combination of his lurking headache, the frustrations of his tenants, the uneasy sensation he'd experienced in his study, that bloody odd whisper, and the fact that he'd acquired a wife who seemed to somehow think that *this* was what passed for a polite greeting, meant that Penvale had had quite enough.

"Last I checked, I do live here," he said peevishly.

"But . . . *here?*" she pressed, an expression of dark suspicion on her face. "In the library? I've never seen you in here before."

"Did you not realize I know how to read?" he asked, causing her scowl to deepen.

"Come to think of it, I've never seen you with a book in your hand."

He flung himself down in the armchair next to hers, reaching for the lone remaining crumpet on a plate that presumably once held several. "I read plenty when I need to," he said, taking a bite. "If I want to learn more about a certain topic, or acquire a specific skill, or need a piece of information."

"But what about for enjoyment?" Jane pressed, looking scandalized. "For fun? A novel, for example?"

"I've never read a novel," Penvale said, and popped the remainder of the crumpet into his mouth.

Jane was gaping at him like a fish; her expression of frank astonishment considerably softened the sharp lines of her face, and she looked almost . . . *pretty*. In the traditional sense of the word, like something pleasant to rest one's eyes upon, as opposed to something more compelling, more challenging, impossible to tear one's gaze from. At least that was how he usually felt when he looked at her. He realized that he preferred the latter to the former.

"What do you mean?" she asked after a moment, apparently having recovered the power of speech. "You must have read a novel."

Penvale paused, considering. "No," he decided. "I really don't think I have. Violet loves them, though, and has convinced Diana to read her fair share, so I *feel* as though I've read one—I've certainly been subjected to many a breathless summary." Jane was looking more indignant by the moment, but he wasn't finished yet. "Which is the one where they hate each other, but then they love each other in the end?" He paused, tapping his chin thoughtfully. "Come to think of it, that could describe about half of them, from what I've gathered, but this one seemed to make a particular fuss of the fact that they *really* hated each other."

"Are you," Jane began in barely more than a whisper, "describing *Pride and Prejudice?*"

Penvale snapped his fingers. "That's the one! Or," he added, "I suppose I could also be describing the story of Diana and Jeremy's courtship. Who can say?"

Jane inhaled sharply. "I should fling this book at your head."

"You wouldn't be the first to make such a threat," Penvale assured her. "But I wish you wouldn't—I've got a devil of a headache."

Jane regarded him thoughtfully, a faint frown creasing the smooth skin of her forehead. "I wasn't joking the other morning," she said after a moment. "I really do think you need spectacles."

Penvale felt a rush of entirely absurd masculine pride and said curtly, "I can see perfectly well. Look at you. Violet eyes. Black hair. Height of a twelve-year-old"—Jane scowled—"and, oh, yes, there it is, that charming smile of yours."

"Fine," she said, tossing her book rather unceremoniously onto his lap. "Read a few sentences from that, if you please."

Penvale lifted the volume and, without even glancing at the title, began to read. "'No one who had ever seen Catherine Morland in her infancy would have supposed her born to be a heroine. Her situation in life, the character of her'—"

"Ha!" Jane said triumphantly before he could read further. "I knew it—look how close you're holding the book to your face."

"This is just how I *read*," Penvale said defensively.

"You and old Mrs. Enys down in the village," Jane said smugly. "Who is *ninety*. Lower the book just so," she added, holding her hand at a distance from her face that Penvale could not fathom being conducive to reading.

He did as instructed and could tell at a glance that there wasn't the slightest chance he'd be able to make out the majority of the words on the page. Rather than admit this, he instead asked, "What book is this, anyway?"

"*Northanger Abbey*—by the author of *Pride and Prejudice*, which you so admire." She paused, an expression approaching glee flitting across her face. Based on his acquaintance with her thus far, Penvale could not imagine anything good following such a look. "Why don't you read it?"

"I wouldn't want to take it away from you whilst you are immersed in it," Penvale said hastily.

Jane wasn't going to allow him to escape that easily. "Oh, I've already read it—it was one of the books I purchased in London and read on the trip back to Cornwall. I can give you this one and a couple of her others to choose between. There's another one I acquired in town, *Persuasion*, that I've just finished, and it's *most* romantic."

"I don't really—" he tried again, and again was interrupted.

"But how can you possibly know you dislike novels if you've never read one?" Her smile was smug, and she was meeting his eyes directly—something he hadn't realized was so rare until he experienced the electric spark of her gaze locking with his.

"I've never been drawn and quartered, and yet I feel fairly confident I would not enjoy that experience," he shot back.

"*I* might enjoy witnessing it, though, if you continue insulting Miss Austen in such a way," she said sweetly, and he grinned before he could stop himself. He saw a flicker of surprise on her face at the sight.

"Say I humor you and read one of Miss Austen's books," he said, leaning back in his armchair as he spoke, slanting a lazy sideways glance at her. "What will you do for *me?*"

"What do you mean?" she asked, her expression guarded.

"If I read one of your bloody books and I don't enjoy it—if I am proved correct after all—what will you forfeit?"

Jane colored slightly, and Penvale realized that her thoughts had taken a much more lascivious turn than his own. Interesting.

"I don't think I need consider anything for this possibility," she said after a moment, "because it isn't going to happen."

"You seem awfully certain."

"That is because I have read a novel before, and therefore I know what you've been missing. However," she added, raising a hand to forestall any protest on his part, "in the interest of fair play, let's say that when we host your friends this spring, I shall smile angelically at your sister every moment we are in the same room."

Penvale let out an incredulous laugh. "I should dearly love to see you attempt this. I'll remember to ask her to be particularly vexing."

"You assume this will ever come to pass," she retorted, but she regarded him thoughtfully as she spoke. She was silent for a moment and then added, "You and your sister . . . you seem like . . . friends."

"I suppose that's what we've become, in some ways," he said, considering. "She's five years younger than I am, but the older she got, the smaller that gap seemed. She always knew exactly what she wanted out of life—to escape our aunt and uncle's home—and she accomplished it as quickly as possible once she made her debut. She married her first husband when she was only eighteen. I suppose I rather . . . failed her." He'd never given voice to this thought—one that had occasionally lingered at the back of his mind from time to time—had never considered sharing it with anyone. How odd that he should now share it with Jane, of all people.

"How old were you when she married, twenty-three?" Jane asked. "And, I gather, without much fortune of your own? I don't see how there's much you could have done to help her. She needed the protection of a rich husband, and she found one."

"I suppose I always treated her as more of an equal—as someone who knew her own mind—than as a younger sister to protect. I don't think she would have wanted it any other way, but I was so busy getting a seat at any table playing a high-stakes game of cards, I doubt I'd have noticed if she did." He could hear the note of bitterness in his own voice—the scorn for the boy he'd been back then.

"It was years ago, I imagine," she said.

"Nearly six," he confirmed.

"Well, it hardly seems fair to hold the man you were six years ago to the standards of the man you are today. You've grown up. Your sister seems very happy in her second marriage, so it all turned out well."

"I suppose," Penvale said, a bit startled—he had not expected such a response from a woman who spent at least half their time together glaring at him.

Their eyes were still locked, something she seemed to notice at the same moment, for she hastily averted her gaze and nodded at the book sitting on his lap.

"I'll look forward to seeing how you get on with that, in any case." Her voice was deliberately light, the moment for sharing confidences clearly over. She left him soon afterward, making an excuse about needing to consult with Mrs. Ash about something, leaving Penvale to his thoughts.

It was only then, staring into the crackling fire in the silence of the room, that he realized it had been entirely one-sided as far as exchanging confidences went. Jane had glimpsed a side of him that he didn't often show, while he was none the wiser about the person who lurked beneath her scowls.

And it was with a faint pang of unease that he realized that he was actually growing curious to learn who, precisely, that woman might truly be.

Chapter Seven

It was a particularly dreary evening, and all was right in Jane's world. She was tucked up in the most worn armchair before the fireplace in the small sitting room attached to her bedroom, a book in hand—this one, written by "A Lady of Ill Repute," was very lurid indeed—and she was just contemplating ringing for a cup of warm milk from the kitchens when, without so much as a knock in warning, the door that connected her suite of rooms with Penvale's opened, and he poked a very irritated head around it.

"What was that?" he demanded.

Jane turned a page of her book. "What was what?"

Penvale regarded her with incredulity. "The *noise*," he said after a moment's silence. "It sounded like someone just dropped an elephant upstairs."

Jane turned another page despite not having read a single word on the previous page. "I didn't hear anything."

Penvale—who by this point was craning his head up at the ceiling as if expecting the answer to materialize there—cast a doubtful look at the walls, which were papered in a delicate blue toile. "I suppose the walls are fairly thick," he conceded.

"And if you heard a noise directly above your room, there's no reason at all that I should have heard it," Jane added, hoping her voice sounded coolly rational. Of course she had heard it—the walls weren't *that* thick, and his elephant comparison had not been entirely inaccurate—but she had already decided not to seem too eager to believe there was something strange afoot, lest Penvale grow suspicious. She had already learned from the experience with her former guardian that she needed to be careful not to take things too far. It was all a rather wearying balancing act—no one had told her that enlisting the help of the household staff of a country estate to stage an escalating series of supposedly supernatural events was so exhausting.

She really should ring for that warm milk.

"I am going to find out what the devil is going on," Penvale announced.

Jane did not have very much experience with the male sex, but what she had gleaned from her reading had informed her that they did seem to have an unnatural fondness for plunging headfirst into every situation, determined to get to the bottom of whatever was afoot. To Penvale's credit, Jane was forced to admit that this did not seem to be his habit, but his usual calm rationality had apparently deserted him.

He even looked a bit disheveled. This was rather shocking; in her entire acquaintance with him, she had seen him look untidy only on the morning she had flung a damp cloth at his head. And even Jane was forced to concede that he could not be entirely blamed for that under the circumstances. But just now he was standing before her in a shirt and breeches, a dark blue banyan clearly tossed on at the last minute for propriety's sake; even with it, Jane could see quite a bit more of his chest than was strictly proper. And his hair—that peculiar hair of his, not quite blond or brown but somewhere in between—was ever so slightly mussed.

The sight of him like this felt more intimate than it should. Jane felt as though she were catching a glimpse of a version of him that she had no right to observe.

"Jane?" Penvale asked, and there was something in his tone that made her think this was not the first time he'd said her name.

She blinked, realizing she'd been so lost in her thoughts that she'd been staring at the sliver of his bare chest visible to her for at least a minute.

"Jane," he repeated, amusement evident in his voice this time, and she quickly pulled her gaze upward to meet his.

"I'll come with you," she said, chiefly to say something before he had the chance to. She rose, only belatedly remembering that she had no dressing gown at hand, though considering that her nightgown had all the seductive appeal of a nun's habit, she supposed it was not too much of an impropriety.

Penvale's thoughts apparently lay along similar lines. "Do you own any nightgowns that don't look like . . . that?" he asked.

"Like what?"

"Like their specific objective is to ward off anyone of the male persuasion who might wish to become better acquainted with their wearer?"

"This nightgown's wearer, as it happens, has no interest in getting 'better acquainted' with anyone," Jane said, though this was perhaps not *entirely* true. Her eyes flicked back to the sliver of his bare chest.

"Well, if she wears it often enough, she won't have any worries on that score," Penvale said, but there was something in his expression that made her think he didn't really mean it.

Her skin prickled under his regard, and she did with this sensation precisely what she did with any other feeling that she didn't completely understand: She ignored it.

"Shall we?" she asked.

"Wait a moment," he said, and crossed to the mantel, where he picked up the rather heavy-looking candelabra that sat there.

Jane frowned. "Do you think you'll need a weapon?" she asked. This could be a good or bad sign, depending—she wanted him to be uneasy, after all, so his desire to arm himself seemed promising. On the other hand, her aim was for him to think that the source of Trethwick Abbey's trouble was supernatural in origin, and while Jane was certainly not an expert, she didn't believe that blunt force was effective against ghosts.

"No," Penvale said dryly. "I think we'll need light." He cast a significant look out the window to the dark sky. "As it is night, you understand."

"Right," she agreed a bit feebly.

Candelabra in hand, he walked to the door and turned to her, repeating her words: "Shall we?"

A couple of minutes later, they were side by side in the doorway of a spare room on the third floor, staring at a wardrobe which had been upended onto its side.

"That's . . . odd," Jane said. She had to play this carefully—she didn't want to give the impression that she was trying to lead him to any particular conclusion, but instead merely hoped that he was intelligent (or at least observant) enough to notice a couple of carefully considered details.

"Wardrobes of that size don't spontaneously tip over," Penvale said, frowning as he entered the room. He glanced down at his feet, about to take another step, and then paused. "And look—there aren't any footprints."

He pointed down at the floor where, sure enough, the dust at his feet lay undisturbed. Jane felt quite pleased with herself—this had been her idea. She'd pointed out that ghosts couldn't very well leave footprints, as she and Mrs. Ash had been going over the specifics of the plan. When Mrs. Ash had suggested they clean the entire room beforehand to eliminate any dust, Jane instead struck upon the idea of enlisting the help of McGinty, one of the stable hands who had often mentioned his eagerness to play a role in the scheme— and who was, crucially, famous across the county for his height. He'd been able to take a long enough step into the room so that his footprint would be in the section of dust on the floor that would be disturbed by the impact from the wardrobe. Then all he had to do was hop back out without brushing away any of the remaining dust. It had been rather clever, Jane thought, and she was pleased that Penvale had noticed.

He shook his head after a moment. "Someone must have been in here," he pronounced.

"But if there aren't any—"

"Wardrobes do not simply topple over of their own accord," he informed her a bit shortly, and she was happy to detect a faint note of frustration in his voice.

"No," she agreed slowly.

"So, logically, someone on staff must have pushed it." He said this with the air of a man who believed that if he spoke calmly and logically enough, everything around him would fall in line with his reasoning.

"Unless . . ." Jane trailed off, biting her lip.

Penvale fixed her with an impatient look. "Unless?"

"Well." Jane folded her hands neatly before her. "It's just . . . there have been so many odd things. Lately."

"Jane." Penvale shook his head. "You cannot possibly think—what, that there's truly some sort of *ghost* lurking in the halls of Trethwick Abbey?" There was an edge of laughter to his voice, and Jane was suddenly very, very determined to see this man unsettled.

"You haven't been here," she retorted. "You don't know what it's like—the long nights, the wailing winds. The moon obscured by clouds. Shadows everywhere. It's downright eerie."

"You've just described a series of weather patterns," he said dryly. "Hardly evidence of a supernatural presence."

"If you can find a member of the household staff who mysteriously doesn't leave any footprints when they walk, I'd be delighted to hear all about it," Jane shot back.

Penvale crossed his arms over his chest, watching her for a moment. Jane darted a glance at his face and saw that his expression was a cross between amused and . . . pensive, somehow. He was regarding her as though uncertain whether to take her seriously. She scowled back at him.

After a long moment, he sighed. "All right. I won't jump to any conclusions about any of the servants—"

Jane breathed a soft sigh of relief.

"—*if*," he added, and she froze, instantly on guard once more, "you will agree to conduct a thorough search of the house with me tomorrow."

She regarded him suspiciously, then offered a stiff nod. "All right, then."

TO SWOON AND TO SPAR

"Excellent." He rubbed the bridge of his nose, his expression suddenly weary. "Then for now, let's see our way back to bed." He gestured in the direction of the door, allowing Jane to pass through it ahead of him, but she did not miss the long, considering glance he gave the wardrobe and the thick layer of dust on the floor before he followed her.

Chapter Eight

It was with an extra spring in her step the next morning that Jane asked Hastey to dress her in one of the new gowns she'd acquired in town—this one made of a fetching red wool, with a cape to match. She had slept well the night before, the evening's excitement sufficiently wearying to ensure a deep, dreamless slumber, and she was eager to continue with her plans. She hastened downstairs to breakfast only to find that Penvale had already dined and vanished; she was just lingering over a final cup of tea after eating when he appeared with ruddy cheeks and the smell of cold sea air clinging to his coat.

"Where have you been?" she asked as he dropped into the seat next to her, leaning forward to fill a cup with coffee from the fresh pot that had just been placed before him on the table.

"Walking," he said. "The cliff path needs some attention—some of the gravel is eroding, and it's a bit dangerous in spots. I'll speak to Cresswick about it."

"That's very industrious of you," she said slowly, taking a sip of tea.

Penvale gave her an inscrutable look. "It's my estate," he said. "It's my responsibility to keep it in good condition."

Jane took another sip of tea to hide whatever expression was on her face. She had not expected, upon meeting him in town, that he would care so much for all the small details that running Trethwick Abbey would entail, and for the people who worked on its land. She'd thought he wanted the house simply because it was his birthright; she had not considered the possibility that he might care for it beyond the status it conferred. This thought made her decidedly uneasy.

Penvale did not seem to find her silence odd. He set his cup down with a clatter and asked, "Do you still wish to help me search the house?"

Jane, avoiding his eyes, merely nodded.

A quarter of an hour later, they were wandering through a series of empty bedrooms on the third floor, Penvale having suggested they begin at the top of the house and work their way down. The attic had offered little of interest, being largely empty; Penvale had looked around the room with a poorly concealed eagerness that soon faded upon taking in its bare state, and Jane had filed this away in the growing mental compartment in which she kept all the things about her new husband that she did not yet understand.

Now they wandered through room after room full of furniture covered by sheets. Mr. Bourne had not been fond of entertaining, and Jane thought it likely that the last time these rooms had been occupied was when the previous viscount and viscountess were still living.

"We'll need to air these out before we host in the spring," Penvale said, recalling Jane from her thoughts with an unpleasant jolt.

"Host," she repeated slowly, mentally cursing; she'd been attempting to put Penvale's sister's promise (or, as Jane viewed it, threat) out of her mind.

"Yes, host," he replied, glancing over his shoulder at her. "You haven't forgotten my friends were planning to visit?"

"Of course not," Jane said. Wishfully attempting to ignore it, more like. "Do you know how long they intend to stay?"

"It's not as though I've sent them an invitation and planned a full itinerary." There was laughter evident in his voice, and Jane stiffened at the sound. It was too familiar from her years at school, when she could never say the right thing or act the right way.

"Why don't you go visit them in town once the Season begins?" she suggested desperately.

"Trying to get rid of me so soon, dear wife? I'm wounded." Some of the laughter faded from his voice when he caught sight of whatever was written upon her face. Jane frowned slightly, not comfortable with the thought that he'd gleaned some of her discomfort from her expression.

"Did you dislike them so much, then?" he asked her more quietly. "I know they can be a bit overwhelming at times—bloody irritating, too—"

There was something in his voice, some forced lightness, that told Jane her response was more important to him than she might have expected.

"I didn't dislike them," she blurted, which was true, for the most part—there had been an awful lot of them, but they'd seemed kind enough and genuinely fond of Penvale. Strict honesty, however, compelled her to add, "Your sister is a bit . . . difficult."

The lines around Penvale's mouth deepened, almost as if he were suppressing a smile. "Diana can be charming when she wants to be and quite lethal otherwise."

Jane hesitated. "She seems protective of you."

This earned an eye roll. "Now that she and Jeremy have settled down to matrimonial bliss, she was hoping I would be her new project."

"Oh." Jane strove to keep her voice neutral before adding, "I take it marrying your uncle's ward solely to purchase a house that should have been yours to begin with was not precisely what she had in mind."

"No," Penvale said bluntly. "But quite frankly, I don't really care. Diana has her life, and she's very happy now, and I'm happy that she's happy, but she can't always understand that what makes *her* happy and what makes other people happy aren't necessarily the same thing." He turned, gesturing at the dusty, gloomy room, and at the view of the windswept hills visible through the windows lining one wall. "Diana would go mad somewhere as remote as this, far away from parties and gossip and her friends—from all the entertainments of town."

"And you won't?" Jane asked skeptically. He hadn't been in Cornwall long, and they had the rest of a lonely winter ahead of them.

"I won't," he said simply.

Jane felt a trickle of unease at the quiet determination in his voice. She had spent so much time worrying about *how* she was going to frighten him away that she'd not paused to consider whether it was right of her to do so.

"And so," he continued before she could ponder this further, "I want to host my friends here—show them the place I've talked about for so long. Prove to them that it was worth it."

Jane did not think of her husband as a terribly expressive man. She had initially thought him a typical society gentleman—or, rather, what she imagined such a man to be: overly polished, idle, entirely lacking in substance. However, the more time she spent in his presence, the more she came to realize that her assessment wasn't quite right. But he was not prone to showing great feeling, so to see him animated when he spoke of Trethwick Abbey—well, she took notice. In that moment, he did not at all resemble the gentleman she had met in that drawing room in London.

And then, belatedly, his words registered.

Prove to them that it was worth it.

It being her marriage, her presence here at what was now his house, not hers. It had never been hers.

"Fine," she said in her frostiest tone, because she had learned long ago that safety lay in that voice, the one that made her sound cold and unapproachable and distant. The one that hinted at nothing of what she might actually feel. "We will host them, then, in the spring, once it's warmer and the roads are passable." She glanced up to meet his eyes. "I expect you'll want to visit them in London, too?" Having been raised in the countryside in a family of a lesser status than Penvale's, she was not entirely certain what gentlemen did during the Season, if they were not in the market for a wife. It occurred to her that Penvale, as a viscount, must have a seat in the House of Lords, and—with a certainty that would have shocked her a fortnight earlier—she was suddenly sure that he attended sessions of Parliament. She was coming to realize that he was not the sort of man to neglect a responsibility.

"Yes," Penvale said a bit distractedly, having resumed his thorough inspection of the room—a fruitless one, as Jane well knew, since there was nothing here that might tip him off as to what was truly afoot. "I expect I'll want to spend some time in town. Parliament will be in session, and I'll want to meet with my man of business, stay at Bourne House . . ."

Live his real life, Jane thought but did not say aloud. She did not know whether he used the singular when discussing these plans out of habit or specific intent—not that it mattered to her either way. She hated London and was perfectly content to be left to her own devices in Cornwall.

Just as if she'd never married at all.

"Shall we continue?" he asked, interrupting her thoughts, and she gave a distracted nod, still so wrapped up in what he'd just said that she didn't even muster an obligatory frown when he took her arm to lead her down to the second floor. She gave herself a stern mental shake as they made their way from room to room, reminding herself that she needed to keep her wits about her. When they entered her morning room, she held her breath, waiting to see if he might notice any of the signs of her plans that were evident in the room, but while he made a fairly thorough examination, he did not pause at any point, and Jane exhaled slowly. He really did need spectacles. From her morning room, they went down to his study on the first floor, and she noticed him straighten slightly as they entered.

"Is something amiss?" she asked cautiously. He had, after all, spent considerably more time here than he had spent in her morning room, and it seemed far likelier that he might notice something unusual about this room now that he was taking the time to examine it carefully.

He shook his head, surveying his surroundings. After a moment, he said, "The other day, when I was in here . . . I felt as though I were being watched."

Jane lifted a brow. "From the windows?"

He shook his head again. "No. From somewhere within the room."

Jane made a show of examining the room slowly. "But . . . there's nowhere for anyone to hide."

Penvale exhaled a frustrated breath. "I know. That's the same conclusion I came to."

Jane began to make a circuit of the room; as she approached a certain section of the bookshelves lining much of the walls, she slowed her pace, hoping he would not notice if she lingered. A quick glance confirmed that the crack in the shelves was not visible even at this distance—whoever had designed this feature of the house had done a very thorough job.

Jane then took several steps along the shelves, casting a quick glance over her shoulder to confirm that Penvale's attention was directed elsewhere—indeed, he was staring out the window, his arms crossed, his brow furrowed slightly as if in thought. At some point, he had rolled up his sleeves, baring an expanse of forearm that Jane willed her eyes not to linger on.

Then, quick as lightning, she reached out, flung a book off the shelf, and shrieked.

Jane was not naturally a shrieker. She had always prided herself on her cool nerves. She had to admit, though, that in the moment, it was rather satisfying—particularly when it caused Penvale to career around, a half-uttered curse escaping his lips.

Exhaling shakily, Jane pressed a dramatic hand to her chest as Penvale turned to face her.

"What the—"

"That book!" She pointed dramatically at the volume in question, lying innocuously on the Persian rug. She considered allowing her fingers to tremble slightly, then decided against it. Best not to take it too far.

Penvale followed the direction of her extended hand, then glanced back up at her, frowning. "It is . . . a book," he offered. "I understood you to be fond of them."

Jane suppressed a sigh. "It—it *flung itself off the shelf*," she declared dramatically. She was not a natural actress, but even she could deliver a single line somewhat convincingly.

Penvale's frown deepened, and he crossed the room quickly to retrieve the book. He scrutinized it—at a very close distance, Jane thought with an internal snort—and then raised his eyebrows. "It appears to be a book about Bloody Mary."

Jane was perfectly well aware of this, as she had not selected the volume at random. "Do . . . do you know if anyone in your family was subject to persecution under her reign?" she asked.

Penvale's brows inched higher. "Are you suggesting that the ghost of a long-dead Bourne ancestor who was fervently devoted to the Protestant cause is now flinging books around three hundred years later because . . . er, because *why*, exactly?"

"I don't know," Jane hedged. She, admittedly, had not given this narrative very much thought, merely seized the likeliest tome to inspire a ghost's displeasure. "I'm not an expert on the religious history of your family."

"Nor, I assure you, am I." Penvale sounded amused as he approached her with the book in hand, then reached out to replace it on the shelf.

"Perhaps your own sinful ways have sparked the ire of a more zealous spirit lingering about the house," Jane suggested, adopting an impressively pious tone, considering she'd never in her life made it through an entire church service without nodding off.

"Let me be certain I understand this," Penvale said, gazing down at her. This close, the difference in their heights was more evident; Jane had to crane her neck slightly to look up at him. His eyelashes were unfairly long, she thought. She noticed that they were a shade lighter than his hair; she noticed, too, that he had precisely three freckles on the bridge of his nose, so faint that she'd never spotted them before. He went on, "You believe that there is a ghost of some unknown religious affiliation lurking in Trethwick Abbey, flinging books around in order to encourage . . . more regular church attendance?"

When he put it like that, Jane had to admit it didn't sound very convincing. Perhaps it was best to abort this attempt at a narrative for their ghost for the moment.

"Well," she said, "I can't pretend to understand the thoughts of a *ghost*, Penvale. I'm not certain they're known for being terribly logical."

"Indeed," he said, crossing his arms again; once more, Jane's eyes were drawn to those accursed forearms. This was extremely irritating. "So perhaps, rather than attempting to comprehend the motives of the"—a skeptical pause—"ghost, we should instead be asking ourselves how the book landed on the floor in the first place."

Jane risked eye contact. She didn't detect outright suspicion in his gaze, which was reassuring; she had known she was taking a risk, attempting something when it was only the two of them in the room, but he did not give the impression of a man about to interrogate her.

"I don't understand it," he admitted, a rueful note in his voice. She could tell that it pained him to admit this, since he was the sort of man who valued calm, rational thought above all else. He didn't like something without an obvious logical explanation. Jane felt oddly pleased to have been the cause of his discomposure.

"Nor do I," she ventured, but he barely seemed to hear her, lost in his own thoughts.

"I don't understand it," he repeated, "but I intend to, at all costs."

He returned to his inspection of the room then, leaving Jane to trail behind him, making a show of doing the same. All the while, she could not help a slightly uneasy thought from crossing her mind: This man might not be so easy to scare away.

Chapter Nine

A week later, Penvale was working in his study after dinner when he heard a faint *tap, tap, tap* against the window.

His desk was situated so that his back was to the set of windows that lined one wall, offering a view of the foggy green hills to the east of the estate. At the noise, Penvale started slightly, the movement sufficient to cause an ink blot to bloom on the letter he was writing, and he sighed in irritation as he turned to look behind him. Given that it was winter, it had been dark for hours, and Penvale had to lean close to the window, his hands cupped around his eyes and pressed against the glass to block the light from his study and offer any view of whatever may lay beyond.

After a moment's futile squinting into the darkness, he decided perhaps the wind had knocked a pebble into the glass, and he turned back to his desk. He stared down at the letter—one to his solicitor in London, asking him to look into revising the leases of his tenant farmers to offer more favorable terms (his uncle had evidently revised the longstanding leases a few years earlier, when they had come up for renewal, and while this had netted a handsome profit for the estate, Penvale could not in good conscience allow the new leases to continue, though the change would be something of a strain on the estate's finances, at least in the short term). He grimaced at the blot of ink, debating whether he could be bothered to start the letter anew, when, once more, there was a *tap, tap, tap.*

He dropped his pen entirely this time, rising from his seat and turning to try to catch a glimpse of anything in the blackness beyond the window. But just as soon as the noise had commenced, it ceased once more, leaving Penvale standing with his face pressed to the cold glass, unable to see much of anything, the only sounds the ticking of the clock on the mantel and the crackling of a fire in the grate.

Tick, tick, tick.

Penvale stared into the blackness for another long moment, suddenly conscious of how he, well lit by the candles and firelight in his study, must be perfectly visible to anyone lurking in the darkness outdoors, and he felt the hairs on the back of his neck rise at the thought.

Tick, tick, tick.

And then, without warning: a bloodcurdling scream.

One that came not from beyond the windows but within the very walls of the house.

Penvale whirled around, his heart pounding a ragged beat in his chest. An empty room—a crackling fire—a ticking clock—

And nothing else. Nothing he could see that could have produced such a sound; no hidden alcove in which someone could have hidden.

One thing he knew for certain: He could not possibly be the only person who had heard that scream. He crossed the room in a few long strides, then set off down the corridor. He had not made it far before he stumbled across a pair of maids, both looking pale and wide-eyed and terrified.

"My lord—the scream—" one of them gasped, her voice tremulous.

"I heard it," he assured her. "Have you seen Lady Penvale?"

"I believe she is upstairs in her morning room," the other maid said, then added, "My lord, do you think there is truly a spirit haunting us?"

Penvale suppressed a sigh. "Not if I have anything to say about it," he told her, and continued down the hall before she could say anything else. He rounded a corner but could make it no farther, letting out a faint grunt as curved, soft flesh collided with his chest and stomach. The glossy black hair provided quick identification. He reached out and seized her by the shoulders to steady her. "Jane."

She looked up at him in surprise. "What are you doing?" she asked in tones of deepest suspicion, making Penvale feel like a burglar in his own home.

"Looking for you, actually," he said, relishing the moment that followed in which she had no satisfactory reply. "Did you hear that scream just now?"

"I did," she said. "It's why I was running. Do you know where it came from?"

Penvale resisted the temptation to offer the first explanation that came to mind—the one that, logically, he knew couldn't be true: that the scream had come from the house itself. Because that was absurd. Houses didn't scream. Humans did.

"I'm not certain," he said grimly. "But I intend to find out. Don't you think it's time we questioned the staff ourselves?"

Jane bit her lip, looking uncertain. "They all think it's a ghost, you know."

"*Most* of them think it's a ghost," he corrected.

"So you truly don't think—" Here she broke off with a shake of her head.

"I don't think . . . ?" he prompted, watching as she searched the corridor around them with an anxious expression, as though certain that a ghost was going to emerge from one of the walls at any moment and bid them good evening.

"You don't think there's even the slightest chance that there might *actually* be something . . . well . . ." She trailed off again, as if searching for the right word. "*Unnatural* afoot?" Her gaze flicked up to him then, fleeting. Their eyes locked for a moment, hers seeming to search his for something, asking some question that he did not know how to answer.

"I do not," he said firmly—more firmly than he would have been able to answer that question five minutes ago, standing in his empty study with his heart racing and the window at his back, acutely conscious of how truly isolated they were out here, on a remote Cornish cliff. In the wake of that shriek, he would have believed all sorts of things about this house.

But the moment had passed. He'd always prided himself on being a practical man, and he had no intention of changing that now. So he added, "Which is why it is time to question the servants."

She frowned. "I don't know—"

Penvale reached out to take her hand, bringing an abrupt halt to her words. Her hand felt small in his, he thought; where his thumb rested on her wrist, he could feel her pulse tapping against his skin like a bird's wing. "Jane. There must be some sort of rational explanation for what is occurring under this roof, and it stands to reason that someone within the household is responsible. Who else would have the opportunity? I intend to work out who that person is."

Jane was very still for a moment, her gaze downcast at her hand, still engulfed in his. Her fingers curled slightly against his palm. "Fine," she said at last. "But I don't want you to speak to them alone—I'd like to be there, too." She glanced up at him. "You'll do your best proud

London gentleman act, and they won't tell you anything, and you'll ruin any chance of learning something useful."

"I wonder that you agreed to marry me at all," he said, feeling her words like a brush of nettles against his skin, surprising in their sting, "if this is your impression of me. Last I checked, I was still capable of basic human interaction without making a complete mess of things, which is more than I can say for you, based on what I've observed."

She slipped her hand from his grasp.

No sooner had the words left his mouth than he regretted them; he'd been so caught up in offering some sort of rebuttal, lessening the unexpected bite of her insult, that he'd stopped thinking too hard about what he was actually saying.

The truth was, he wasn't accustomed to having to think much about anyone's feelings other than his own. For so long, his only family had been Diana, his closest friends two men who had known him practically since boyhood. These were people whose presence he took for granted and about whom he'd never wasted much time worrying. He was not in the habit of keeping a mistress, either—mistresses were an unnecessary expense that a man in his position could ill afford. He supposed that once he felt assured of the estate's finances, he could afford a mistress at last, since he'd no longer be hoarding every spare penny, but the thought of such an arrangement now that he was married to Jane seemed unexpectedly distasteful.

Jane.

Jane, whom he had just grievously insulted without really meaning to, because he'd never learned not to be careless when it came to others' feelings. Or, at least, he'd never learned to be terribly *careful*. In truth, he'd spent a fair amount of time congratulating himself on managing to acquire a home and a wife without having to change much of anything about his life other than his residence. And he realized all at once that this was . . . insufficient.

He, at the moment, was proving to be an entirely insufficient husband.

He looked at her, and her face was curiously unreadable, nothing in her expression giving evidence that his words had affected her in any way. She wasn't quite meeting his eye, though, and it was only now that he realized he'd grown used to her doing so more frequently over the past few weeks.

"Jane. I apologize. I didn't mean that."

She crossed her arms. "Of course you meant it." There was something protective in her stance, and Penvale suddenly felt as though a great distance separated them, despite the fact that they stood only a foot apart.

"All right," he said. He knew somehow that sweet words would not serve him well in this moment—not that they ever did with Jane. "I did mean it. But I didn't mean to say it aloud, and certainly not like that, and I apologize."

She regarded him for a moment that stretched between them, growing tighter with each second that she did not speak. "All right," she said, echoing his words. "That was honest, at least." She nodded her head once, sharply. "I take it you'll let me join you for the interviews, then." She said this flatly, as if his response were not really in question; Penvale supposed that, under the circumstances, it wasn't.

"Fine," he said, pressing his lips into a firm line, acknowledging defeat. "Shall we begin tomorrow morning?"

After the second hour spent interviewing members of his staff, Penvale was beginning to get the impression that they didn't like him very much. There were only so many times a man could be gazed upon with abject wariness before he grew a touch concerned.

"Tell me," he said to Jane after a pair of kitchen maids departed, sparing warm smiles for her and solemn stares for him, "have I murdered someone recently and forgotten about it?"

Jane, who had a cup of tea raised halfway to her mouth, paused. "If you have, I'm even more concerned for your mental faculties than I am for your eyesight."

"Jane."

"Penvale."

"The staff seem terrified of me."

She waved a dismissive hand. "You're being hysterical."

"*Hysterical!* They look at me the way—" He broke off abruptly before he could finish that sentence.

"Yes?" she asked in a dangerous tone of voice.

"They look at me the way you do half the time," he said, throwing caution to the wind.

"And how is that?" she asked, her voice deceptively sweet—a sound that Penvale found rather chilling.

"As though you'd like to push me off the cliff path the next time we're on a walk together," he said quite honestly.

"We haven't *gone* on a walk together."

"And can you blame me, given the possible outcome?"

"Don't be absurd. If I were going to murder you, I'd work out something much sneakier and easier than pushing you off a cliff." She paused to consider. "Poison, for example, seems like it would work nicely."

"It's very odd that you and my sister don't get along, because you sounded remarkably like her just then," he said darkly, and was pleased to see her blanch.

"In any case," she said after a brief, appalled silence, "I think you are imagining things—I've not noticed anything out of the ordinary."

"Of course you haven't," Penvale said, exasperated. "They all love you. It's nothing but blissful smiles for you."

"Perhaps because I am not treating them like criminals," Jane said, frowning. "Do you have to commence the questioning the moment they enter the room?"

The room in question was the library, where they'd had a tray of tea and biscuits sent up to offer the servants some refreshment and perhaps put them more at ease, though it had not been a terribly successful strategy. The staff had seemed disconcerted to be offered food by their employers, as if they were guests invited to tea, and Penvale was beginning to wonder if the biscuits weren't doing more harm than good.

He leaned forward to select his third.

On top of all this, they'd managed to learn nothing of use—predictably, everyone had professed ignorance of the screaming and the tapping at the window and any other strange occurrences around the house. Penvale, lacking any evidence suggesting anyone's guilt, could hardly start in on accusations, but there was a persistent voice at the back of his head reminding him of one undeniable fact:

Houses simply did not haunt themselves.

"Who is left?" he asked wearily, feeling as though he'd come through several wars.

"Mrs. Ash, I believe." Jane consulted the list she had drawn up in her neat handwriting. "I think we've spoken to everyone else."

"Thank God," he muttered.

"Need I remind you that this was *your* idea? You've no right to complain."

"You're right," Penvale conceded, in part just to see the surprised expression that flickered across her face. "Shall we ring for her, then?"

This proved unnecessary, as the woman in question entered the room at that moment. "My lord, my lady," she said solemnly, curtseying. "Did you need me to fetch someone else?"

"No, thank you, Mrs. Ash," Penvale said politely. "Won't you take a seat? We were hoping we might have a few minutes of your time."

Looking as though she expected to be struck by lightning at any moment, their housekeeper lowered herself into an armchair opposite Penvale and Jane. She sat in it stiffly, looking exquisitely uncomfortable; evidently, Jane noticed this as well, for she leaned forward in her seat and said gently, "Mrs. Ash, may I pour you a cup of tea?"

The older woman's expression softened at these words, and something niggled within Penvale—some half-formed thought that had been lingering at the back of his mind, trying to bump its way to the front.

Jane was *different* when she spoke to the servants, he realized, and not in the unpleasant way that most aristocrats were when speaking to their social inferiors. The prickliness, the temper that always seemed so quick to spark whenever she was in conversation with him—those were absent. Her voice was soft, easy, in a way that it rarely was with him. Even her ever-present scowl was gone, replaced by a gentle smile. He did not understand her at all, this mysterious creature he had married, but he could not help thinking it reflected well upon her that she spoke to her servants with more kindness than she used when addressing her equals.

Though Penvale did still hold a cherished hope that she might one day converse with his friends and family with something less akin to open hostility.

Jane finished pouring a cup of tea for Mrs. Ash and leaned forward to hand it to her. Relaxing back in her chair, she said, "Lord Penvale is attempting to understand everything strange that has occurred at Trethwick Abbey of late, Mrs. Ash, and he would like to ask you a few questions."

"All right," Mrs. Ash said reluctantly, with the air of a woman about to attend her own funeral.

"I wonder if you might recall," Penvale began in a brisk tone that earned him a glare from Jane, "when, precisely, you first observed anything unusual occur."

Mrs. Ash made a great show of being deep in thought. "I suppose it was last summer," she said at last. "That was when we first heard the wailing."

"Wailing," Penvale repeated, curious. His uncle had not provided many specifics regarding the events that had led to his sudden desperation to sell the house.

"Oh, yes," Mrs. Ash said gloomily. Next to him, Jane shifted in her seat but did not say anything. "In the middle of the night, we first heard it—an uncanny sort of shrieking. It sounded as though it came from within the walls . . ." She trailed off, shaking her head.

"Hmm," Penvale said, regarding her steadily; this did, in fact, sound remarkably like what he had experienced the day before. He turned to his wife. "Jane, did you hear the noise?"

She looked surprised to be asked her opinion on the subject. "I . . . I did," she said, lifting her chin.

"And were you not alarmed, as my uncle presumably was?"

"I was," she agreed readily.

"But not so alarmed that it put you off the idea of living here?"

"I like to think that I am made of sterner stuff than that."

"Sterner stuff than my uncle, at least?" he asked.

"Yes." She met his eyes defiantly.

"I agree," he said simply, flashing a quick smile at her before turning back to his housekeeper. "What about you, Mrs. Ash?"

"My lord?"

"Were you not also alarmed? The noise you describe sounds terrifying indeed—one could hardly blame you for being spooked."

"Well, I thought it might be the wind at first—"

"But you no longer think that?"

"No, my lord. It quickly became clear that the wind was not to blame, when we kept hearing it on otherwise quiet nights."

"So what, then?" he pressed.

"Then there was the matter of the bloody christening gown." She said this with a degree of ghoulish satisfaction that Penvale found somewhat disturbing.

"I beg your pardon?" he asked, nonplussed.

"Oh, yes," Mrs. Ash said with relish. "The master was going to bed one night—late, naturally," she added with contempt, as though this were some sort of moral failure, and Penvale was at once glad that he had adopted country hours since arriving at Trethwick Abbey. "And suddenly, he was yelling loud enough to wake everyone in the house, because . . ." She paused dramatically.

Penvale caught himself *just* as he was about to lean forward in his seat.

"He claimed that there was a christening gown in the bed," Mrs. Ash finished.

Penvale blinked. "A christening gown."

"They go on babies, when they are christened," Mrs. Ash explained helpfully. "At a church," she added, clearly doubtful that a godless man from town could possibly know anything of this ritual.

"Thank you, I am indeed familiar with the custom," Penvale said.

"And there was *blood* on it," Mrs. Ash added.

"Blood," Penvale repeated. "How much blood, precisely?"

Mrs. Ash rubbed her hands together eagerly. "Enough."

"Enough for . . . what?" Penvale was growing more perplexed by the moment.

"Enough to give the master quite a fright," Mrs. Ash said with grim satisfaction.

Penvale turned to Jane, who was calmly eating a ginger biscuit despite the mildly stomach-turning nature of the conversation. "My uncle found a *bloody christening gown in his bed?*"

"Allegedly," Jane said coolly, taking another bite.

"What the devil do you mean, 'allegedly'?" Penvale asked, growing more horrified the longer he contemplated the matter. "Either he did or he didn't, I don't see how there could be much ambiguity about it."

"His valet disposed of it, so no one else saw the blood," Mrs. Ash explained. "He left it for the maids to scrub the following day, but by the next morning . . ."

"The blood was gone," Jane finished.

"Clean and dry," Mrs. Ash intoned.

"Out, damned spot!" Jane added helpfully.

Penvale turned to her, incredulous. "Do you mean to imply that you think my uncle had some sort of mental break in which he started imagining bloody spots where there were none?"

Jane shrugged, seeming remarkably unconcerned. "I wouldn't dare venture a guess," she said meekly, leaning forward to select another biscuit. "In any case, that was when he decided to sell the house and go to London."

"I can't imagine why," he murmured. At that moment, however, out of the corner of his eye, he thought he detected something decidedly odd in Jane's expression. He couldn't define it specifically, but he had the impression that she was watching him very carefully. Almost as if she wanted to see how he would react.

And, all at once, deep in his bones, he knew: Jane *knew* something. Penvale was not much of an expert when it came to the ways of young, innocent Englishwomen, but he was absolutely certain that they did not sit calmly eating biscuits while mysterious, allegedly bloody christening gowns were discussed, not unless they knew something more was afoot. Now, her desire to help him search the house and interview the servants seemed more suspicious. Why did she suddenly wish to spend so much time in his company? It certainly could not be due to any great affection on her part.

Jane had lived at Trethwick Abbey for years, had come to know these servants—if she did know who the culprit was, her first instinct would not be to inform him, nor would it have been to enlighten his uncle, for whom she'd already mentioned her distaste. No, she would take pity on the person, try to persuade him or her to stop, perhaps, but with equal energy would attempt to ensure no consequences for the actions.

While Penvale was sympathetic to the dislike his servants might have felt for his uncle, his sympathy did have its limits. And he was discovering that one limit was a perhaps bloody christening gown in a bedchamber.

However, he did not say any of these thoughts to Jane—not yet.

He merely turned back to Mrs. Ash and said, "Is there anyone on staff that you have noticed behaving oddly?"

He half-listened as she shook her head and made a number of protestations about the upright moral character of every person in her employ; this was no more than he had expected, so he paid little mind to it. Instead, he thought about the woman sitting next to him and how he was going to convince her to tell him what she knew.

He recalled their earlier conversation and Jane's casual utterance: *We haven't* gone *on a walk together.*

It was, he thought, high time for that to change.

It was time he got to know his wife.

Chapter Ten

"Jane," Penvale said a few days later, "would you like to come with me into the village?"

Jane glanced up from her toast. Penvale was seated opposite her at the breakfast table, looking uncommonly cheerful, and she frowned slightly. She didn't know what could give him cause for good cheer this morning, since she was nearly certain that his sleep had been interrupted by a bit of eerie wailing the night before—*hers* certainly had been, though at least she'd had the advantage of knowing that the source of the wailing was Hastey, who had a taste for theatrics and had been alarmingly eager to take a turn playing the role of a mournful ghost.

And yet here he was at breakfast at his usual virtuous hour, despite the fact that it was a blustery, gray sort of day—the clouds in the distance looked as if they might even foretell snow.

"Why are you going into the village?" she asked.

"I thought to eat luncheon at the inn, just to make the villagers more familiar with me, and perhaps offer my custom at a few of the shops. I've visited on a couple of errands but have yet to spend much time there, and I thought I ought to remedy that."

St. Anne's, the seaside village closest to Trethwick Abbey, was intimately linked to the viscountcy and had been for generations. Penvale's land abutted the edge of the village, and the majority of its population relied in some fashion upon the largesse of the estate. For all that, Mr. Bourne had rarely ventured into the village and had never seemed overly concerned with what the villagers thought of him. Jane said as much to Penvale, and he frowned.

"I rather hope the standard of behavior I am being held to is somewhat higher than that of my uncle," he said curtly, pouring a splash of milk into his coffee, and Jane realized that she had offended him. Until that moment, she hadn't even realized that she had the power to do so.

"I . . . I didn't mean . . ." she began, the words awkward on her tongue. She wasn't accustomed to having to apologize to anyone, because she wasn't used to her words mattering enough that they would have the power to wound. She paused, took a breath. "I don't mean to compare you to your uncle—I am well aware that you're very different men." She hesitated. "Your uncle . . . I mean to say . . ." She sighed, frustrated that, as ever, the words would not come out in a configuration that matched what she felt. "I do not mind your company, most of the time," she said in a rush, surprising herself as soon as the words were out of her mouth. *That* wasn't what she'd meant to say at all.

And yet she thought that perhaps it might be true.

"We're not very good at this yet, are we?" Penvale asked. He'd remained silent, watching her carefully as she'd struggled to get her apology out. At some point, his mouth had quirked into an odd half-smile, and his gaze had warmed as she'd spoken. His eyes were hazel, more brown than green most days, but the flecks of green stood out to her this morning as she looked back at him, not feeling remotely tempted, for once, to look away.

"Neither one of us wanted this marriage," he continued, "and we're not making much of a success of it yet. We've both said things we didn't mean—or at least that we didn't mean in precisely the way that we said them—so let's call it even, shall we?"

"All right," she said slowly.

"If," he added, and she slumped back into her seat, waiting to see what his condition would be, "you come to the village with me today."

Jane, recognizing when a battle was lost—or no longer worth fighting—merely nodded.

St. Anne's was, Jane supposed, an exceptionally lovely little village, resembling nothing so much as a particularly idyllic scene from some sort of sentimental novel. It was all right, if one liked that sort of thing.

"That sort of thing" being narrow, winding cobblestone streets lined by whitewashed buildings set into a steep hillside that descended to a small cove. It was the sort of place where everyone knew everyone else, where families had run the same shops for generations, where it was impossible to so much as walk down the street without getting sucked into a series of seemingly endless exchanges of pleasantries and gossip.

It was, in other words, Jane's nightmare.

It was also entirely counterproductive to her purposes at the house. How much better it would have served her plans had St. Anne's been a grim, eerie sort of place, populated by buildings exclusively made of gray stone, plagued by a mysterious, improbably omnipresent mist. Instead, it looked downright cheerful today; the sun had even been disobliging enough to put in an appearance after the morning's clouds. An implausibly adorable, rotund cat sat in a shopwindow, flanked by a pair of oversize, exceptionally fluffy kittens. Somewhere, someone was baking something that smelled of cinnamon and sugar. Jane heard the distinct sound of a child's delighted giggle. A church bell chimed the quarter hour.

This was all highly distressing.

"Atmosphere," she muttered mournfully as she trailed her husband down one of the inconveniently picturesque streets. "What does one have to do to get a bit of *atmosphere* around here?"

"Did you say something, Jane?" Penvale asked, turning; seeing that she'd fallen behind, he paused, extending an arm as she reached his side. She took it reluctantly, determined not to notice its reassuring strength under her hand. How *dare* anything about him be reassuring? The nerve of the man.

"Nothing," she assured him sweetly, which—in a credit to his intelligence, inconvenient as that particular trait might be—he appeared to find unsettling.

"Are you all right?" he inquired as they paused to look at hats on display in a shopwindow. "You look a bit unwell."

"Perfectly fine," she said through gritted teeth, attempting something approaching a smile—an attempt that was evidently unsuccessful, as he paled slightly at the sight.

"I think frowning might be your best option, if that's what one of your smiles looks like."

"Lovely," she muttered, and that was the last word she spoke for quite some time as Penvale commenced their tour of the village.

At first it was tolerable. Jane would never use the word "charming" to describe Penvale—he was lacking in a certain easiness, a particular gleam in his eye and lilt to his smile. But he was compelling all the same, she realized. He spoke politely to everyone they met, real warmth evident in his voice, and he listened carefully to questions, answering as best he could any concerns they raised. She wondered that she had ever thought him a typical overly smooth aristocrat; there was nothing in his manner that suggested he thought himself superior to any of the villagers. He made no effort to hold himself at a remove, as might have been expected of a haughty lord from town.

At one point, a young mother struggling to wrangle a naughty toddler while also juggling an extremely chubby baby unceremoniously plopped said baby into Penvale's arms while she got a better grip on the would-be escapee. Penvale, who clearly had not been expecting to suddenly have an armful of baby, looked startled. He held the infant out before him and surveyed him.

"How do you do?" he asked the child solemnly.

"Eeeee," the baby responded.

Penvale looked helplessly at Jane, who shrugged.

"I don't speak baby," she told him.

"What am I supposed to do with it?" he asked.

"Try . . . cuddling it?" she suggested.

The look he gave her implied that she may as well have suggested climbing into bed with a lion, but he gingerly pressed the baby to his chest. He looked at Jane. "Now what?"

"I've seen people pat them before," she said helpfully. "On the back, I believe?" She reached out a finger to stroke the baby's fuzzy head, which was improbably soft.

Penvale patted the baby gently on the back. The baby made a sort of gurgling noise, which seemed promising.

"I think it likes that," Jane said encouragingly. A moment later, the baby spit up onto Penvale's shoulder, and he cast her a look of wounded betrayal as the mother—having wrestled her other child into submission—rushed back over to reclaim her younger offspring and offer a litany of apologies for the state of Penvale's jacket, which he waved off with good humor. Once the woman was out of sight, he removed a handkerchief from his pocket and attempted to wipe away the disturbing substance glistening on his shoulder.

"Have I got it all?" he asked, and Jane took the handkerchief from him, standing on her tiptoes to wipe the rest of it away.

"Not the sort of mess that handkerchief usually has to clean up," he said, giving her a grin that reminded her of the pirates from some of her books, and which made her nearly certain he'd just said something inappropriate that she didn't understand. She paused to consider the things she had gleaned from her reading and shook her head, reflecting that even those works had occasionally cast a bit of a veil over the proceedings. Sometimes being a woman—or a *lady*, at least—was very tiresome.

She had little time to dwell on this thought, given the whirlwind pace at which Penvale conducted their tour of the village. Following a lengthy conversation with Mrs. Rowe, the widow who ran the bakery and who did not stop badgering Penvale until he professed his preference for cinnamon buns (which she promised to have on offer the following week), Jane watched as Penvale fished a pencil stub and a small notebook out of his jacket pocket. He scribbled something hastily in the notebook.

"What are you writing?" she asked curiously.

"A note to myself to stop by the bakery next week for one of those buns," he said, pocketing the notebook. Jane looked at him for a long moment and he coughed, seeming almost embarrassed. "If she's going to the trouble of making them, the least I can do is stop by to purchase a few."

"You could send someone on staff to do it," Jane said.

"I could, I suppose," he agreed, offering her his arm once more.

But he wouldn't. Jane didn't know how she was so certain, but she knew without a doubt that he would come into the village to purchase the cinnamon buns himself.

For her part, Jane was doing her best—she answered questions that were asked of her, she made introductions when warranted. She wished desperately that she was better at asking questions, though—this was an aspect of conversation that had always given her some trouble. It wasn't that she was disinterested in the answers, merely that she could never think of the right thing to ask. It was so much easier when people just spoke unprompted, at length, and she could listen without much being expected of her. But this—trying desperately to think of things to inquire about, pleasantries to exchange . . .

It was exhausting.

Her interest was piqued at one point, however, when they stopped by the village's small school just as the children were fleeing in a disorganized horde, as though Lucifer himself were at their heels. When the crowd of small bodies had cleared, it revealed merely a frazzled-looking schoolmistress who appeared to be only a couple of years older than Jane and seemed in a decidedly foul mood. Jane, contrary creature that she was, rather appreciated this; it was nice to encounter at least one person in the village who didn't dissolve into paroxysms of delight at the sight of the viscount and his viscountess.

The schoolmistress gave a weary sort of sigh and bobbed a curtsey at them, her arms full of books. She had dark hair and eyes, a nose scattered with freckles, and a sharp look in her eyes that Jane noted with respect.

"My lord, my lady," she offered.

"Miss—" Penvale paused. "I apologize, but I don't think we've been introduced on my previous visits to the village, which now seems like a grievous oversight."

"Trevelyan," the lady supplied. "I was likely holed up attempting to instruct those monsters you just witnessed departing."

"They did seem rather . . . spirited," Penvale said diplomatically, stepping forward to relieve Miss Trevelyan of some books. "Where are you bound with these? We're happy to escort you there."

"Just to my cottage," Miss Trevelyan said with a grateful nod, turning to lock the door of the schoolhouse behind her. It was a small, rather ramshackle building with ivy creeping up its walls that Jane imagined was glorious to behold in the summertime. "Those are a few books from my personal collection that I brought in for the children to read, and we've finished with them."

Jane, who had thus far contributed nothing to the conversation, frowned as they set off along a narrow side street behind the schoolhouse. "Are the children in need of reading material, Miss Trevelyan?" she asked. The words sounded awkward and abrupt even to her own ears, but she was pleased she'd got them out nonetheless.

Miss Trevelyan glanced at her. "Always, Lady Penvale. The village doesn't have any sort of lending library, and the school's collection that I inherited from my predecessor was a bit pathetic, so I've been supplementing with a few of my favorites from when I was a girl."

"I have a number of books from my own childhood that I saved and brought with me to Cornwall," Jane said, the words tumbling out of her mouth before she realized what was happening. "I would be more than happy to bring them to you on my next visit to the village, if you would like them."

Miss Trevelyan smiled at her, the crease between her brows easing. "Thank you, Lady Penvale, that would be most welcome."

Jane felt oddly . . . pleased. It was nice, she reflected, to feel as though she had something to offer someone. Something to contribute.

And, even though she could not bring herself to admit it, equally nice was the flash of a smile, bright and fleeting, that Penvale gave her over his shoulder before he turned back and inclined his head to whatever Miss Trevelyan was saying.

By the time they had deposited Miss Trevelyan—and her books—at her small cottage on the outskirts of the village, the sun had already passed overhead and was beginning its slow descent over the course of the afternoon. Penvale suggested they stop for luncheon, and Jane, wearied by the day's activities so far—and the effort of keeping a somewhat pleasant expression on her face for so long—eagerly agreed.

"Would you like to use the private room, my lord?" the innkeeper asked upon their arrival at the village's lone inn, a respectable, timbered establishment in the center of St. Anne's. Jane saw Penvale hesitate—undoubtedly, he would prefer to mingle among the other patrons of the inn; after all, if the objective of this trip into the village was to see and be seen, there was little point in sequestering themselves in a private room to eat their meal. Jane was just mustering up the energy to attempt to look politely acquiescing when, with a glance at her, Penvale said, "Yes, please. A private room would be perfect."

Jane didn't say anything as they were led to a small room with windows facing out onto the bustling street before the inn, nor as the innkeeper departed with promises of ale (Penvale) and tea (Jane). It was only once they were alone again that Jane said—somewhat unenthusiastically—"We could have dined in the public room."

Penvale ignored this half-hearted suggestion. Instead, he fixed her with a steady look and said, with the air of a man who has made an important scientific discovery, "Jane. You're *shy*."

Instantly, Jane felt her cheeks warm. She glanced down at the wooden surface of the table, tracing the pattern of the grain with her index finger. "Congratulations," she said. "Do you want some sort of prize for working out something so blindingly obvious?" Penvale grinned, opening his mouth to reply, but Jane wasn't finished yet. "Of course I'm shy, any fool can see that. Have you truly only now realized it?"

Jane felt almost offended. Did he really pay her so little attention that it had taken him over a month of marriage to notice something so fundamental about her character?

Penvale was undeterred by her outburst. "I don't think it's as obvious as you think it is," he said. "I personally just thought you were misanthropic."

"Did you have to look that word up in the dictionary?" she asked him peevishly, trying her best not to be charmed when he let out a hoot of surprised laughter. The sound was nothing at all like what she would have expected to hear from him.

"I think people just think you're unfriendly," he said, leaning forward to rest his elbows on the table as he spoke. "But I watched you today—I could practically see you squirming when you were trying to think of something to say, or when the attention of the group landed on you." He laughed again, shaking his head. When he laughed, she noticed, the lines at the corners of his eyes, normally barely visible, deepened. She liked them and didn't like that she liked them. "I can't believe I've spent the last month thinking you hated me."

"If you continue this conversation much longer, I promise you I will."

He smiled at her. "I feel as though I should write to all of my friends and tell them not to worry."

Jane frowned. "Were they worried?"

The innkeeper returned at this point to give Penvale his ale and Jane her pot of tea, and Penvale waited until they were alone to respond. "Now that they've all settled down to matrimonial bliss, they were exceedingly concerned by the terms of our arrangement."

"Because ours was not a love match."

"There was that, yes, and the fact that they were somewhat convinced you actively despised me." He paused, his mouth twitching. "I can't imagine what could possibly have given them that impression."

Jane rolled her eyes as she poured a steaming cup of tea. "Yes, well, you've found me out, so they needn't fret."

"I'd already convinced myself that you didn't hate me," he assured her. "I'd simply come to the conclusion that you are like my sister and express affection primarily through antagonism. Indeed, under that assumption, I instead began to fear that you were desperately in love with me."

Jane regarded him coolly before giving up and allowing him a small smile. "You're funnier than you seem, you know," she informed him.

"Am I?"

"When I met you, you seemed a bit . . . detached, I suppose. Not the type of man to joke. You just seemed so desperately focused on Trethwick Abbey . . . almost as if that drowned out everything else."

He stared down into his drink. When he glanced back up at her, there was something raw and vulnerable in his expression that made Jane, in that moment, terribly grateful that she had grown comfortable enough around him not to avoid his eyes. It felt like a privilege, some sort of precious secret, to see his face like this.

"I suppose it did," he said quietly. "Drown out everything else, I mean. It's all I've wanted since my parents died. Diana was only five when it happened, so I don't think she remembers much about them or Trethwick Abbey, but I do. I remember my mother and father—I wanted to be just like my father. And then he was gone, and we were sent away from here to live with relations who didn't really want us, and I spent all my time just wishing—"

He broke off, and Jane offered hesitantly, "Wishing to come back?"

He shrugged helplessly. "What I really wanted was my old life back, but since that was impossible, I wanted the next best thing, and that was the estate. So as soon as I left Eton and went to Oxford, I started playing cards—it's one of the few acceptable ways for a gentleman of my standing to earn an income, and a bunch of foxed university lads were easy enough marks. By the time I left Oxford, I was good enough that it began to feel like a real possibility, that I really could win enough money to, if I was careful with it, amass enough of a fortune to buy Trethwick Abbey. And for years, I didn't think about much else."

"And now?" she asked.

"Now . . . ?"

"Now what do you think about?"

He was silent for a moment. "The house. Our mysterious ghost. How to ensure the estate remains profitable." Another pause, even longer. "How to avoid ruining the only thing I've ever truly wanted."

But what, Jane wondered suddenly, was he going to do now that he had it? Because his answer—all the thoughts that weighed on his mind—were not, she thought, enough to sustain a man for the rest of his life. He'd spent years with a single goal, but what did he want now?

She pondered this question as the innkeeper reappeared and presented them each with bowls of a hearty beef stew, along with a loaf of crusty bread. And she continued to ponder it as Penvale dove into his food like a man who'd been starved, rather than one she'd witnessed eat an entire rasher of bacon that very morning.

She was so lost in thought that it took her much longer to finish eating than it did him, and she looked up at one point to find that steady hazel gaze of his regarding her thoughtfully.

"What is it?" she asked, a bit self-conscious; she wondered how long he'd been watching her.

He shook his head, smiling slightly. "Would you like to go home?" he asked, ignoring her question entirely.

Her brow crinkled. "Don't you want to linger in the village? Meet more people?"

He shrugged, a lazy, effortless gesture that somehow encapsulated the comfort he felt in his own body that she had never felt in hers. "The village will still be here next week," he replied. "I've had enough for today."

Jane couldn't help but think that if she had not been with him, he would not have returned home so early.

Which meant he'd done it for her—because of whatever he'd observed of her that morning, whatever greater understanding he had gained.

And she wasn't at all certain how she felt about this fact.

Chapter Eleven

In light of recent events, Jane decided it was time to go on the offensive.

She had felt unsettled for a couple of days after their trip into St. Anne's and their lunchtime conversation, and she was certain that spending too much time in Penvale's company was not wise, so she began making excuses to avoid him—having her breakfast sent to her bedchamber rather than dining in the breakfast room with him, spending long hours on walks around the estate when she knew he was at home. She wasn't sure whether he noticed—he hadn't said anything, and some small, easily denied part of her gave a pang at the thought that her absence hadn't even been noted—but the important thing was that all this time alone gave her the opportunity to think.

It was time to escalate the haunting.

She was pleased that her scream in his study that day had seemed to rattle him, and it had been useful, in a sense: It had illuminated the fact that Penvale's suspicions lay firmly on the staff rather than on her. Wasn't this always the way of aristocrats? Blaming their underpaid workers for something when they couldn't pin the blame on anyone else?

(Jane had noted reluctantly that Penvale had increased the salaries of every member of staff by a considerable degree as soon as he'd taken a look at the account books, but she chose to ignore that in favor of righteous indignation. This was her prerogative, after all. As a lady.)

All of this did give her pause; she didn't want him to become so suspicious that he let go a member of the staff. She'd never forgive herself if someone lost a position because of her. It was therefore imperative that he be made to believe that there truly *was* a ghost, immediately.

And then, conveniently, it began to snow.

It was late for snow, which itself was something of a rarity in Cornwall, and rarer still now that they were past the first week of March. It had been a cold winter, and one that was apparently determined to keep them in its grip, so what started as a few flakes soon turned into a steady snowfall. Jane was in the sitting room attached to her bedroom, making her way through a pot of tea, wrapped in her oldest and rattiest shawl as she perused a weeks-old newspaper that had been sent down from London. She glanced out the window and caught sight of the falling snow and paused, letting her newspaper fall to her lap. She loved snow—there was, as far as Jane was concerned, nothing more pleasant than the feeling of sitting down with a cup of tea beneath a cozy blanket to watch the snow fall gently and quietly outside.

"Snow," came Penvale's voice from behind her; he muttered it more like a curse, and Jane jerked her head up, not having heard him enter the room.

"Where did you come from?" she demanded, clutching her shawl to her chest for reasons that escaped her, considering the gown she was wearing beneath it was so modest that it likely would have made a maiden aunt's wardrobe look daring by comparison.

"I knocked," her husband replied. "Three times. When you didn't respond, I became concerned and opened the door."

"Oh," Jane said, a bit flustered. "I was distracted by the snow."

"As am I," he said, irritation evident in his voice, and Jane realized that his hair was slightly damp, as was the wool of his coat.

"Were you outdoors?"

He gave a short nod. "I beat a hasty retreat once the weather turned, but I wasn't quick enough." He glared out the window at the softly falling snow as if it had caused him personal offense.

"Penvale. It's just snow."

"I *hate* snow."

"It's just water," she pointed out.

"No." He shook his head vehemently. "It's *frozen* water. That's an entirely different thing. Not to be trusted."

"Are you angry because you'll need to fix your hair?" she asked innocently, and was rewarded by his appalled look. Unable to help herself, she added, "Perhaps you would have been able to tell it was about to snow if you had spectacles."

"Jane," he said warningly, taking a step toward her.

"I'd heard London gentlemen were fussy," she continued, "but I always try to be generous of spirit and therefore assumed it was simply an unfair stereotype."

"Jane, so help me God—"

She rose from her chair and darted behind it, using it as a sort of shield. "Are you worried that your coat will be ruined, too? Is there a bit of mud on your boots causing you concern?"

He reached the opposite side of the chair and leaned forward very deliberately, bracing his hands on the arms of the chair, his face quite close to her own. Jane's breath caught in her throat; the air between them seemed thick and alive. This close, she could make out more of the green flecks in his eyes, smell the sandalwood scent that clung to his skin, mingled with the smell of cold air and snow and woodsmoke that he had brought indoors with him.

She leaned back, shaking her head slightly as if to dispel a bit of fogginess, and said very deliberately, "Did you need me to find some lavender oil for your bath? To ensure your skin remains soft and smelling of . . . of . . ."

"Of lavender?" he supplied, a laugh escaping him before he could contain it. Jane felt almost giddy with her own power and the heady rush that came from making someone—or at least *this* particular someone—laugh. He said, "No, thank you," so dryly that Jane could not prevent an answering smile from flitting across her face, and then he added, "But I *am* going to take a bath now."

As the afternoon progressed, the snow began to accumulate in great mounds. Jane couldn't recall a snowfall like this in the three years she'd lived here, and she wandered from room to room, admiring the views of the snowdrifts accumulating on the hills to the east of Trethwick Abbey, and of the fat, heavy flakes falling over the gray sea to the west.

In the ballroom, she found Penvale. This was not a room that Jane frequented—it had never been used for its intended purpose in the entire time she had lived at Trethwick Abbey, standing empty and, in the winter, quite cold, thanks to the enormous windows that lined one wall. A couple of sets of French doors led onto a terrace that, in fine weather, offered dramatic views of the ocean and cliffs but today would undoubtedly be a windswept misery. It was bitterly cold in the room, the imposing stone fireplace that occupied much of the southern wall lying empty.

Penvale was standing before one of the windows with his back to her, one arm braced against the glass. This stance caused his shirt to stretch tightly across his shoulders—his jacket was nowhere in sight, and he was wearing a gray waistcoat over his shirt that did nothing to hide the shift in muscles each time he moved his arm. He must have been freezing, but he gave no sign of discomfort, standing utterly still as he stared out at the falling snow.

"The roads will be in bad shape after this," he said, startling Jane; she hadn't realized he'd heard her approach. "It might be a few days before we're able to make it off the estate."

"Perhaps it will rain and melt it all away," she said as she drew closer to him, crossing her arms over her chest against the chill. She came to a halt next to him; he glanced sideways at her, then moved a step closer, until she could feel the warmth of his body even without touching him.

"Perhaps," he said, his tone indicating deep skepticism. "We may be trapped, though. I bloody *hate* snow," he muttered.

His aversion to snow was beginning to strike Jane as rather odd. "Why are you so bothered?" she asked curiously. "It's not as though we've anywhere we desperately need to go."

Absurdly, she found herself feeling almost . . . *defensive*, as though he were criticizing this place that she loved so much, and she felt wounded at the slight despite the fact that—as she sternly reminded herself now—anything that made him regard Trethwick Abbey with even a slightly reduced degree of affection was certainly to her advantage.

"It's . . . it's inconvenient," he said, sounding so indignant that Jane was tempted to laugh. "What if one had plans and then one was stuck at home? What if there was somewhere you badly needed to be? It's a bloody headache."

Jane glanced at him, and then her gaze lingered for a moment. He was so terribly practical, utterly unsentimental. What did the loveliness of softly falling snow matter if it got in the way of whatever he had planned for the day? How could such a man, she wondered, ever truly appreciate the wild beauty of this place?

Despite the chill, Jane remained in the ballroom for several long minutes after Penvale murmured an excuse and departed, contemplating the realization she had made. If they were likely to be trapped at Trethwick Abbey for a few days, with no one able to reach them, this was a perfect opportunity—the best she was likely to receive, in fact.

She turned on her heel and set off with brisk steps in search of Mrs. Ash. It was time for their ghost to become a bit more active.

Penvale had retired early, in a dark mood. It had snowed all afternoon and well into the evening, though the rate of snowfall appeared to be slackening once he returned to his chamber and drew his curtains tight against the night. He'd dismissed Snood, his valet, after changing into a shirt and breeches, and stood moodily before a roaring fire, a glass of claret in hand.

The wind gave a particularly fierce howl outside, and the fire emitted a loud crack. Penvale took a sip of wine, staring unseeingly into the flames. There was another howl, louder this time, sounding almost human in its mournful wail. Penvale felt the hairs on the back of his arms stand up. He lifted his wineglass to his mouth again, then froze as another howl began, even louder and closer.

And he realized after a moment that this noise was not coming from the direction of the window, as might be expected, given the storm outside.

No, this howl came from behind him—as if from deep within the house's walls.

Penvale turned slowly, not moving from his spot by the fire, and surveyed the room before him. It was quiet and still, a few candles flickering in sconces on the walls.

And then, with no warning, that same eerie wail.

Penvale frowned and took a few steps in the direction he thought it had come from before the connecting door burst open and Jane tumbled through.

"What was that?" she gasped. Penvale couldn't be certain in the dim light, but he thought she looked paler than usual. She was already dressed for bed in one of her damned high-necked nightgowns, though this one, at least, wasn't flannel, and she had a violet dressing gown thrown over it that brought out the startling shade of her eyes. "Did you hear that noise?"

"Last I checked, my ears were still attached to my head," he said dryly, "so yes."

She gave him a dark look, but he felt pleased that, for once, he was not the only one wandering the house in pursuit of odd noises, half certain he was losing his mind. This noise, just now, he had assuredly not imagined; Jane's appearance merely confirmed that fact.

"Where did it come from?" she asked, walking farther into the room and turning in a slow circle to take in her surroundings.

"I'm not certain—that direction, I think," he said, nodding at the wall on the far side of the room, beyond which lay the hallway. Jane inclined her head to one side as if to catch the sound of some sort of supernatural presence. "You needn't strain yourself," he said. "If it happens again, I promise you'll be able to hear it." He hoped his tone masked the slight unease that lingered, despite the fact that he currently had a steady mental monologue informing him that there had to be a rational explanation, one that most likely involved a bored servant. He crossed to the door, opening it and poking his head out into the hallway, which was, predictably, dark and still.

He turned back to Jane. "I'm going to take a walk—care to join me?"

This time she was the one who seized the candelabra.

They had proceeded only a few feet down the hall when they heard it again, more clearly this time: a long eerie wail, louder than the storm howling outdoors. Penvale tilted his head, then turned on his heel, making for the doors to the library at the end of the hall. "Don't you think it came from this direction?" he asked over his shoulder as Jane trailed him at a slower pace.

"I . . . I believe so," she said, sounding a bit uncertain. Penvale flung open the doors to the library and entered the room, dark and full of shadows cast by the looming shelves and various pieces of furniture. On clear nights, the moonlight spilling through the windows lining one wall offered a fair degree of light, but in tonight's storm it was difficult to see much beyond the pool of light cast by the candles in Jane's hand. Penvale stood in the center of the room, turning in a slow circle, and then—

"Aaaaaaaooooooooooooo."

Jane jumped, making the candlelight flicker; this was gratifying, given that Penvale had started quite violently himself. The noise had come from the interior eastern wall.

"What could possibly have caused that?" Jane asked, sounding a bit unnerved.

"I don't know," Penvale admitted. He slowly approached the wall he'd focused his attention on, which was papered in a rich shade of green, featuring a faint pattern of leaves in a lighter green that repeated in intricate detail every few feet. Feeling somewhat foolish, he leaned forward and pressed his ear against the wall.

"Do you hear anything?"

Jane's voice was in his ear, close enough that he could feel the warmth of her breath against his neck. Penvale—being a skeptical, dignified sort of man—jumped approximately a foot in the air and said, "*Jesus Christ.*"

"Sorry!" Jane said, holding up her hands defensively as he turned to glare at her. "How could you possibly not have heard me behind you?"

"I was *listening,*" he informed her, his heart thudding unpleasantly in his chest.

"For what?" she asked.

"For . . ." He trailed off, realizing he didn't have a good answer. For ghosts? For mice? What, precisely, did he expect to hear as he stood here with his head pressed against a *wall,* of all things? "For suspicious noises," he finished, a bit pathetically.

Jane barely seemed to hear him. "This always happens in books," she muttered. "Someone is listening intently for a mysterious noise, and then someone creeps up behind them . . ." She looked almost cheerful, which Penvale found mildly disturbing. "It's so nice when things actually work out the way they do in novels, isn't it? So satisfying." She paused, mock-thoughtful. "Oh. I don't suppose you'd know, would you?"

"Jane."

"Right. Sorry." She looked entirely unrepentant. "Did you hear anything, then?"

"I didn't get the chance to, did I?" he asked irritably. "Before you crept up behind me like . . ."

"A ghost?" she suggested.

He cut a glare at her.

She gazed back at him, straight-faced.

He turned back to the wall, as if it were about to reveal all of its bloody secrets under the strength of his glare. It looked . . .

Like a wall. Obviously.

"What is your plan here, exactly?" Jane inquired.

He tossed her another irritated look over his shoulder. "I don't know," he admitted through gritted teeth. He wished—absurdly, pointlessly—for his father. His father, who had been dead for nearly two decades. His father, who never got around to teaching Penvale all the things he needed to know to be the viscount, to be in charge of this land and this house and everyone within it. Not, he supposed, that his father ever had to contend with a damned haunting, of all things.

As if on cue, another shriek, so loud it sounded as though it were directly on the opposite side of the wall.

Penvale jumped back with a muffled curse—at this rate, he would never get within five feet of a wall ever again—and, after taking a moment to allow his heart to resume beating, he took a couple of quick steps to the left, where he yanked open the door to the adjoining room, which revealed a small drawing room. It was dark and still, no sign of having recently been occupied, but an interior door was ajar, leading to a bedroom, and another beyond it, all connected by interior doors that allowed one to quickly travel through the rooms without going into the hall.

"Jane," Penvale said quickly, "go into the hall and make sure no one enters it. I'll meet you in your morning room." He then set off with quick, quiet steps, listening intently; had he imagined it, or did he hear the faint sound of running footsteps? He increased his own pace as much as stealth would allow, until he finally reached the end of the series of interconnected rooms, the last of which was Jane's morning room. It was at the very edge of the house, directly above his study, both within a turret featuring curved walls.

The room was empty.

He turned in a circle, listening carefully, but whatever footsteps he had heard—or imagined he'd heard—were gone, the only sound the wind.

The door to the hallway opened, and Jane burst in. "Did you—"

He shook his head. "No," he said shortly. "There's no one here."

"Oh," she said, and something odd flickered across her face for half a second, gone before he could identify it. "Shall we return to bed, then?" She sounded almost eager at the prospect, not that Penvale supposed he could blame her; it was late, and this had been a bit of a wild-goose chase. He led the way silently back through the halls until they reached his sitting room, and he exhaled a long breath as the door to the hallway shut behind them.

No sooner had they entered the room and taken a moment to stand in peaceful silence than the window clattered open and a gust of snow blew in.

"Of course," Penvale muttered after his heart had resumed beating once more; prior to moving to Cornwall, he had not considered himself an easily startled man by nature, but he was becoming down-right twitchy. If Diana were here, she would no doubt mock him mercilessly, but he could not help sparing a dark wish that his mysterious ghost would make an appearance in his sister's bedchamber when she visited in the spring. He had years of grievances filed away, waiting for the moment he could exact his revenge.

"Are you going to close that?" Jane asked, interrupting his contemplation of ways he could torture his sibling, and he spared a sheepish glance for his wife before crossing the room to close the window, squinting slightly against the snowflakes pelting his face, carried into the room on the strong wind gusting off the ocean. He slammed the window shut, then regarded it thoughtfully. It latched securely, with no wiggle or sign that it was becoming loose; Penvale had latched it earlier just as firmly. How had it opened? It was windy, to be sure, but not *that* windy.

"Is the latch broken?" Jane asked as he turned to face her, and for a fraction of a second he paused, taking notice of something in her tone. He couldn't put his finger on what it was—hadn't even realized that he knew her well enough, had paid close enough attention to note such a thing—but all at once he was certain, down to his bones, that this was not the innocent inquiry it appeared to be.

He took slow, deliberate steps toward her; she did not move, that violet gaze locked with his, but a faint hint of color appeared in her cheeks. Jane was many things—shy, an awkward conversationalist, and frequently openly hostile toward her spouse—but she was not much of a blusher.

"The latch is not broken," he said calmly, watching her carefully. "The latch appears to be functioning perfectly, and I myself was the one who latched it not an hour ago, when I stuck my head out the window to see how hard it was snowing."

Jane frowned, her blush fading. "Why on earth would you do that?"

"I wanted to see if it was letting up." He came to a halt before her.

"And you couldn't have merely looked out the window?" She looked utterly perplexed.

"It was . . . foggy," he said. "From the warmth," he added, nodding sagely, as if he had the faintest idea what he was talking about. He didn't want to admit what he'd really been doing—trying to get a better listen to the wind outside, when he'd first heard it begin to howl. Because to admit that would be to admit that he was, perhaps, only slightly, a little bit . . . well, rattled.

"I wanted to see how deep the snowdrifts were," he added hastily, and then plunged on before Jane could ask any further questions, as if anything he had just said made any sense whatsoever. "The point is, I closed that window myself, and I do not believe I am such a spoiled London gentleman that I'm incapable of latching a window properly."

"Hmmm," she said with great skepticism, but before she could opine at length about his need for spectacles or something else similarly lowering, he continued.

"I can see perfectly well enough to close a window, Jane."

"How did it open, then?" she asked, a trace of unease evident in her voice. Penvale was once again alert. He could not say what it was in her manner that raised his suspicions, beyond the fact that she was not a terribly good liar. She was skilled enough at hiding her true feelings behind her customary ill humor, that much was true, but proper lying—or, in this case, putting on a show of a woman frightened by a supernatural event—was another matter entirely.

"Who can say?" he said solemnly, then immediately regretted it as her eyes narrowed upon his in suspicion. He had to tread carefully here; he couldn't very well go from being an avowed skeptic to seeming to believe in ghosts. He had to lull her into a false sense of security, and then, when her guard was lowered, he would strike.

He felt like he was trying to capture an extremely shy cat—although it must be noted that the cat he had the most recent first-hand experience with (an extremely scrawny, fluffy kitten that Emily and Belfry had adopted, and which seemed to be constantly lurking underfoot whenever he visited their home on Duke Street) was not the slightest bit shy.

"It just seems odd, is all," he amended hastily. "I know I latched it properly. It's . . . strange."

There. He thought that would do—he didn't sound so rattled that he would draw her attention to his uncharacteristic unease; perhaps just credulous enough that she would begin to think him an easy mark.

Happily, this strategy seemed to work, for her eyes widened once again and she nodded, perhaps a bit too eagerly. "Very strange," she agreed.

"Perhaps, then," he said slowly, leaning in closer to her; was he imagining it, or did her breath hitch slightly as he did so? For his part, he almost immediately realized that this was a mistake: This close, he could smell the citrus scent of her skin. It must be her soap, he thought distractedly; this, too, was a mistake, because he was immediately flooded with thoughts of Jane bathing, Jane not wearing any of those high-necked nightgowns—Jane not wearing anything at all, in fact. And these sorts of thoughts were not at all helpful at the moment.

"Yes?" she asked, the slightest breathless edge to her voice.

"Perhaps I should sleep in your room tonight," he murmured.

"You—what?"

"I just worry, you see," he explained, his tone calm and rational, "that the ghost may appear in your bedroom next, and I wouldn't wish to leave you alone to face it." He was so close to her now that her eyes occupied most of his field of vision. That meant he was too close—too close for anything other than kissing her.

And clearly, he wasn't going to do *that*.

But the thought was unexpectedly compelling. And while Penvale certainly wasn't a monk, it had been a long time since he had found a woman truly compelling. He hadn't had time or mental energy in the past few years, so focused on his pursuit of Trethwick Abbey that women had become something of an afterthought, an occasional pleasure but nothing he'd allowed himself to devote too much attention to. Diana had often asked him why he didn't simply marry an heiress with a fortune large enough to allow him to purchase the estate—marriage to a wealthy man had been her method of escape from their aunt and uncle, after all—but he'd been stubbornly determined to do this himself, on his own terms.

And yet here he was, with a wife he'd been more or less forced to wed.

Jane was baffling, and maddening, and didn't even seem to *like* him the majority of the time, and yet he found himself all at once . . . interested.

Which was why it was probably for the best that she said, "I don't want you to sleep in my room." He should, he knew, breathe a sigh of relief at this rebuttal, but before he could do so—and before he could interrogate why, exactly, he didn't feel like doing so at all—she added, "But I'll sleep in your room."

"Will you?"

"I believe your bed is larger than mine," Jane said with a sniff, "and I already know how dreadful you are to share a bed with."

Well, that was sufficient to kill any semblance of romance or seduction about the proceedings. That was of little import; as long as he had her in his bed, he could keep an eye on her.

And if she knew anything about what the bloody hell was happening in this house, he would very soon find out.

Chapter Twelve

This was an unfortunate development, but Jane was determined not to allow it to ruin her plans.

Jane was a suspicious person by nature, and she could not help wondering at Penvale's sudden solicitous concern for her fragile nerves. He'd never seemed terribly worried about her before—had she been that convincing earlier? She hadn't wanted to protest too much at his suggestion, though—surely a young, innocent wife uninvolved in staging elaborate, supposedly supernatural mishaps at a manor house would indeed be frightened by these strange events and would welcome the calm, soothing presence of her husband in her bed at night, and his ability to exert his manly strength and frighten away any spirits.

Or something.

So it was that Jane found herself tucked into Penvale's enormous bed, which smelled of him in a disconcertingly pleasant way (what *soap* did he use? Did all men smell like this?) and which was almost irritatingly comfortable. More comfortable than her own bed, in fact. How was this possible? The staff didn't even *like* him.

Did they?

She eyed the bedspread with suspicion. Was it fluffier than hers? She gave it a furtive pat and wondered if she would sound truly deranged should she inquire as to where the bed linens had come from so that she might procure a set from the same shop. She then realized that Penvale surely did not have the faintest notion of the origin of his sheets.

In any case, here she was, preparing to share a bed with her husband, all in order to keep his suspicions at bay. At least she'd had the sense to quickly suggest that they share his bed rather than hers, since his presence in his own bedchamber was a key element to the success of the plans Jane had hastily enacted for tonight. The window blowing open had gone perfectly—Snood, Penvale's valet, must have been impressively sneaky if he'd managed to unlatch it without Penvale noticing.

The next part of the plan—and the reason it was so crucial that Penvale remain in his own bedroom—was a night of thoroughly interrupted sleep, and while Jane was not precisely thrilled about her own sleep being disrupted as well, she was willing to make a sacrifice for the cause.

At that moment, Penvale walked into the room—he'd been in the dressing room adjacent to his bedchamber, evidently removing his clothing, because he approached her in a nightshirt, the sight of which, oddly, made her want to burst into hysterical laughter. It seemed so strangely ill-suited to him, and she had a flash of curiosity: What did he *normally* wear to bed? She was certain it wasn't this; she couldn't have said why, but she somehow knew that this was for her benefit.

He paused and gave her a strange look. "What are you doing?"

Jane glanced down and realized that she was in the midst of patting the bedsheets as though they were a beloved pet. She attempted to think of some sort of explanation for her behavior that would sound remotely sane, then abandoned this as fruitless. "Examining the quality of the bed linens," she said.

"All . . . right," he said, sounding mystified.

"Have you been bribing the servants?" she asked suspiciously.

"For . . . better sheets?" His look of confusion—evident in the line forming between his brows—only deepened.

"Precisely."

"I have not," he said slowly, continuing to approach the bed. "Are yours dissatisfactory?"

"I didn't think so until I felt these," Jane informed him, at last ceasing her patting and leaning back against the pillows, tugging the sheets up to her neck. She tried to subtly turn her head to catch a faint pleasant scent on the pillowcase—was it lavender? *Her* sheets were not lavender-scented.

Apparently, she had not been sufficiently subtle, because a look of faint satisfaction spread across Penvale's face. "Smells nice, doesn't it?"

Jane froze. "It's fine," she said coldly, permitting herself one last surreptitious sniff.

"Like a summer day in the south of France, I expect," he said cheerfully as he climbed into bed, offering Jane a quick flash of calf and thigh. She'd never spent much time thinking about what a man's legs would look like under breeches, but she'd had a brief glimpse of muscle and surprisingly golden skin. Why would the skin of his legs be golden? Surely he wasn't in the habit of going about . . . *nude*.

Outdoors.

And then, because evidently she no longer had even the faintest ability to guard her tongue when she was in his presence—though he was probably the person she should be guarding her tongue around most carefully of all—she asked, "Do you prance around naked outdoors?"

Penvale, who was in the process of tucking the sheets neatly around his waist, froze. "What a question," he said conversationally, turning to face her. Even though his bed was positively enormous, it seemed considerably smaller now that he was in it, fixing her with that odd hazel gaze. It didn't seem particularly piercing at first, nothing like the icy blue or green gazes of heroes in some of the novels Jane had read, but she'd come to realize that it was uncomfortable to be trapped beneath for very long. He was not a terribly intimidating man, her husband—he was tallish but not imposing; athletic in build but not heavily muscled—and yet she had the sudden impression that he saw far more than she had realized the first afternoon she had met him, and when he fixed his eyes on her, she was almost certain he was seeing more than she would wish him to, as if she were a puzzle that he was desperately trying to work out.

Jane didn't like it—or, rather, she didn't dislike it, even though she knew she should, and it was this fact that vexed her more than anything else.

"May I ask why you are inquiring?" he continued.

And Jane—who all at once decided that she would simply have to brazen this out—said, "Your legs look as though they've seen sunlight at some point within memory."

He let loose a surprised laugh that lit up his face, making his eyes come alive, erasing the creases from his forehead that he had no doubt earned through many a lifting of an ironic brow. For certainly they could not have come from *frowning*. What did this man have to frown about?

"Fair enough," he said, still chuckling, turning fully onto his side to face her, a movement that Jane mirrored before she could stop herself. "They have *seen sunlight*, as a matter of fact—I like to swim." Seeing her appalled expression, he added, "Not here—not yet, at least. It's a bit cold even for my tastes. But in a couple of months, I expect I'll start swimming in the sea in the mornings."

"It will still be freezing," Jane said, very skeptical about this plan. "It's England. We're not known for our balmy seas."

"No, we're not," Penvale said with a faint grin. "But in London, I swim in the Serpentine until the first frost. It's bracing."

"When do you go?" Jane asked curiously; one of the things that had struck her about London was how *busy* it was. She loved Cornwall because she could bundle herself up and strike out on a walk and, if she walked in the right direction, not see a single other person. How did you find that same sense of peace, of space, in London?

"In the morning," Penvale said. "One doesn't have to rise terribly early to be awake before the rest of the *ton*, so I just got into the habit of rising to go on a morning swim. In the country, I don't have to be quite so clandestine, so I can swim whenever I want."

"Where in the country do you go?" Jane asked; after all, until a couple of months before, the country property that was his by ancestral right had not belonged to him at all.

"Jeremy and Audley both have country houses," Penvale said, the sound of his friends' names warm and affectionate. Jane found herself strangely curious about these men who had been like brothers to her husband for so long. She had spent a little bit of time with their wives but not with the gentlemen themselves, though she didn't suppose she would have been comfortable around them, anyway. Not for the first time, Jane wished for some sort of cloak of invisibility she could fling over herself so that she might observe all the people around her without being expected to participate in any of their conversations.

"Well," Penvale added, "Audley *had* a country house—he gave it up last year, gave it back to his father."

"Why on earth would he do that?" Jane asked. She couldn't imagine willingly giving up a country escape and resigning oneself to a life spent in town.

"Audley and his father . . . don't get on," Penvale said, a strange twist to his mouth. "He was proving a point, shall we say. And his father's quite unpleasant, make no mistake about it. But I just . . . " He paused, long enough that Jane wasn't certain he'd continue, before he finally said, "Well, I miss speaking to my own father, that's all."

He said these last words very quietly, though in the silence of the room, they were perfectly audible. It was a simple enough sentence, so why did Jane feel like she'd been granted a glimpse of something important?

In response to her silence, Penvale offered a rueful laugh, as though embarrassed to have shared so much. "I'm sorry, I'm blathering," he said.

"You're not," Jane said quickly—too quickly, probably, but she was desperate for him not to think that he'd burdened her with this confession. It occurred to her that she was not the only one who had sacrificed something in this marriage; after all, he had given up any hope of a love match, of having someone he might trust with his thoughts. She could not make their marriage a love match—at the moment, she couldn't think of the right way to describe their marriage at all—but she could . . . listen.

"I don't mind listening to you," she said, feeling stupid as the words left her mouth. "I mean to say—I know I'm not a very good conversationalist—but I like talking . . . to you."

Something in his face softened as he gazed at her from his side of the bed. "I suppose all I meant to say is, I've felt very far away from my own father for a long time," he said. "And it always struck me as sad that Audley's father is living, and they barely speak."

"You and your father were close, then?" Jane asked tentatively, fearful that any word she spoke would land wrong, as her words so often did, and would break whatever spell had crafted this fragile peace between them.

"I'm sure, had he lived longer, we would have butted heads as I got older, but as a boy, I idolized him. He inherited the title just after I was born, and the estate was in bad financial shape—he was making improvements, but that's the reason that the death duties were such a blow when he died, and we had to sell. But I remember how much he loved this place." He shook his head ruefully. "I suppose, in some way, the promise of this house has always been that it would . . ." He trailed off.

"What is it?" Jane asked.

His gaze flicked to hers and held it for a moment, almost as if he were asking her some sort of unspoken question. Whatever answer her eyes gave was enough for him to sigh, rub a hand across his face, and say, "I suppose I always thought that Trethwick Abbey would give me a place to go where my memories would feel more . . . alive. Where I'd feel less at risk of losing them as time passed."

Silence fell in the wake of this confession; in the soft candlelight of the room, his expression was starker, more open, than usual.

She reached out a hand and placed it gently on the bed between them, close to where his was resting, but not quite touching. "That's an awful lot to expect of one house," she said softly.

She said nothing else, and neither did he. Then, so slowly and gently that it was almost possible to believe she was imagining it, he nudged his hand toward hers and allowed their little fingers to brush.

"It is," he agreed just as softly.

And the thought struck her that, for all this man had been surrounded by friends, by a sister who clearly loved him, loneliness was just as familiar to him as it was to her.

And then the clock chimed the hour, the brush of his finger was gone, and the spell was broken. Penvale shook his head as if to clear it and said in his normal tone of voice, "In any case, Audley gave his house back to his father, meaning I've one less country lake to swim in, but Jeremy's house in Wiltshire has a spectacular one which I took advantage of for a few weeks this summer. One morning I discovered him and Diana out there—I think they'd sneaked away for some sort of open-air tryst" —at this, his voice was tinged with mild horror—"and we came perilously close to running into each other when we were *all* unclothed, which would have been an experience so traumatizing I expect I'd have drowned myself in the lake and you'd never have even met me."

"And what a loss that would have been," Jane murmured, pleased that her voice came out sounding normal, despite her pulse still pounding an erratic beat in her throat. Her hand tingled where it had brushed against his. She wasn't certain whether she meant to be sarcastic; her tone evidently conveyed it, because Penvale gave her one of those sideways grins that she found herself, despite her better judgment, growing oddly attached to.

"All this is to say, that's why my skin is not quite as pasty as that of the average Englishman," he concluded. "Do you swim, then?"

Jane blinked at him. "Did you miss the bit where I informed you how cold the ocean is here?"

"Surely in the summer it's not so bad," he pressed. "On a sunny day, I'd imagine it would feel like something of a relief."

"I have dipped my toes in on days like the one you describe, and I think they were numb within fifteen seconds."

"Only your toes?" he asked, and there was some note in his voice, some dark undercurrent, that made Jane's breath catch in her throat. "Jane, we'll go swimming this summer. We'll have a picnic on the beach in the cove, and after we've been sitting in the sun for long enough to thoroughly ruin that lovely complexion of yours, we'll be so hot that we'll plunge in."

Jane was momentarily distracted by the fact that he had just called her complexion lovely, but soon enough she realized that, at some point, she would have to admit something, so she may as well do it now.

"There's just one problem," she informed him. "I don't know how to swim."

"But," Penvale said, and then paused, considering, "you live by the *sea*."

"I'm aware," Jane said coolly, inclining her head toward the windows, which, during the daylight hours, did offer a rather spectacular view of that very sea.

"But," he said again, "*how?*"

Jane sighed, irritated. She'd known this would be his reaction, but since she didn't wish to spend the entire summer coming up with excuses to avoid swimming with him, it had seemed easiest to come out with it. Although, if all went according to plan, he would no longer be here this summer, meaning she might have just avoided telling him altogether.

Odd how the prospect of his absence—the very thing she was spending a considerable amount of time and energy trying to achieve—had been lately in the pesky habit of fleeing from her mind after only a few minutes in his company.

"I never had anyone to teach me," she said crossly. That crease appeared in his forehead again, deepening the faint lines there, but he didn't say anything. She was aware all at once how pathetic that must sound to a man who had just spent several minutes describing his friends.

"No one?" he asked, surprise evident in his voice. "I think Diana and her friends knew how to swim by the time they were wearing long skirts."

Jane didn't doubt it—but then she suspected that her younger days had been nothing like his sister's. It was not that she'd been entirely friendless; while some of the girls at the finishing school she'd attended for a few years had been cruel, teasing her for her shyness and her inability to converse with ease, others had been kind enough, and there had been a regular set she'd taken her meals with, gone on occasional walks with into the nearby village. But they hadn't had the sort of connection Penvale seemed to share with his friends— Jane was too shy to find herself easily sharing confidences—and she'd lost touch with them as soon as they left school, she being whisked away to Cornwall, the other girls going on to marry and settle down to lives of quiet domesticity. She'd never been much of a correspondent, either—the contents of a letter that were considered acceptable for a well-bred lady to pen were so tiresome and dull that Jane could not be bothered to attempt them.

She didn't wish to admit any of this to him, so she merely shook her head.

"But your father was in the *navy*," Penvale said, sounding more indignant by the moment.

"Yes," Jane said sharply. "Which meant that he was very rarely home to teach me much of anything."

A brief silence fell, in which Jane could see him absorbing the picture that single sentence had painted, of a lonely, friendless childhood.

"Well," he said, his frown smoothing away, "I shall simply have to teach you."

"You'll—what?" she asked. This was not what she had been expecting; she'd assumed that once she shared her lack of ability with him, he'd accept that she would not be a likely companion for sea-bathing excursions, and he'd leave her in peace.

"I'll teach you," he said easily. "It's not so difficult. Children can do it."

"I am not a child, in case you hadn't noticed," she informed him, sitting up in bed. "Children also crawl around in the grass and jump in muddy puddles, and I can assure you I don't do those things, either."

"But those aren't useful skills," he pointed out practically. "You live on a cliff next to the ocean—hell, it's not even *safe* for you not to know how to swim."

"So long as I don't plan on jumping off the cliff, I don't see why it matters!"

"Ah, yes," he said thoughtfully. "Since I'm the one in danger of being shoved off a cliff, it only matters that I can swim."

"What you should really be concerned with is the thickness of your skull," Jane muttered. "In case I am tempted to bash it in."

The words came out suitably coldly, but beneath, she felt something bubbling within her: an almost insuppressible desire to laugh, of all things. She gazed at him, wide-eyed at this realization, and she saw that the corners of his mouth were twitching, too. Her eyes caught his and held them, and her heart stuttered in her chest. The silence between them took on a strange, heavy quality with each moment that it lingered, and she was acutely aware of every single inch of space that separated them in that enormous expanse of bed.

He reached up his hand, and it hovered in that neutral territory between them, and just when she thought that he would reach toward her—

"Aaaaaaaaoooooooooooooohhhhhhh."

Jane and Penvale both jumped, despite the fact that Jane had been perfectly aware this was going to happen. This was the reason she had been determined to sleep in Penvale's room, after all, rather than risk missing the carefully choreographed series of ghostly wails. But for the past few minutes, she had entirely forgotten the reason she was lying there in his bed.

"Jesus bloody Christ," Penvale said, sitting bolt upright and shoving back the bedsheets. He sprang from bed with athletic grace and, wearing nothing but his nightshirt, sprinted across the room in three great strides, coming to a halt just before the wall opposite the bed. Head tilted slightly, he was clearly listening intently, and then he sighed, turning back to her.

"Should we ... do something?" she suggested hesitantly, aware that she needed to play this very carefully indeed.

Penvale turned and regarded her for a long moment, his expression unreadable. Jane suppressed the urge to fidget, wishing she could crack his head open and peruse his thoughts like the pages of one of her favorite books.

"No," he said at last. "Let's ... go to sleep. Try to get some rest. We can deal with this in the morning."

Jane frowned. It seemed unlike him not to wish to investigate further, and she knew a pang of unease deep within her—was it possible that he suspected something? Suspected *her*?

He climbed into bed and reached over to extinguish the candle on the bedside table. He glanced over his shoulder at her, his expression strangely inscrutable. "Try to go to sleep, Jane—it's too bloody late and cold to wander the halls in search of a ghost."

"Right," she said slowly. "You're right, of course." With that, she burrowed down beneath the blankets and shut her eyes tight, trying very hard to ignore the large, warm body a few inches away.

But it was not long before the wailing commenced again—not so frequent as to become predictable, that was a point she had stressed—and after an hour or so, Jane abandoned any pretense of sleep, instead lying with her arms folded neatly across the bedspread, staring up at the darkened canopy. Next to her, Penvale was silent, but it was a very *wakeful* sort of silence; there was no sign of the deep, steady breathing that indicated sleep.

After a while, the wailing ceased for good—it was growing late, and Jane hadn't wanted anyone to lose a full night's sleep over this plan, although several members of the staff had been alarmingly eager to participate—and she felt her eyes grow heavy at last. Knowing that she had several hours of uninterrupted sleep to look forward to, she burrowed even more deeply into her nest of blankets, basking in the warmth and listening sleepily to the sound of the cold wind howling outside.

This is very nice, she thought.

It might have been a minute, or an hour, or several hours later when she was awoken by the sound of a loud bang.

There was some rather creative cursing from next to her as Penvale emerged from his own pile of blankets, looking grumpy and mussed and far younger than usual. Jane stared blearily at him in the dark, shadowy room, then belatedly realized it was not merely the chill air of a room with a banked fire that was causing her to shiver—it was an *actual* gust of cold air. From outdoors.

Because there was an open window.

Really, now, this was taking things a bit far, Jane thought as Penvale scrambled out of bed once more and bolted across the room to secure the windows. She hadn't instructed them to undo the latch in the bedroom, merely the sitting room—though she supposed she could not complain if Snood had got carried away in a fit of enthusiasm for his role in this drama. Snood was not a fan of country living, as it transpired, and was most eager for his employer to return to town, where life was more civilized, and he could spend his time on the all-important task of perfecting the waterfall knot for Penvale's cravat.

"The wind here, it ruins everything," he'd informed Jane mournfully when she had taken him into her confidence and given him a role to play in her plan for supernatural mayhem.

"That must be . . . very frustrating?" she had offered, and he had given a long-suffering sort of nod, obviously gratified to have someone appreciate his tale of woe.

In any case, he had clearly become overly enthusiastic about his task, which was why Jane was lying in a bed in the middle of the night watching snowflakes blow in through the window Penvale was struggling to close. She loved snow, but she ultimately preferred it to remain outdoors.

After a moment, Penvale got the window shut and returned to bed, muttering darkly all the while. "Strangely uncooperative windows this house seems to have," he said as he climbed back into bed; in the dark,

Jane couldn't make out his expression, but there was a wry note to his voice that set her on edge.

"Mmm," she offered noncommittally.

He rolled over immediately and gave all appearances of having fallen back into a deep slumber, but Jane lay there studying the line of his back and the breadth of his shoulders for quite a while before sleep found her again.

Chapter Thirteen

The first night, it was irritating. The ghostly moans, the mysteri-
ously malfunctioning windows, the interrupted sleep—an annoyance,
undoubtedly. But Penvale was capable of handling annoyances. This
time a year ago, he'd have given his left foot to deal with any manner of
annoyance if he could do so at Trethwick Abbey.

By the second night, it surged past irritating to downright infuriat-
ing. The snow had abated that morning, but a quick trip out to survey
the state of the roads confirmed that they were well and truly snowed
in. Great drifts obscured the landscape, turning it unrecognizable, the
tenants' cottages looking like little gingerbread houses beneath a layer
of white. It was pretty, in its own way, if one appreciated idyllic scenes
of wintertime coziness.

Which Penvale did not. Not when they were so damned inconvenient, at least.

And then, late in the afternoon, it started to snow *again*, which
did his mood no favors. Jane had made as if to retreat to her own bedchamber that evening, but he had wordlessly gestured her through the
doorway into his—he wanted her where he could keep an eye on her,
despite the purple shadows under her eyes.

Soon after they retired, the noises started: the wailing, the strange thumps from overhead (in rooms that Penvale knew perfectly well were unoccupied). He resolutely ignored all of this, though it kept him awake for the better part of the night; he was certain that if he did not offer any sort of a response, the parties responsible would eventually give up and abandon their efforts.

But it was undeniable that he spent a considerable portion of that night simmering in his own anger as he listened to the wails commence and subside and resume. He was not, as a general rule, a man prone to anger; he was, however, a man who enjoyed sleeping, and being deprived of it for two nights running was more than he could stand.

By the third night, he was beginning to grow downright unhinged. He had spent a considerable portion of the day outdoors, the snow having ceased once more and the sun even having begun to make faint, largely unsuccessful attempts to peek from behind the heavy iron clouds that scuttled across the sky. He returned home—having slogged his way through snowdrifts in the company of his steward to ensure that all the tenants were safe and warm—feeling damp, cold, and wearier than he ever had in his life. It took a lengthy bath for his toes to regain feeling—he made a mental note to acquire better boots at the earliest opportunity—and he and Jane dined largely in silence.

"For heaven's sake, go to bed," Jane said in exasperation before the dessert course had even arrived. "I'll join you later," she added, and if Penvale were a more suave, charming sort of man—if he were his brother-in-law, in other words—he would have taken this opportunity to offer some sort of sly innuendo. But he was too bloody tired to consider it, so he took himself upstairs and apparently wasted no time sinking into a deep, dreamless sleep, because he didn't realize Jane had joined him until some indeterminate amount of time later, when he awoke in the pitch dark of midnight to the sound of, of all things, a baby crying.

And this—for some reason, *this*—was finally too much.

"Jane," he said curtly, rolling over and prodding none too gently at the lump of sheets and blankets that contained, somewhere within, his wife.

"Mphlmph," said the blankets.

"*Jane*," he repeated more insistently, because, by God, if he had to be awake for this nonsense, so did she. He reached over and shook her by the shoulder.

Jane poked an indignant head out of her nest of sheets. "*What?*" she demanded, blinking at him in the dim light of the bedroom.

"There's a baby," he informed her shortly.

"I beg your pardon?" she asked, looking entirely—and perhaps understandably—perplexed.

"At least I presume it is a baby," he amended, and inclined his head to the side, falling silent. They regarded each other without speaking; Jane opened her mouth to reply, but Penvale reached out a single finger to shush her, resting it against her lips. She exhaled softly, her breath warming his skin, and at that precise moment, Penvale wasn't certain he could have moved his hand—that single index finger—if his life depended on it. She looked at him with those violet eyes, and their gazes held each other's as silence stretched between them, growing taut with each passing second.

After nearly a minute had passed, they heard the noise again. Penvale, happily, did not consider himself to be much of an expert on babies, but he was fairly confident in his ability to identify a baby's cry when he heard one. And that was almost certainly what he was hearing. He raised his eyebrows at Jane, who looked . . .

Entirely puzzled.

Penvale fought the urge to frown. He wasn't certain what Jane knew about the events transpiring around the house, but she did not present the image of a woman who had any clue what was currently happening.

Still turning this over in his mind, he climbed out of bed, shivering slightly in the chill. He darted into his dressing room and snatched up the first pair of breeches he saw, hastily flinging them on before seizing a banyan and then returning to the bedroom to find Jane out of bed, knotting a dressing gown around her waist. She ran a distracted hand through her mussed hair, watching as he lit a candle and picked it up before approaching her to offer his arm.

"Shall we investigate our apparently haunted house, Jane?"

For all his light tone, Penvale had to admit that he was beginning to feel a bit unsettled as they quietly made their way up and down the deserted hallways of Trethwick Abbey. The house was old—very, very old—and the worn wooden floors of the corridors creaked occasionally and unpredictably, though Jane had a knack for avoiding these spots, a testament to the fact that she knew the house considerably better than Penvale did.

As yet.

The house was deserted, all the servants long abed, candles extinguished. The small circle of light provided by the candle Penvale carried only allowed them to see a couple of feet before them, leading to the unnerving feeling that they were walking into some sort of dark labyrinth, one with unknown dangers ahead. Which was absurd, since the only dangers Penvale expected to encounter were perhaps a pair of servants with too much time on their hands.

And a baby? Where the hell did they get a baby, of all things?

Although common sense urged him to do otherwise, Penvale recalled the conversation he'd had with Jane and Mrs. Ash about the mysterious christening gown in his uncle's bed. His imagination took this as a sign that it had been given free rein, and he envisioned all sorts of ghostly baby apparitions wafting around the halls of Trethwick Abbey by night, wailing ghostly baby wails.

He was feeling a bit nervy.

Beneath his foot, a floorboard gave a particularly loud *creak* and Penvale jumped as though he'd heard a gunshot.

Jane regarded him with an expression he could only honestly describe as vaguely patronizing.

And then: a wail.

He set off at a brisk pace in the direction from which he thought it had come; they had made their way to the opposite wing of the second floor from their bedrooms, which was where they had gone on their fruitless chase a few nights earlier. He thought the baby's wails might have been coming from the far corner of the floor, where Jane's morning room was—it received lovely morning sunlight, and Jane had once remarked that she felt rather like a cat basking in the sun when she was curled up in the window seat reading. Penvale, more charmed by this image than he cared to examine—or even fully admit—had filed away this description in the mental dossier he was keeping on his wife, one which grew fatter and more distracting by the day.

The cry had stopped as abruptly as it had started, and the only sounds were his footsteps on the floor, the whisper of Jane's dressing gown against the floorboards. Penvale halted outside the morning room, listening intently. "It came from here, didn't it?" he asked Jane, shutting his eyes and listening hard.

"I . . . I think so," she whispered, and he cracked an eye open to see that she was leaning forward slightly, her gaze focused ahead, though Penvale couldn't guess what might have her attention, given their limited pool of candlelight. "It sounded . . . terribly *real*, didn't it?" she asked softly, and he detected a note of unease in her voice that mirrored the feeling creeping up his spine. He was forcefully aware of how little they could see of their surroundings, just the two of them and a candle in this enormous, dark, empty house. He was suddenly conscious of the remoteness of the house, set atop a windswept cliff, surrounded by snowdrifts, even the small comforts of the nearest village as unreachable as the moon.

"It did," he said, equally softly, and at that moment the baby—or whatever the hell it was—let out another unnerving wail, this one so close that Penvale knew, beyond a doubt, if he were to reach out and seize the doorknob just to his right, open the door to the morning room, he would find it within.

Jane beat him to it. She took two hasty steps forward and flung the door open.

As one, they peered into the dark room—it was brighter here than it had been in the hallway, thanks to the large window above the very seat that Jane was so fond of, through which moonlight spilled into the room. Not seeing any evidence of a person, Penvale took a step forward, Jane clutching his arm. Was he imagining it, or had her grip tightened? In the combination of moonlight and candlelight, the room appeared full of hulking shadows, which, upon drawing near, vanished to reveal pieces of furniture. They made a slow circuit of the room, finding no evidence of any presence, ghostly or otherwise.

Penvale had a strange sensation, however, of being watched. The hairs along the back of his neck rose, as if there were a pair of eyes on him, and he turned sharply, holding his candle before him, its meager light revealing nothing but a settee against the far wall, bracketed on either end by a pair of mismatched end tables, atop one of which tee-tered a stack of books.

"What is it?" Jane breathed, as if she, too, sensed some strange other presence within the room that she was hesitant to disturb.

Penvale shook his head and, without fully realizing what he was doing, tugged Jane closer to his side, so that he could feel the soft press of the side of her breast against his arm. *Not* a terribly helpful thing to notice at the moment, it must be said, but . . . well.

Well.

He led her toward the window seat and sank down upon it, draw-ing Jane down next to him, and leaned back against the cold pane of glass, his gaze alert on the room before him.

All was quiet and still. After a minute or so of contemplation of his surroundings, he felt Jane's eyes on the side of his face, and he turned to look at her. He opened his mouth to ask if she detected anything amiss, but before he could do so, a rending wail split the silence.

Jane jumped as badly as he did this time, her breath coming in great uneven gasps that matched the pounding of his pulse. As one, they hopped to their feet, making for the north-facing wall, where the noise had originated from.

There was absolutely nothing obviously amiss.

Penvale spent a good deal of time scrutinizing that stretch of wall, searching for something—anything—that might explain why he'd just heard a baby's cry as loud and clear as if it were in the room with them. But there was nothing visible that suggested that the wall was anything other than a wall.

By this point, the clock above the fireplace was chiming the one o'clock hour, Jane was stifling a yawn, and Penvale was growing too weary to care if there was an entire nursery's worth of invisible crying babies. In unspoken agreement, they retreated from the room, back down the corridor, and to the western wing, not speaking until they were within the warmth and comfort of Penvale's bedchamber. Jane removed her dressing gown, neatly laying it across the tufted bench at the foot of the bed, while Penvale—without even sparing a thought for her maidenly virtue—removed banyan, breeches, *and* nightshirt until he was wearing nothing but his smalls, a sight which caused Jane's eyes to momentarily widen as she glanced over at him while climbing into bed. He followed suit, settling down and extinguishing his candle, and rolling over to face her just as she rolled to face him, so that they wound up a bit closer together than either of them had likely intended, only a few inches of bedsheet separating their faces.

Penvale looked at her, her features slowly coming into focus as his eyes adjusted to the darkness. A stubborn lock of dark hair had fallen onto her cheek, and without thinking—without even realizing what he was doing, as if his hand had a mind of its own and was inexorably drawn toward her skin like a magnet—he reached out and tucked that strand of hair behind her ear.

His hand grazed her cheek as he withdrew it, and her eyes were wide on his as she let out an exhale that was not *quite* steady. Somehow, it was only the sound of that slightly unsteady exhalation that made him realize he was holding his own breath.

His hand burned where it had touched her skin.

"Where did the noise come from, Jane?" he asked, his voice soft.

"I don't know," she replied.

He held her gaze as if searching for something, some answer, though he couldn't have said what it was. He believed her.

He nodded at her, just once, and he could tell she understood.

TO SWOON AND TO SPAR

"Good night, Jane," he said, softer still, and he turned onto his other side and tried very hard not to listen to her breathing, not to wonder how long it took her to fall asleep.

Try as he might, he could not exert *that* much control over his ears, and so he knew that, despite his exhaustion, he lay awake long after her breathing had slowed to an even, steady pace, his mind full of questions.

Chapter Fourteen

Despite Penvale's dire mutterings about suffocating in a snowbank or being concussed by a falling icicle, the snow did eventually melt in the face of the relentless damp of a Cornish late winter, and March progressed slowly, wet and blustery.

Jane had been somewhat rattled by the mysterious baby in the night and had wasted no time in making inquiries with Mrs. Ash.

"A crying baby," Mrs. Ash repeated, frowning. "Are you certain?"

"Entirely," Jane said, crossing her arms.

"Perhaps it was a fox?" Mrs. Ash suggested.

"A fox *inside* Trethwick Abbey?" Jane repeated incredulously. "Mrs. Ash, you cannot be serious."

"No, I suppose not," the housekeeper agreed slowly. "But I must confess, my lady, I heard nothing, and none of the other members of staff have mentioned it, either." She paused, a canny gleam in her eye. "Perhaps you and his lordship were imagining things? I do understand your sleep has been disrupted of late."

Jane fought the urge to blush, though nothing in Mrs. Ash's tone indicated that she intended a double entendre. "Perhaps," she said, flustered, and left the butler's pantry convinced that Mrs. Ash thought she was losing her mind.

In any case, Jane called a brief pause to their activities, fearing that Penvale was beginning to suspect something of her, which was not untrue—she had not missed several lengthy, thoughtful looks he had given her the week of the snowstorm—but which was also, undoubtedly, a convenient excuse.

Because Jane was feeling rather muddled. Her inquiries among other members of the staff regarding the baby noises had been fruitless; every servant she spoke to professed innocence, just as Mrs. Ash had, all with such seeming frankness that Jane was torn between feeling unnerved—*was* there actually a ghostly baby crawling about the halls at night?—and questioning her own sanity. Had she imagined it? If Penvale hadn't been with her that night, she would have begun to think so.

She had been glad that he'd been with her, and she didn't know what to do with this feeling, nor did she dare examine it too carefully.

She had expected that he'd wish to return to their investigation with renewed fervor in the days following the storm, but a series of small crises involving the estate's tenants occupied much of his attention over the next week. A few cottages had sustained damage from the wet, heavy snow and gusting winds the storm had brought to shore, requiring temporarily housing an entire large, rather boisterous family in one of the spare rooms of Trethwick Abbey while their roof was mended. Then there was a bridge that his steward thought was in need of repair, which resulted in several rides out to inspect it, from which Penvale returned damp, muddy, and in decidedly ill humor. Once the roads cleared, too, a sizable backlog of correspondence from town arrived, almost all for Penvale, the contents of which kept him confined to his study, but to Jane's surprise, there was a letter for her as well.

When Crowe had presented it to her at the breakfast table, her heart had sunk, fearing it was some attempt on the part of Penvale's uncle to make contact with her, though she couldn't imagine why he would possibly wish to do so. The handwriting, however, was neat and feminine, and when she'd opened the letter and glanced down at the signature, she was astonished to realize it was from her sister-in-law.

Jane cast a furtive glance across the table, where Penvale was absorbed in his own stack of letters, which he was regarding at a worryingly close distance with a furrowed brow and a faint squint. Suppressing a sigh, Jane returned her attention to her own letter and read:

Willingham House, Fitzroy Square, 4 March

Dear Jane,

I've decided it would be absurd for me to address you as Lady Penvale, in part because I'm still not accustomed to there being such a person, and in part because if we are to manage some semblance of sisterly affection, starting in writing seems as good a place as any, so I hope you won't be bothered by my informality of address. And if you are bothered, you're hundreds of miles away in a drafty old house no doubt having your complexion slowly ruined by the sea breeze, meaning there's nothing you can do about it, anyway.

This has been a fairly dull winter here in town; I am already looking ahead to spring, and Lord Willingham and I were discussing our desire to pay you and Penvale a visit as soon as the weather warms a bit and the roads dry out. If you would please write back with the dates that would be amenable to you, we can begin planning our journey.

I've sent a letter to my brother with a similar query, but he's never been a terribly reliable correspondent—please remind me to show you a sample of some of the abysmal excuses for letters he sent me whilst he was at school and university, in which he considered, for example, "Hello sis, hope you haven't got too many new freckles in this hot weather we've been having" to be a perfectly acceptable opening. I must confess it is a relief to have a woman to correspond with now.

I will await your reply and look forward to seeing you both in the spring. In the meantime, I am sending along some of my favorite cream for my complexion, as no doubt yours will need it after the ravages of a windy winter on the coast, and I do not expect the village shops will have much to offer in this regard.

Yours, etc.
Diana

Jane set down the letter, unsure whether she wanted to crumple it up and roll her eyes in irritation or burst into an unseemly fit of laughter. Diana certainly did not stand on formalities in her correspondence, which Jane supposed should not come as a surprise. She was not entirely looking forward to having her sister-in-law under her roof for a few weeks this spring, but she supposed it couldn't be avoided.

"I've had a letter from your sister," she said, and Penvale, who was still squinting—Jane made a mental note to inquire as to whether there was anyone capable of crafting spectacles in the village—at the letter before him, glanced up at her, faint surprise registering on his face.

"Have you?"

"She wants to know when she and the marquess can come visit."

"Typical Diana," he muttered, running a hand over his face. "She couldn't just wait for a bloody invitation."

"Shall I send invitations, then?" Jane asked, striving for a neutral tone. She couldn't bear for him to realize just how uncomfortable she found the thought of playing hostess to his sophisticated London friends, even if some part of her—buried deep within—had grown rather intrigued by the idea of observing her husband in the company of those who knew him best.

Because the fact was, the more time she spent with Penvale, the more she wanted to know about him. She found herself *curious* about him in a way she had never been curious about anything else, unless she counted the house she lived in. When she had first arrived at Trethwick Abbey, eighteen years old and newly parentless, a single trunk of possessions to her name and nothing to occupy her time, she had spent days wandering the halls of the house, familiarizing herself with each room, each hidden staircase, each tapestry that concealed a door. This practice had been quite useful, as it turned out; who knew that haunting an old manor house would require such familiarity with secret passages?

Now she felt the same urge with Penvale, who was not a static, unmoving, immutable building she could wander through slowly, but someone who himself was undoubtedly changing every day that he spent here, and she felt a sudden piercing ache to know him better, to witness those changes herself, rather than from a remove.

And she could not help but think that if she wished to know her husband better, knowing his friends better was not a bad way to go about that endeavor—those noisy, cheerful friends she had found so intimidating in London.

"Yes," Penvale said slowly. "To Diana and Jeremy, of course, and Audley and Violet, and Belfry and Emily. West and Lady Fitzwilliam, too."

Jane frowned. "Have I met those friends?"

Penvale, who had been staring thoughtfully into the middle distance, glanced at her with faint surprise, almost as if—Jane thought grumpily—he had forgotten that he hadn't been speaking to himself. "They were at the wedding, you were introduced—don't you recall?"

"There were an awful lot of people there," Jane said testily.

"Jane." Penvale's voice was amused. "There were a dozen people at most."

"Well, it felt like more at the time," Jane said, glaring at him. She deliberately laid the letter opener—which she belatedly realized she still clutched—on the table before her plate, hoping her message was clear: *Irritate me further, and I will stab you with this.*

"West is Audley's brother." Penvale leaned back in his chair, still looking faintly amused and seeming unconcerned for his own safety, which Jane thought was a bit overly confident of him, given her mood.

At his words, Jane conjured a memory of a tall, serious-looking man who bore a strong resemblance to Violet's husband. "He had a walking stick?" she asked uncertainly.

Penvale nodded. "He was in a curricle accident several years ago—one that killed Jeremy's elder brother, the previous marquess. West broke his leg badly, and then a fever set in—they weren't certain he'd survive."

"Oh," Jane said. She'd never been good in moments like these, when it felt as though some sort of response were required, one that needed a bit more social skill than she possessed.

Penvale, fortunately, did not seem to notice her awkwardness.

"Lady Fitzwilliam was at the wedding, too, though, from what I recall, she took particular care to ensure that she was as far from West as possible the entire time."

Jane thought again. "She was a . . . redhead?"

Penvale laughed. "No, that was Belfry's sister. We may as well invite her, too—add the Earl and Countess of Risedale to your list," he said a bit imperiously, as if Jane were his secretary. She resisted the urge to roll her eyes. "Lady Fitzwilliam—you'll hear Diana and her friends call her Sophie, and I'm sure she'll give you leave to do so as well—is an old flame of West's, and I'm fairly certain my sister is hell-bent on matchmaking the pair of them. If we don't invite her as well, Diana will never let me hear the end of it." He said this with the tolerant affection of an elder brother.

Jane's head was beginning to spin a bit at the litany of impressive titles he'd just rattled off. "All right," she said, her heart thumping in her chest at the thought of a house party of this size. She held up her fingers one by one as she recited the names back to him. "Lord and Lady James, Lord and Lady Willingham, Lord and Lady Julian, Lord and Lady Risedale, Lady Fitzwilliam—" She looked at him inquiringly.

"Bridewell," he supplied.

"Lady Fitzwilliam Bridewell, and We— Sorry, what is West's actual name? What is that a nickname for?"

"His courtesy title. He's the Marquess of Weston."

"And the Marquess of Weston," she said, holding up a final finger. "Anyone else?" *Please, let there be no one else.*

"Belfry's brother, perhaps—the Earl of Blackford."

Jane frowned. "Then our numbers will be uneven." She tried to keep a hopeful note out of her voice.

Penvale cast a long-suffering look at the ceiling. "Let's invite Lady Fitzwilliam's younger sister, then. Sophie is the eldest of several, and the middle sister was widowed a few years ago—no doubt she'll be glad of a change of scenery, now that she's out of mourning."

Jane suppressed a sigh with some effort. "What is this sister's name?"

Penvale paused for a long moment.

"Penvale! You want to invite her to our house party, and you don't even know her name?"

"Sophie has a lot of sisters," he said defensively. "Four, I believe. And they're all married now, so I struggle to remember their . . . Ah!" He snapped his fingers triumphantly. "Mrs. Brown-Montague. She married the younger son of a viscount, if I recall correctly—he was in the army. Died at Waterloo, I believe."

"Mrs. Brown-Montague, then," Jane said with her best attempt to sound deeply enthused at the prospect of entertaining a horde of houseguests, all of whom were of a considerably more elevated background than her own, a sizable chunk of whom she'd never exchanged more than a word with, and a few of whom she'd never met at all. "Anyone else to add to the list, before I start on the invitations?"

"No," Penvale said slowly, but with a faint frown. "Perhaps I ought to write the invitations, though."

Jane immediately stiffened. "Why would you do that?" she asked. "I'm not an expert on these things, but I think sending the invitations would be well within my responsibilities as the viscountess."

"Well," he said, "you've never hosted a party like this, and I know you're uncomfortable in situations like this, so I want to make sure my friends feel truly welcomed—"

"And why," Jane broke in sharply, "don't you think I could manage that? Do you not think I'm capable of writing a letter of invitation without insinuating that I despise them?"

Penvale waved a hand dismissively, which did nothing to improve her temper. "Of course not. It's just that— Well, you've not spent much time with my friends, have you? So I thought they might be more inclined to accept an invitation if it came directly from me."

Jane went still. Placed both of her hands in her lap, where she folded them neatly, out of sight. Leveled an even look across the table at her husband. "You mean to say that you think I have been so unfriendly toward your friends, in our almost nonexistent acquaintance, that they would not accept an invitation if it came from me?" She was trying very hard to keep her voice calm, but that was growing more difficult by the moment.

Penvale straightened in his seat, clearly sensing that he'd waded into dangerous waters. "I didn't mean to imply that you were ever deliberately unkind—just that they don't know you terribly well yet. You're not particularly . . . warm, you know."

Jane felt his words like a blow. She was aware of her own shortcomings. She was aware of her discomfort around people she did not know well, and that she was hardly a skilled conversationalist—at least not when the conversation turned to the sort of idle chatter that polite society seemed to find so vitally important and which Jane found so desperately dull. But she did not think she was unkind—and she knew that she was perfectly capable of sending an invitation without implying that its recipients were unwelcome.

She was merely *shy*—not completely hopeless.

Except perhaps her husband thought she was—and it was not a terribly pleasant realization to make, not when she was already feeling entirely out of her depth with a large house party to host for a group of near-strangers.

"Is that what you think of me, then?" she asked, meeting his gaze without blinking. How odd to think that she had found it so difficult to meet his eyes for so long and that she should find it so easy to do so now. How odd, indeed, that this time two months ago, she was just making his acquaintance, while now he was becoming so frightfully familiar to her, in a way that most people had never been—most people had never had the chance to be, for that matter.

She was more comfortable around him than she had been around any man—or woman—her own age whom she had ever met. Perhaps this was why she felt the sting of his words so sharply.

She had been coming to . . . *trust* him.

How unutterably foolish.

"I think this may have come out wrong," he replied, not breaking her gaze, his voice as quiet and serious as her own. "I didn't mean to cause offense."

"Of course not." She shook her head once. Sharply. "I do not believe it was intentional at all—but you *did* cause offense, all the same. At least now I know. Now I know that you think I am so awkward, such an embarrassment, that I cannot even send a polite letter to your friends without frightening them off. I know—" Here, for the first time, her voice wavered a bit, but she pressed on all the same. "I know that I am not like your sister and her friends and doubtless countless other women you've known in London, all your mistresses, all the ladies you courted who batted their eyelashes at you and bantered and flirted and said frightfully clever and amusing things. I'm not like that. I'll never be *charming*."

"I know that." Something about his tone caused a small trickle of warmth to course through her—there was an appreciative note to his words, one that did not sound as though he regretted any of the things she had just said about herself, the qualities she had reminded him she did not possess.

But she mustn't dwell on that warmth.

"I have other qualities," she said. "I don't plan to host balls for the *ton*, or to try to mingle in the finest circles—I'd fail in any such attempts, and I don't *want* to. But I—I can be a good wife, and a good mistress of this estate, and I thought you had conversed with me enough to know that even if I can't discuss the weather and so-and-so's new dress and which coiffure is at the height of fashion, I can . . ." She trailed off before finishing quietly, "I can discuss the things that matter. And I can send a bloody invitation, for heaven's sake." Before he could respond, she pushed back her chair and announced, "If you'll excuse me."

And then she fled.

Chapter Fifteen

Penvale was not accustomed to apologizing.

It was not that he thought himself so perfect, so above reproach, that he never did anything that warranted apology. It was more that the need scarcely arose because he never had conversations serious enough to put himself at risk of offending whomever he was conversing with, not even Diana, Jeremy, and Audley.

But Jane was not his sister or his friend.

She was his wife.

He had spent much of the past year watching his friends play out their own romantic dramas, and often it had been so obvious to him what needed to be done—what simple conversations needed to be had. Why could his friends not see it?

He was finding, however, that it was considerably easier to sit and offer opinions as an idle observer than it was to make a success of his own marriage. One thing, at least, was clear: He'd been an ass, and he needed to apologize.

But in order to do that, he needed to find Jane.

At first he'd made a beeline for the library—it was her favorite room, after all. But he'd entered it, confident that he'd guessed correctly, only to find the room empty, no sign that anyone had recently been within. So then he'd tried the morning room—no—and her bedroom—still no—and, eventually, lowered himself to asking Mrs. Ash if she'd seen Lady Penvale.

"Last I saw her, she had her pelisse on and was heading down the stairs" was the woman's solemn reply, as if to imply that she never expected to see Jane again. How one could look *quite* so mournful while polishing a banister was beyond him.

So Penvale fetched his coat and set off.

It was a wet, blustery day, and no sooner had he stepped outside than he was hit with a blast of salty wind in his face. The main entrance to Trethwick Abbey faced away from the ocean, and he stood in the gravel driveway, gazing at the rolling green hills in the distance, deep in thought.

Where would Jane have gone?

He turned seaward, recalling their discussion about the cliff path.

The path in question was a narrow strip of dirt and gravel, bordered on the western edge by only a couple of feet of wind-torn grass and the dramatic jagged rocks of the cliff face. Below, there was nothing but open air and crashing ocean. The path wound behind Trethwick Abbey and continued along the sea cliffs to both the north and south of the house—if one walked far enough to the south, the path would begin a gentle descent into St. Anne's, while to the north, it eventually descended to a cove with a small beach and clear, cold water perfect for sea bathing.

Penvale set off to the north, reasoning that if Jane were upset and didn't wish to encounter anyone, she'd likely walk away from the village rather than toward it. While the wind was cold, during the rare moments when it died down, the air itself was reasonably mild, the first day in ages that had felt as though spring might be beginning to make its presence known. After only a few minutes of walking, Penvale spotted Jane, her red pelisse standing out like a beacon against the gray sky and ocean. She was perched atop a large boulder with her knees tucked up under her chin, her arms wrapped around them, her gaze fixed steadily out to sea.

If she heard his approach, she gave no indication, and she did not turn to acknowledge him as he hoisted himself up onto the boulder next to her. He turned to look at her, even as she kept her eyes relentlessly focused on the waves—indication, if he'd needed any, that she was not going to make this easy for him.

"I'm sorry," he said, his voice just loud enough that the wind couldn't steal his words. She cut him a sideways look but didn't reply, clearly waiting to see what else he had to say.

"I speak carelessly sometimes. I don't often think about what others will think of what I say—if what I say might hurt them. I'm not accustomed—" He broke off, drew in a deep breath, wishing he could physically crawl out of his skin, so uncomfortable did this admission make him. But he would do it. She deserved honesty from him, at least.

"I'm not accustomed to my opinion mattering enough to cause offense," he said, and now she did turn to look at him, the wind whipping the tendrils of dark hair at her temples that had escaped from the braided knot at her nape. Her eyes were wide, more blue than violet today, and there was color in her cheeks from the cold wind.

"But—your sister. Your friends." She seemed incredulous, and Penvale wondered, in a flash, how she saw him—what she thought of his life, as she had come to know him. He was not used to wondering what anyone else thought of him; what he thought of himself had always been enough.

What, then, had changed?

"I love my sister and my friends," he said evenly, and she leaned closer to him so that his voice carried to her ears above the gusting wind. "But they have their own lives—their own marriages, now—and I know that mine is not the most important voice in their ears, if it ever was. And this is as it should be, of course."

He looked at her and reached out a hand to seize hers, warm in his grip even through the gloves she wore. "I know that ours is not a marriage that either one of us would have chosen"—why did it cause him a bit of a pang to utter those words?—"but it is still a marriage, and I have no right to treat your feelings carelessly. Not when I should treat them with more care than anyone else. Not ..." Here he hesitated, not wishing to do further damage, then took a breath, trusting that she would take his meaning. "Not when others, I suspect, have not been so careful in the past."

A flicker of her eyes was the only sign that he had guessed correctly, and she glanced down to her hand, held tightly in his.

"I know you are perfectly capable of sending a polite invitation, and I know you can host my friends without insulting them. I was being an ass by suggesting otherwise." He paused, choosing his words carefully. "I watched you in the village the other week, with the villagers—I know you were trying. And I know you will try when my friends visit, too, and I was not giving you enough credit when I implied that you would offend them. It was ... well, it was very badly done, and I wish I'd taken three seconds to think before I opened my mouth." The confession made him feel raw and exposed, but it was not untrue, and she deserved this, and much more, from him.

She looked up at him now, the dark lashes framing her eyes impossibly long and thick, and considered him for a long moment. Penvale had the sense that she was taking his measure, and he felt a rather desperate wish to know what she thought as she regarded him.

"I know that I am shy," she said. "And I know that I . . . am not at ease, to say the least, when I am around people I do not know well. And I know—I know that I seem ill-tempered and rude in these situations, and even as I am doing it, I cannot work out *why* I am doing it or how to behave any other way. But I do not wish to embarrass you or make any of your friends uncomfortable. And I . . . I apologize if my behavior in London has made our marriage difficult for you or made you feel that you have something to prove to your friends."

"Hang my friends." His voice came out sharper than he intended, but she did not flinch. "I don't care what they think about our marriage. I only care what *you* think."

And, even as he spoke these words—these words that he had not intended to say at all—he realized that they were true. He did care what she thought—of their marriage, of *him*.

When had he started caring?

He reached up with his free hand to cup her cheek, cold and soft. He was drawn toward her as if by some peculiar gravity.

"What—what are you doing?" Her voice was scarcely more than a whisper, one he felt against his skin.

"I don't know," he said, and then he kissed her.

When his lips first touched hers, she went rigid with surprise, but after another second, her mouth softened beneath his, and he deepened the kiss, his hand sliding down to cup her jaw, angling her head to the side.

Her hand landed tentatively on his shoulder, then slid up to his neck, and he felt her lips curve into a smile against his own.

"What is it?" he asked, drawing back just enough to speak but not far enough that he could see anything other than the vivid blue-violet of her eyes as he rested his forehead against hers.

"You need a haircut," she said.

"Why," he asked, slowly winding a curl of her hair around his finger, "are you so concerned with my appearance? First you want me to wear spectacles, now a haircut?"

She drew back far enough that he could tell she was scowling at him. "I want you to wear spectacles because you can't *see*, you absolute idiot," she said, and he was laughing before he could help himself, a laugh that was cut short when she abruptly tugged his face down to hers.

And then they were kissing again and their tongues were tangling, and someone gasped, and for the life of him, Penvale wasn't certain which one of them it was, and she was pressing closer to him, freeing her other hand from his grip so that she could wrap it around his shoulders, pressing the softness of her breasts against his chest, and Penvale was just beginning to become aware—truly, painfully aware—of how long it had been since he'd last taken a woman to bed—

"*Squawk!*" said a seagull, quite close at hand.

"Good *God*," Penvale swore, breaking away from Jane and turning to catch a glimpse of the bird in question, which was several feet away, watching the proceedings with considerable interest.

"*Squawk?*" inquired the seagull.

Penvale eyed it warily.

"Er," Jane said from behind him; at some point, she had removed her hands from his neck and shoulders, and Penvale felt a cold wind blowing across the suddenly exposed skin at his nape. He glanced back at her, though he did not like to leave his back exposed to the seagull for very long. "Is there a problem? You look a bit pale."

"I'm fine," he informed her.

"*Squawk!*" said the seagull, and Penvale whirled back around, maneuvering onto his knees so that he might be prepared to . . . well, to do what, he wasn't precisely certain. But he thought it best not to be caught unaware by a large seabird.

He and the seagull exchanged a look heavy with meaning—on Penvale's part, at least, and that meaning was more or less *Stay the bloody hell away from me or I will encourage one of my well-paid employees to come shoot you.* Until, that is, said meaningful look was interrupted by the arrival of a second seagull.

"*Squawk?*" asked the newcomer.

"*Squawk!*" said the first seagull joyfully.

Penvale turned to Jane, unsettled. "Are the seagulls *bigger* in Cornwall?"

Jane, for her part, appeared to be trying not to laugh. "I am hardly a seagull expert, but I don't think so."

He glanced back at the birds. "I think they're bigger," he said definitively. "Those seagulls could eat Cecil as an appetizer."

"Cecil?" Jane asked blankly.

"Emily's kitten," he informed her. "No doubt you'll make the little bas—little fellow's acquaintance when they come to visit, as I'm sure she'll bring him with her."

"I see," she said, and he was fairly certain that she was still close to laughter.

"Those are unnaturally large birds, is what I'm saying," he said, keeping his eyes fixed on the seagulls as he sprang to his feet. He turned to offer a hand to Jane, pulling her to her feet as well.

"Do you think they'll let us pass them? Or might they attack?" she asked, a slightly apprehensive look crossing her face.

Penvale, gratified by her sensible wariness of their winged companions, said—as calmly as he could manage under the circumstances—"Don't worry. I'll approach them first—I think if we walk slowly, and avoid any sudden movements—"

At this juncture, he was forced to break off, because Jane was giggling so hard that he doubted she could even hear him.

"Ha, ha," he said acidly as she dropped his hand and strode past him, offering the seagulls a cheerful "Hello, ladies!" as she passed them. Penvale took a slightly more circuitous route, one that involved slipping and sliding up and down a grassy knoll and through a mud puddle before he rejoined Jane on the path and they continued their progress back to the house.

"Far be it from me to mock one's very real fears," Jane said as they walked, "but I was wondering if it was all birds, or seagulls specifically, that inspire such terror in you?"

Penvale reached out to grasp her by the elbow and steer her past a slushy puddle. "If you must know, it's seagulls specifically. I'd forgotten how damned large they are here; a whole world of suppressed childhood memories came flooding back."

"Ah," Jane said solemnly. "Mauled by one, were you?"

"Not quite," he hedged.

"Oh, now I *must* know," she said, something close to glee in her voice. And Penvale realized that—despite the fact that Jane would undoubtedly use this highly embarrassing story as ammunition against him for some time to come—he wanted to do whatever was within his power to keep that happy note in her voice.

"I was . . . mobbed. By a flock of seagulls."

Jane, admirably, did not laugh. Yet. "That must have been traumatizing."

"It was, thank you. I was eight. I had stolen Diana's scone during tea in the nursery and run away so that I might eat it in peace before someone caught me—she was screaming bloody murder, and I doubt it will surprise you to learn that, even at three, she had an impressive pair of lungs."

"Shocking," Jane murmured.

"Anyway, I came outside and hid along the back of the house, thinking it might take long enough to find me there that I could enjoy the scone in peace, and I was just about to take a bite when they descended." He could not prevent a shudder.

"How many seagulls, precisely, are we discussing?"

"Hundreds."

Jane gave him a skeptical look.

"All right, perhaps six," he amended reluctantly. "But I can assure you, when they swoop down upon you with their wings flapping, it *feels* like hundreds." Out of a desire to preserve some shred of dignity, he added, "I put up a fierce fight—even managed to get a small bite in before they snatched it away. But ultimately, I was left sconeless. And then I was banned from having dessert for the rest of the week, on account of stealing the scone from Diana in the first place."

"A true tragedy."

"To an eight-year-old, it was. I can still remember my father informing me that future viscounts did not steal scones—or anything else—from ladies. To which, naturally, I replied that chubby little sisters didn't count as ladies, and then he advised me to stop talking before he changed his mind about thrashing me." He shook his head ruefully at the memory. "In any case, I've disliked seagulls ever since."

Jane reached out to seize his hand. "Thank you for sharing this dark memory from your past. I hope, now that you have voiced it, it will lessen its grip on you and torment you no longer."

"Jane," he said, attempting sternness but failing to pull it off, betrayed by the smile that insistently tugged at the corner of his mouth. As they approached the house and she laced her fingers through his, he knew that at some point in the past hour—whether it was due to his apology, or his kiss, or possibly just his sharing a traumatic past with seagulls—she had forgiven him.

And he could not deny the wave of relief that washed over him.

Chapter Sixteen

It was toward the end of March that Jane realized something in the village had changed.

She had traipsed into St. Anne's alone that morning, a basket over one arm and only a tentative plan in mind. Penvale was occupied with meeting a surveyor who had come to assess the bridge in need of repair. Jane had sent a couple of deliveries of books for Miss Trevelyan a few weeks earlier, in the wake of their previous meeting in the village, but she had continued to dwell on the schoolteacher's plight, particularly each time she whiled away an evening in the library at Trethwick Abbey, surrounded by more books than she could possibly ever hope to read. Slowly, an idea had come to her—one she had not yet mentioned to Penvale— so she had come into the village today to make a few discreet inquiries.

Every village could use a library, after all, and she was in need of an occupation; while she did have her haunting to orchestrate, that hardly occupied all of her time. Initially, in the wake of Penvale's kiss on the cliffside a week earlier, Jane had wavered, her thoughts lingering on the feeling of his mouth on hers, the warmth of his hands on her skin.

This was a dangerous weakening on her part; Jane had not thought herself the sort of woman to allow a single kiss to distract her from her purpose.

It had, however, been interesting from an intellectual standpoint—her books had a lot to say about kissing, and she'd grown curious to see how the real thing compared to the fictional ones. But now she knew that even her most scandalous books had come nowhere near describing the sensation of Penvale's tongue tracing her lips, his hands on her skin, the thoroughly shocking way her pulse had seen fit to take up residence in a certain unspeakable part of her body. So she could sleep peacefully at night, having satisfied her curiosity, and certainly would not lie awake replaying said kiss in her mind for more nights in a row than she cared to admit.

She had just begun to wonder, with a lack of enthusiasm that was frankly alarming, whether she really ought to be getting on with haunting the house again when a conversation with Penvale over the breakfast table had given her an awfully clever idea.

"Have you sent the letters of invitation yet?"

She glanced up from the toast she was buttering. "No, not yet." She suppressed a sigh before adding, "Did you have more friends to invite?"

"No," he said quickly. "I just thought to glance at them before you have them mailed—I might add a couple of notes to the bottom of the letters, if you don't mind." He glanced up at her. "Not to correct anything you've written—it's just that I'm not a very reliable correspondent, and I owe notes to a few of my friends."

She returned her attention to her toast, relieved that at least he wouldn't be increasing their numbers even more—and believing his assurances, despite their previous argument. She didn't wish to spend too much time examining why, precisely, she was so ready to believe him. "As you wish. If you could see that they're posted once you've done so . . ."

"Certainly," he said, and she glanced up at him as she lay her knife down, surprised to find that he was watching her with an odd expression.

"Is something wrong?" she asked uncertainly, suddenly self-conscious.

He shook his head. "No—no." He pushed his chair back and rose. "I'd better go write those notes, then. I'll want to warn everyone not to come if they're particularly afraid of ghosts." He shot her a grin as he departed, clearly finding himself vastly amusing, but Jane sat rooted to her seat, an idea taking hold in her mind.

It was *perfect*. Why hadn't she thought of it sooner?

There was one way to ensure that this awful house party didn't take place: make Penvale so nervous about their haunted house that he canceled it. For if he was truly convinced that a ghost was wandering their halls by night—well, surely he'd warn all his friends off of visiting.

Jane rose from her seat, eager to confer with Mrs. Ash on the next stage of her plan, and resolutely ignored the fact that her desired outcome was now entirely focused on ridding herself of Penvale's friends rather than Penvale himself. And the fact that Penvale's absence no longer seemed nearly as appealing as it once did.

Jane and her accomplices had ceased their midnight wails, solely because the staff were sacrificing sleep (and, truth be told, so was Jane). Instead, they resorted to a simpler program of events, including mysteriously vanishing and reappearing objects from various rooms of the house, strange thumps from the ceiling at dinner every other day (except Sundays, of course; even spirits seemed to have a healthy respect for the Lord's day).

Today, however, Jane was going to the village, and she carried with her a basket full of books.

Her first stop, once she made it to St. Anne's—her hem a muddy mess from the walk along the cliff path and her bonnet trailing behind her on its ribbons, the wind long since having knocked it from her head—was the village school. She had found in the library an illustrated dictionary that she thought might interest the children, and had tucked it among the other books that she carried.

"My lady!" Miss Trevelyan seemed surprised when Jane tapped at the door; Jane had deliberately timed her visit for the afternoon, when she knew the children would already have been dismissed, so that she wouldn't interrupt a lesson, and so that Miss Trevelyan was alone. "The children have enjoyed the books you sent along—we already had an incident with a child sneaking one home and returning it with a few spots of raspberry jam on the pages." She looked vaguely guilty. "We, er, did our best to wipe the jam off."

Jane waved a dismissive hand. "I don't need those books back, so feel free to spill as much jam on them as you please." She paused, considering. "Or perhaps not—I suppose it might attract ants after a while."

Miss Trevelyan's mouth twitched, but she merely said, "We're very appreciative, at any rate—and if I might add . . ." Here she trailed off, looking a bit hesitant. "We're so pleased by the buns the viscount has sent over regularly as well."

Jane frowned. "I beg your pardon?"

Miss Trevelyan smiled. "You needn't tell him that we know it's him—I understand that he swore Mrs. Rowe to secrecy when he asked her to ensure that a box of cinnamon buns was delivered to the school twice a week, for the children to enjoy as a treat. We're ever so grateful, and we'll never let on that we know it's him, but . . . I wanted to tell you, at least, how kind I think it is."

Jane was torn between astonishment and irritation. Would Penvale never have the decency to behave as she expected him to? Why, oh *why*, could he not be the unfeeling London gentleman she had been so certain she was marrying? She had no qualms about haunting that man. But this one! A man who delivered baked goods to children! It was . . . well, it was simply unfair. Why had she had the bad luck to marry a man who seemed determined to make her like him?

Miss Trevelyan was regarding her with something approaching concern. "Are you quite all right, my lady? Should I not have mentioned it? It's just that I can't say anything to Lord Penvale directly, but I didn't want it to go unacknowledged—"

"No, no," Jane assured her, waving a hand. "Lord Penvale is very . . . thoughtful." She paused, eyeing the schoolmistress, before tentatively adding, "And you might call me Jane, if you wish."

Miss Trevelyan opened her mouth, likely to protest, and Jane felt as though she'd badly misstepped and hastened to make amends. "I mean, you don't have to, not if it makes you uncomfortable. It's merely that I was thinking—well, we're of an age, and there aren't many ladies of our age in the village—"

At this juncture, mercifully, Miss Trevelyan interrupted her. "Jane."

Jane fell silent, having only the vaguest, most horrified notion of any of the words that had just come out of her mouth.

"I'd like that. I'm Louisa." She hesitated, shifting the dictionary from hand to hand, then added, "Perhaps you might care to come to tea sometime?"

Jane, who belatedly realized that she should have been the one to extend such an invitation, as the viscountess and mistress of a large estate, but couldn't figure out a way to decline now without sounding even ruder, simply said, "I—I'd like that."

Miss Trevelyan—*Louisa*—smiled at her and said, "I'm a bit out of practice at making friends, but I've no doubt we can muddle through together."

And Jane, recognizing these words for the gift that they were, managed a smile in return.

A short while later, as she made her way from the schoolhouse farther into the village, her thoughts returned to her husband, and what Louisa had told her, and the word Jane had used to describe him in reply: thoughtful.

He *was* thoughtful, she realized, her mind lingering on the memory of their previous visit to the village together, and his request for a private room for their meal, his willingness to return home far earlier than he would have preferred. All because he could tell—without her uttering a single word—that that was what *she* preferred.

She also had the oddest feeling that he would deny such an adjective being used to describe him. She puzzled over the strange, contradictory man she had married as she continued making her way around the village—popping into the haberdasher in search of a new hat for the springtime; getting fitted for new boots at the cobbler; stopping in at the bakery, because she had walked all the way from Trethwick Abbey, after all, and she thought she deserved a treat for her trouble. As she continued her afternoon in this pleasant fashion, she could not help but notice that the villagers had changed ever so slightly in their manner toward her.

Coming into the village as the ward of Mr. Bourne had always been a rather fraught experience for Jane; her guardian, unsurprisingly, had not been popular, and she always felt anxious, as if some of the villagers' dislike for him was going to rub off on her. So she'd done what she had always done whenever she felt anxious or uncomfortable: gone very, very quiet and very, very cold in the hope that no one would notice how awkward she felt. This meant that whatever sympathy the villagers might have felt for her, as a young lady stuck alone in a drafty old manor house with an unpleasant guardian, quickly faded.

And Jane had no one to blame but herself.

But today was different. She didn't pick up on it at first, being caught up in her own thoughts, but as she made her way along the village's narrow streets, she noticed smiles and friendly nods from the villagers, as opposed to the curious stares she was accustomed to on her infrequent visits. When she stopped at the bakery, a man went out of his way to rush to hold the door open for her, and when she thanked him, he asked her to give his best to her husband.

When Mrs. Rowe at the bakery slipped a couple of extra cinnamon rolls into a bag for Jane to take back to Trethwick Abbey "since his lordship is so fond of them," Jane paused before again expressing her thanks.

When Jane popped into the cheesemonger, who had a particularly advantageous location in the very heart of the village, to inquire if she could leave her basket of books—along with the carefully handwritten placard reading *Please take as many as you wish,* with her name signed beneath—at the far end of the counter near the door, the shopkeeper gave her a smile of such warmth that she was tempted to peer over her shoulder to ensure he wasn't smiling at someone else.

And when a pair of sisters skipping down the street paused to ask her if it was true, as the viscount said, that Jane read three books *every week*, Jane was sufficiently surprised that a laugh nearly escaped her.

By the time Jane had concluded her errands and begun her solitary trek back to Trethwick Abbey, she could only draw one conclusion: The villagers were determined to *like* her.

And she was fairly certain it was all Penvale's fault.

It was odd, Jane thought, since, upon her first meeting with Penvale, she never would have guessed that he was the sort of man capable of inspiring such loyalty among the populace.

But the truth was, the more time that passed, the more Jane came to realize that her impressions of Penvale at their first meeting had borne only a passing resemblance to the man he actually was—and she was beginning to suspect that he loved Trethwick Abbey just as much as she did.

Many of Jane's fondest memories took place in the library: rainy afternoons spent before the fire, a book and a pot of tea at hand; the first time she'd entered the library at Trethwick Abbey, never having seen so many books in a single place; the evening recently when she'd chucked a volume of poetry at Penvale's head as he was particularly irksome (marriage was causing him to finely hone his ducking skills). But all of them paled in comparison to the sight before her eyes just now, upon her return from the village.

Penvale was sitting bent over a novel—a *novel!*— in an over-stuffed armchair before the fireplace, sniffling in a highly suspicious manner.

Jane—so gleeful that she worried it was possibly injurious to her health—crept into the room to get a better look at him, her presence unnoted. He was near the end of his book, a lock of hair partially obscuring his expression.

"Dusty in here, isn't it?" Jane observed airily.

He jerked his head up, revealing red-rimmed eyes. "How long have you been standing there?" he asked her warily.

"Only a minute or so," she said. "You seemed so engrossed in what you were reading that I didn't wish to disturb you." She tapped her chin thoughtfully. "Is it something about crop rotations?"

"Jane—"

"Irrigation systems?" she persisted. "I understand irrigation is very emotional."

"So help me—"

"Perhaps it's about sheep?" She batted her eyelashes, then almost immediately regretted it, as it made her feel like she had some sort of strange eye twitch. "We do have an awful lot of sheep around here. So much baa-ing."

"It's your bloody *Persuasion*, as you are perfectly well aware," he burst out, brandishing the book with what Jane considered to be a reckless disregard for the integrity of its spine.

"That book was quite expensive, and if you can't treat it with the proper respect—"

"I'll buy you another bloody book—I'll probably have to do so anyway, since this one has caused me to actually *shed tears*." He sounded appalled; Jane, naturally, was delighted. "Over a letter, of all things!"

"Ooooh. Captain Wentworth's letter." Jane sighed dreamily, sinking down onto the arm of Penvale's chair and pressing a hand to her breast. "Isn't it lovely? 'Half agony, half hope'! It's the most romantic thing." She peered over his shoulder at the page before him. "You've wept on the page!"

"I know," he said through gritted teeth. "That's why I said I'd have to buy you a new one. This is horrifying."

Jane huffed. "It's all right for gentlemen to *cry*, you know!"

"I'm perfectly aware," Penvale said indignantly, although Jane guessed he likely had not shed a tear in years. Jane herself was not prone to excessive displays of feeling, except with regard to events within the pages of her favorite novels. "I simply don't wish to cry over a *book*. A *novel*, of all things."

Jane poked him in the shoulder. "So you like it, then?"

Penvale once more looked furtive. "I— Perhaps. It's all right."

Jane bit the inside of her cheek to prevent herself from smiling— the sight of which would likely only cause him to dig in his heels further, stubborn man that he was. "And yet here you are, when doubtless you have plenty of other business with which to occupy yourself, unable to tear yourself away from the pages of Miss Austen's work."

"It's a dreary day," he hedged. "Awful weather. Can't get anything done outdoors."

(A quick glance out the window assured Jane that she had not lost her senses entirely and that it was, indeed, still a bright, sunny spring day.)

"Of course," she agreed solemnly.

"My study is terribly dark and chilly, you understand," he added.

(His study was, in fact, warmed by a fire and had the benefit of an almost unseemly number of candles and lamps.)

"Frightful," she said, nodding.

"My eyes were struggling to read the fine print in some documents my solicitor sent me, so I thought to give them a rest."

(He must truly be desperate for an excuse if he was willing to risk her suggesting he get spectacles, she thought.)

"By . . . reading something else?" she inquired.

"The text is larger."

(The text was quite small.)

"This all sounds very serious," she said. He watched her carefully, clearly waiting for some sort of unforeseen attack. "But not as serious as the fact that you won't admit you were wrong!"

She jabbed an accusatory finger into his chest, which was surprisingly firm for a man she had supposed to be an idle aristocrat, and she was reminded of his fondness for swimming. She then hastily tried very hard *not* to be reminded of his fondness for swimming, because that conjured up an entire litany of mental images involving very little clothing and a lot of . . . activity.

"Fine!" He reached up and caught her hand in his and looked directly at her. "I was wrong. I've spent days thinking about Anne Elliot and Captain Wentworth and . . . well, I was beginning to grow concerned that they weren't going to work it out!" He clutched her hand more tightly as he said this, and Jane had to try very hard to keep herself from smiling.

"I knew you'd like it," she said. "Would you like to try *Northanger Abbey* next? I purchased it in the same set, you know."

"I believe that one was in the stack you forced upon me, so it's likely already on my bedside table," he reminded her.

"You should read it," she urged. "It involves a possibly haunted house. Perhaps you will experience feelings of empathy for its heroine."

"I doubt that," he said darkly, but his gaze on her turned thoughtful, and Jane instantly wished that she hadn't brought it up. She was very careful when it came to discussing the supposed haunting of Trethwick Abbey—and she did not wish for him to suspect that she might have been inspired by any of her reading.

"In any case," she added hastily, "I will sleep the happiest sleep of my life tonight, knowing that you have come to realize the joy of novels."

"Jane." He now sounded reluctantly amused. "I've discovered that I enjoy one novel. *One.* I don't know that you should get too carried away in your excitement."

"Oh?" she asked. "Did you care to wager on the likelihood that you'll like another one I select for you?"

"Interesting you should mention our wager," he said, resting his head against the back of his chair and allowing his eyelids to lower lazily as he regarded her. "I don't recall that we'd worked out what *I* was going to do for *you* if you won."

"We . . . didn't?" Jane asked uncertainly, realizing as she spoke the words that he was correct. *She* had promised to behave sweetly to his sister, should she lose—she reflected cheerfully on all the energy she would save in May, not having to keep that particular promise if her plan to frighten off their houseguests proved unsuccessful—but they'd never discussed what *he* would do if he were the loser.

"Is there something you wish me to do for you, Jane?" he asked her, and Jane suddenly felt warm. She cast a glance at the fire, which had not instantaneously doubled in size and strength to explain the sensation.

All at once, she could think of nothing but the moment the week before, when he had kissed her in the open air, the wind whipping around them. She wondered what it would be like to kiss him here—indoors, where there were no people who might see them, where they were not wrapped up in layers of coats and gloves, where it was quiet and warm and still.

She licked her lips.

She also wondered what he would do if she *asked* him to kiss her.

Or if, better yet, she did it herself, without asking—if she took what she wanted instead.

She rather thought she might like to find out.

She reached a hand down to his face, the stubble on his cheek rough against her palm in a way that she found strangely pleasant. He tilted his head back, pressing his cheek into her hand, and then turned his face so that he could press a soft kiss to her palm. His gaze upon her was unwavering as he did so, and Jane felt her pulse in her throat, then the slow, heavy slide of warmth within her, seeming to pool in the base of her stomach.

She swallowed once, and then she leaned down and pressed her mouth to his.

It was a soft kiss at first, tentative and searching, and Jane let her eyes fall shut, seeing nothing, her entire world becoming the feeling of his lips on hers and the warmth of his cheek against her hand, the sudden press of his fingers at her waist—as though he were anchoring her to him. And Jane, who had never felt particularly tied to anyone or any place other than this old house, found she liked the feeling of being tethered to him, however gently.

Tentatively, she pressed her tongue to the seam of his lips, and he opened his mouth with the faintest guttural sound that sent the pool of heat settling even lower, between her legs, in a way that she was not unfamiliar with, but which she'd never thought to experience with anyone so mundane as a *husband*.

The husbands in her books were solid, dull sorts—it was the kidnappers, the pirates, the incorrigible rogues that sent the blood racing in her veins and her pulse pounding in parts of her body that she hadn't even been aware it was possible for a pulse to take up residence.

But then, when she had imagined a hypothetical future husband, she hadn't imagined anyone like Penvale. He wasn't solid and dull—but neither was he a rake or a rogue or a seducer.

He was . . . complicated.

Jane was coming to find that she *liked* complicated.

And she certainly liked everything about the way he kissed her, with his other hand at the nape of her neck, the warmth of his palm on her bare skin sending sparks coursing up her spine. His fingers slid into the silky mass of her hair, pinned back in a windswept knot, and she heard the faint *plink* of a hairpin falling to the floor.

Even as his fingers were busy, he continued to kiss her, his tongue sliding against hers, and Jane, despite all her reading, had not realized that kissing could feel like *this*—this needy, this utterly consuming, this intimate.

Her mouth curved against his in a smile—there was no need to be clever or witty, to converse easily, to make jokes, to offer a tinkling false laugh. Here, there was just her mouth and his tongue and his hand brushing the underside of her breast, setting all her nerves ablaze, and the low sound in her throat that she knew should have embarrassed her but which she could muster no shame for, not when she felt his mouth curve against her own in reply.

His hand left her breast, and Jane would have objected, would have voiced some protest, if she could have drawn her mouth away from his long enough to do so, but then it was at her waist, his other hand joining it there, and he was pulling her down so that she was straddling him in his chair, and—oh.

He bore her weight down upon him, and she could feel him beneath her, stiffening in his trousers, and Jane was very, very grateful for all the reading she had done that was not at all appropriate for an unmarried lady, because otherwise she would not have had the faintest clue what was happening.

He drew back, placing a series of kisses along her jawline, and she tilted her head back, marveling at the knowledge that *she* had caused that ragged edge to his breath, the color riding high in his cheeks. She might not be at home in a drawing room or at a ball, but *this*—this way of communicating, in which no words at all were necessary—

This, she liked.

His mouth continued its progress down her throat as his hips shifted beneath her, causing friction that sent a rush of sparks shooting down her spine. "Don't you think it absurd," she said, barely aware of what she was saying, awash in sensation, "that the only reason I know what *that* is"—she allowed her hand to drift, rather daringly, toward his lap—"is because I've read a lot of inappropriate books?"

Jane had always thought the word "splutter" was one of those things people did in books but not in actual life. And she would not have expected to use the word to describe the noise and gestures made by a man like her husband, collected and polite, every hair in place. And yet, in that instant, Penvale was decidedly spluttering.

"Are you having some sort of fit?" Jane inquired solicitously.

"I am *not*," he said after recovering enough to regain his powers of speech. "I'm just attempting to convince myself that we are actually having this conversation."

"I don't see why it should be improper, given what we were just doing."

"Well, doing and discussing are different things," Penvale said.

"One does not discuss the marital act, then, even with one's spouse?" Jane frowned. It was very irritating when she found a topic she *did* wish to converse about, only to be told that it wasn't proper. "That feels a bit prudish, I must say."

Penvale let out a huff of laughter. "It's not that we can't discuss matters of the bedchamber," he began.

"Not only the bedchamber, apparently," Jane felt compelled to note. "As we are currently in the library."

"The metaphorical bedchamber," Penvale amended.

"Oh!" Jane was extremely pleased. "Has your newfound appreciation for novels given you a love of metaphor?"

"Jane." Penvale pinched the bridge of his nose, and Jane was disturbed to note that she liked it when he did that—she found it charming, in fact. Jane found few things charming and almost never anything about gentlemen. They tried far too hard to be charming—it made her naturally distrustful instincts rear their heads. But this was unintentionally charming, and Jane was finding that was an entirely different class of charm, one she was alarmingly susceptible to.

"It just seems to me that if one is removing one's clothing with another person, the normal rules of polite society might not apply, which is why I was surprised to hear you say that one didn't discuss such things!"

"That's hardly what I meant."

"So people *do* discuss such things?"

Penvale reached up a hand to tuck an errant curl behind her ear. Why did the brush of his fingers against her ear make her feel as though she couldn't take a deep enough breath?

"They do. You caught me by surprise, but you're correct—there's nothing wrong with discussing this. And there are plenty of things you could say in these situations that I'm quite certain I'd enjoy." Something in his tone shifted as he spoke, his eyes sparking with a devilish light that Jane willed herself not to find appealing.

"Such as . . . ?"

"A bit of lewd banter in the bedroom can be very enjoyable," he said simply.

Jane regarded him with suspicion. "Lewd banter . . . in what way?" she asked slowly. She didn't like to admit to ignorance, but there was no denying that he knew a lot more about these matters than she did.

"I could tell you what I'd like to do to you."

"Oh," Jane said, and she felt her pulse once again make its presence known in a delicate location. "And you'd . . . like that?"

"I would," he said, and though he spoke easily enough, a certain renewal of interest on his part was impossible for her not to notice, given her position atop his lap. He *would* like it.

"But then what was it I said that was wrong?" she asked in frustration, coming back to the original reason the proceedings had halted—her expression of what she thought was perfectly reasonable indignation about the state of young ladies' sexual education.

He regarded her, and she was tempted to look away, because

something in his eyes was too frank, too knowing, for her comfort. This was why she'd never liked to meet people's gazes directly until she knew them very well—doing so always gave her the uncomfortable feeling that the other person was somehow learning something about her that she'd rather he or she didn't.

"Nothing," he said after a moment of this uncomfortable silence. "Nothing you said was wrong. It just— It surprised me. It was very . . . frank."

Jane rolled her eyes in exasperation. "This is why I hate polite society! There are so many rules, and you're always meant to be saying two things at once, but then half the time, something I say is wrong somehow!"

"And so you don't try at all," he finished, still watching her closely, his tone indicating that she was some sort of puzzle he was slowly solving.

And Jane didn't *want* to be solved. She didn't want to be treated like something to be worked out, to be understood—she just wanted to be herself.

Jane meant to make an elegant, stately departure at this juncture, but at that moment, she came to learn a truth—perhaps not universally acknowledged but undeniable all the same: It is impossible for a lady to extract herself from straddling a gentleman's lap with anything approaching grace.

"For heaven's sake," she muttered as she flailed. Jane was not very tall, but she suddenly seemed to have far too many limbs, a fact that was not aided by the pesky skirts getting in her way. At last, Penvale— acting out of gentlemanly chivalry or perhaps a self-preserving desire not to get kneed in a sensitive portion of his anatomy—took matters into his own hands, literally, and hoisted her bodily from the chair and set her gently on the floor.

"Thank you," Jane said, in exceedingly ill temper by this point, and swept from the room without giving Penvale even the slightest chance to reply.

Chapter Seventeen

As they moved from March steadily into April and the reality of
the approaching house party loomed larger in Jane's mind, she realized
that she was running out of time.

"Have you mentioned anything about our ghost to your friends?"
she asked over dinner one evening in the second week of April, having
that afternoon received a scrupulously polite acceptance of her invitation from the Marquess of Weston.

Penvale laid down his fork, regarding her consideringly. *Too* consideringly. She didn't like or trust it. "I haven't," he said slowly. "I didn't
think it worthy of note—a few noises in the night, a bit of lost sleep.
Hardly newsworthy."

He spoke casually, but Jane was on her guard. Something about
the way he was looking at her made her decidedly uneasy, and she
thought it best not to press the matter.

"Of course," she agreed, returning her attention to the roast pheas-
ant on her plate. Clearly, if Penvale didn't even think it worth noting—
yet—then it was time to escalate things. It would be May before she
knew it, and she'd have a houseful of unwanted guests.

It was time to resort to a possibility Jane had held as a last resort:
She would have to impersonate a ghost.

"You're going to do what?" Mrs. Ash asked, extremely skeptically, when Jane confided this plan the following afternoon.

"I'm going to be a ghost," Jane said, stirring her tea. They were tucked away in the butler's pantry, enjoying a pot of tea and a plate of rather delicious cakes. Penvale was occupied with tenant visits that afternoon, meaning they could speak freely without any risk of being overheard.

"And how, precisely, do you intend to convince your husband that he is seeing a ghost and not merely his wife in an old nightgown?" Mrs. Ash asked, taking a sip of tea.

"I'm not going to let him get a proper look at me." Jane was pleased to have a ready response. "I will lure him from his bedroom with my ghostly wails—"

"This, I look forward to hearing."

"—and then once he is in a dark corridor, I will allow him to catch a glimpse of me vanishing around a corner."

"Won't he immediately think to check your bedchamber to see if you are safely asleep and not roaming the halls?"

"That," Jane said smugly, "is where the hidden staircase comes in."

The staircases: the key to their entire plot. The hidden staircases that Jane had lived in fear of Penvale discovering, the ones that had allowed mysterious ghostly noises to emanate seemingly from the walls themselves. The ones that would permit her, if she chose her location very, very carefully, to easily make it back to her bedchamber before Penvale did.

Because the convenient thing was that there was an entrance to one of these staircases in Penvale's bedroom.

Jane had discovered the staircases the first year she'd lived at Trethwick Abbey; with her guardian often absent, leaving her to her own devices, she hadn't had much to do other than explore her home. The fact that it wasn't truly hers made this quest all the more exciting; she felt as though, by learning this house better than the man who owned it, she was making it hers in this one small way. She might not own this house, but she *loved* it, and she *knew* it.

And, less nobly, she now knew it well enough to aid in the staging of a haunting. This had not been her original intent, but it was an undeniable benefit. And the fact that there was a matching set of hidden staircases within the interior walls in opposite corners of the house—evidently built to make it easier for servants to move from floor to floor rapidly, but which had at some point been abandoned—was quite convenient when it came to said haunting.

Mrs. Ash, meanwhile, was regarding her with a considerable degree of skepticism, but all she said was a doubtful "Whatever you think is best, dear," which was not quite the rousing show of support that Jane had envisioned.

Jane decided to pick her moment carefully, not wishing to leave anything to chance. First were the practical considerations: She'd want to choose a night that wasn't very clear, just to ensure the corridors of Trethwick Abbey were as dark as possible. The house boasted a series of mullioned windows at the eastern end of various hallways that, under ordinary circumstances, Jane was fond of, providing as they did lovely views of the hills, but they undeniably made the halls brighter, particularly on nights when the skies were clear and moonlight was allowed to spill through the windows unobstructed by any clouds.

As her luck would have it, April was uncommonly mild that year, full of lengthening days resplendent with afternoon sunshine, clear evenings with a low-hanging moon and thousands of stars twinkling overhead.

Jane was very irritated.

Or, rather, as irritated as it was possible to be when one was emerging from a gray Cornish winter into a world of green grass and bleating lambs and soft breezes under sunny skies.

Penvale, for his part, seemed inordinately cheerful. He was often gone from early in the morning until late in the afternoon, visiting tenants, observing lambing, trudging around the muddy lanes in boots that had lost almost all their London polish.

"My bootmaker will be appalled when I'm next in town," he informed her. "I've never gone through a pair so quickly in all my life."

"That is because you were an indolent, useless sloth," Jane retorted. Lately, she had taken to being deliberately provoking and was continuously nettled when all he did was grin at her by way of reply. It was a boyish grin, one that made him look several years younger and gave Jane the uneasy feeling that he knew precisely what she was doing.

And what *was* she doing?

A voice at the back of her mind told her, in smug, superior tones, that she was trying to keep Penvale at as much of a remove as possible, lest she find herself weakening toward him once more—her mind had lingered upon that kiss in the library far more often than was wise—or perhaps even admitting to herself that a lifetime spent sharing this house with him would not be so terrible a fate after all.

But Jane had come too far to allow such thoughts to hold much sway, so she pushed them firmly from her mind. It was time to become a ghost.

Penvale was not, as a rule, an overly observant man, which was why he was puzzled to find himself so utterly convinced, in the days that followed, that something was amiss with Jane.

Recently, she had been strange around him, and he couldn't work out why. He'd been busier than usual, it was true; as the weather had improved, he'd found himself spending long days out of doors, working alongside his tenants in the sunshine. All anyone could speak of was the uncommonly warm and sunny spring they were enjoying, and he was soaking up every moment of it. Here he was, home at last, toiling away outdoors, always a problem to solve or complaints to hear. It was precisely what he'd dreamed of.

And yet, as the days passed and Jane's strange manner toward him continued, even the long, tiring hours he spent outdoors were not enough to lull him to sleep at night with a blissfully blank mind. Instead, he lay awake long past midnight, staring at the darkened canopy above his bed, trying not to reflect on the fact that he occasionally caught himself thinking longingly of the nights Jane had spent sleeping next to him. Nights when he'd barely been able to snatch any sleep at all, what with all the wailing and window banging and various other absurdities. There was no excuse whatsoever for thinking back upon those nights with anything approaching longing.

And yet.

Now Penvale found himself lying awake, and it was more pleasant to reflect on Jane—this curious, mercurial creature he had married—than it was to dwell upon the other thoughts that weighed heavily on his mind. Namely, the fact that he had all the things he once thought he wanted above all else—and yet . . . he still felt dissatisfied.

Penvale had spent the entirety of his adult life convinced that if he could just accomplish this *one* thing—reclaiming Trethwick Abbey, his birthright, the place he belonged—then everything else would fall into place. And yet here he was: He had Trethwick Abbey; he'd even married, as he was expected to do.

And he still felt as though he were waiting for something.

He was slowly coming to realize that the house was not enough. Managing the estate brought him a sense of purpose, of intention, that he relished—but it was not enough on its own. Within a few weeks, his friends would arrive, happy in their marriages, secure in the affections of their spouses, and God damn it, but Penvale was jealous, and he was furious with himself for feeling this way, and for the first time in his life, the person he naturally thought first to turn to regarding a matter of great import wasn't Audley or Jeremy, it was *Jane*, of all people. At some point, he'd grown accustomed to her presence, her willingness to listen to whatever happened to be on his mind, even if she often responded with a sharp word. He'd stopped minding her sharp words, he realized.

It wasn't so odd that he should think to unburden himself to Jane first, he reasoned—she was there, across the breakfast table in the mornings, in the library on rainy afternoons, a mere room away at night. He'd grown used to having her around, was all. He *liked* having her around. It was nothing more complicated than that.

But Jane was the very person he couldn't speak to about this.

Not when she was, he suspected, trying to be rid of him.

He wasn't certain of this—he wasn't certain of anything about Jane, maddening creature that she was—but the more he thought about the ghost and how its presence had so neatly chased away his uncle, the more he thought it would be just like Jane to employ said ghost to be rid of the husband she'd never wished to marry in the first place.

As luck would have it, this suspicion was strengthened not ten minutes later, when he was yanked from his thoughts by the decidedly odd occurrence of a ghost materializing in his room.

Penvale was lying abed, still miles away from anything that

approached restful slumber, when, out of the corner of his eye, he noticed a flicker of white. He turned his head sharply but saw nothing other than complete and total darkness; it was a cloudy night, and there was little light coming into the room, even though the curtains were only partially drawn. He sat up in bed, wishing he were wearing something more than his drawers. He stared into the darkness for a long moment, not seeing anything, and then, once more, there was that bloody unearthly moan.

Penvale sprang out of bed, silent as a cat; it sounded as though the moan had come from directly behind him, and he spun around, feeling like a madman as he stared at the wall, his heart pounding in his chest. In that moment, he thought quite longingly of the silent and unhaunted walls of Bourne House in London, and wondered if country living was really all it was cracked up to be.

He stood there for long enough, shivering and staring, that his heart had time to return to something approaching its normal pace, but then, again—

"*Oooooaaaaaahhhhhhoooooooohhhhhh.*"

This time, the noise was more distant, but it was distinct enough that Penvale was certain its source was nearby. He seized the nearest article of clothing to hand—the breeches he'd tossed on a chair hours earlier, his valet already having been dismissed for the evening—and raced for the door, bursting out into the hallway outside his bedroom to find . . . nothing.

He stood there, staring first left, then right, and just as he was preparing to pick a direction at random and hope for the best—

"*Ooooooohhhhhhhhaaaaaahhhhhhhhh.*"

The moan came definitely from his left, the eastern portion of the house, and Penvale took off at a run, skidding around a corner just in time to see a flicker of white vanishing around the corner at the far end of the hallway. He set off in hot pursuit as she—whoever she might be, this ghostly figure in white—led him on a merry chase, around corner after corner, down hallways, up a flight of stairs, until at last Penvale rounded a final corner he had seen the flicker of white skirt pass around mere moments earlier—

And he skidded to a halt.

He was in the gallery, which stretched along the entirety of the southern side of the house on the third floor. And it was empty. He turned in a circle, feeling as though he were losing his mind— there were no doors, barring the one he had just careened through, only walls full of framed paintings and portraits, a few marble statues occupying some of the vast expanse of floor.

There was no one else here.

This was it. He'd finally lost his mind. All this time in a house perched upon a godforsaken cliff, surrounded by those damned moors—he'd lost it. He probably needed to return to London and seek medical attention. Diana would be positively gleeful; he was never going to hear the end of it . . .

His mind was full of such thoughts as he made his way back to his bedchamber, still half-expecting to turn the corner and find someone lurking in the shadows, waiting to jump out and scare the ever-loving hell out of him, but nothing of the sort occurred, and within a short amount of time, Penvale was standing before his own bedroom door once more, reaching out a hand to open it—

And then he paused.

He looked to the right, at Jane's bedroom door.

He should let her sleep, he told himself. Jane was many things, but he didn't think she'd taken to vanishing into solid walls, so she reasonably could not be to blame for tonight's events. It wasn't her fault she'd had the bad luck to marry a madman.

But still . . . curiosity beckoned.

And so, not feeling very gentlemanly at all, he reached out and, without so much as a knock announcing his presence, opened her door.

The sitting room was dark, the fire banked, and through the open door, he could see the foot of her bed, barely visible in the gloom. He crept forward on tiptoe, barely daring to breathe, until he stood in the doorway leading into the bedroom, peering toward the bed, and realized—

Jane was asleep. He stood in the doorway, processing the sight before him: Jane, curled up on her side in bed, that heavy fall of dark hair tumbling over one shoulder. Her arm was curled around her pillow, partially obscuring her face, but this *did* give him a clear view of the nightgown she wore:

Plaid. A particularly hideous green-and-yellow plaid. Nothing remotely ghostly or ethereal about it.

Penvale felt like clutching his head in despair.

And then, as he turned to leave, he saw it:

A white nightgown, balled up and shoved beneath the cushion of an armchair.

He jerked his head around and regarded the sleeping figure in the bed for a long, silent moment before retreating silently from the room, and in the hours before sleep found him, he was unsurprised to note that the ghost did not moan once.

Chapter Eighteen

Being a ghost was exhausting.

Jane had newfound respect for all the spirits that inhabited the Gothic novels she'd read—the lost sleep! The running! The sepulchral wailing! It was, quite frankly, a lot for one person (or spirit) to juggle.

After three nights of leading Penvale on a midnight race through the halls of Trethwick Abbey, she was sorely ready for a bit of rest. The first night had been the most wearying—he'd been particularly relentless in his pursuit, and she'd begun to worry that she'd not be able to put enough distance between them to allow her to slip through the hidden door obscured by some rather clever paneling in a dark corner of the gallery. The next two nights had been a bit less draining. She'd kept the program of events largely the same—put on an old nightgown, waft carefully around the door of his bedroom until he caught sight of it, and then hastily scamper off, offering ghostly wails all the while—but he'd seemed less fervent in his pursuit after the first night.

Perhaps he was growing nervous at last? This was a promising development, if true; their house party was only a little over a fortnight away, and if she wished to make Penvale uneasy enough to call it off—or to perhaps confide in his friends regarding his ghostly troubles, thus discouraging them from visiting—then she had little time left.

She wondered how many more evenings she'd need to don her white nightgown before her plan succeeded; Jane was not terribly athletic by nature and would be perfectly happy to never run again. Especially not in the dead of night, when she'd much rather be slumbering peacefully in her bed.

"Something wrong, Jane?"

Jane glanced up, having been so immersed in her thoughts that she hadn't even heard him come in. She was in the library, sifting through stacks of books, trying to find ones that she thought the villagers might like. It was a beautiful, warm afternoon, and she'd opened the French doors that led out onto the terrace so that the salty sea breeze could blow in.

Penvale stood a few feet away, surveying her with a slight frown. He looked sun-kissed and a bit weary; his jacket had been discarded at some point, and he was clad in a shirt and waistcoat, the sleeves rolled up to the elbows. He tugged at his cravat to loosen it, and Jane's eyes caught on this movement.

"No, nothing's wrong," she said, his question belatedly registering, even as her gaze remained stubbornly fixed on the skin at his throat that was now visible. "Why do you ask?"

"You were frowning," he said, and she looked up at him in surprise, waiting for whatever joke was about to come out of his mouth—about how that was nothing out of the ordinary; about how he didn't know why it should strike him as unusual; et cetera—but instead he looked faintly perplexed as he added, "It . . . it was different from your usual frowns." He coughed a bit awkwardly as soon as he uttered this sentence, his eyes roaming around the room rather uncomfortably.

"I was just . . . thinking, I suppose." She sat back on her heels, smoothing the skirt of her gown—a new one she'd acquired in town, made of white lawn. Penvale's eyes followed the motion of her hands, and it only belatedly occurred to her that this gown was ever so slightly similar in appearance to the white nightgowns she'd worn for haunting purposes.

He took a few steps toward her, then lowered himself to the floor as well. This close, she could see a smudge of dirt on his cheek, and she wondered what he had been busy with outdoors.

"Are these for the village library?" he asked, plucking a book from the top of a teetering stack; it was a natural history of Cornwall, and he flipped through it, his brow furrowing faintly as he skimmed its pages. Jane liked that brow furrow, the faint line that was visible even when he wasn't frowning.

"Yes," she said. "The other books have been well received, so I thought I'd bring more. I inquired about the lease on one of the empty storefronts in town . . ." Here she trailed off, and Penvale glanced up inquisitively. "Well," she said. "Apparently, the building belongs to you."

Amusement sparked in his gaze. "*Does* it? Should I drive a tough bargain in leasing it to you, then? I'm not as flush as I once was, you know—the extra coin could be helpful."

She crossed her arms. "Penvale."

His grin widened. "I'll write to my solicitor in London—he has copies of all the deeds to various buildings that the estate owns. Once we have it in hand and can make certain there's nothing odd about it, or an outstanding lease that needs to be sorted out, then it's yours to do with as you wish."

"I—" She broke off awkwardly. "Thank you," she said a bit feebly, because what else did one say to a man who had just given one an entire building? Her childhood dreams had been sufficiently modest to match her upbringing: She supposed she would marry and raise a family, though she had little familiarity with what a happy, close-knit family life would look like. If she did not wed, she might become a governess—it was one of the few respectable professions open to a woman of gentle breeding but limited funds. Never had she imagined the grandeur of her life at Trethwick Abbey; even after she had come to live there, it had not seemed possible that it could one day be her home in truth. She had thought that prospect too marvelous to contemplate, until she had determined to make it so—and to now be granted this additional gift, one she had not even thought to dream for herself . . .

She didn't quite know what to say.

He regarded her for a long moment. "You are my wife, Jane," he said simply. "If there is something you wish of me, you need merely ask."

There was something about his tone that set her on edge—some wary, watchful quality to his voice, or his demeanor, or both. She got the impression that he was saying one thing but intending to convey a whole host of other things at the same time.

She opened her mouth to reply, to perhaps ask him what, precisely, he meant—

When there was a sudden bloodcurdling scream.

Jane and Penvale both jumped; for a moment, there was no sound beyond their breathing, coming considerably quicker as they sat frozen in place, staring at each other, wide-eyed.

"What was that?" she breathed, her heart still pounding fiercely in her chest.

"You don't know?" he asked her, and she lifted a brow at him in reply, daring him to outright accuse her of something.

With that single question, she understood one thing with complete clarity:

He *knew*.

Of course she should have realized it. What sort of fool was she to think she could convince a man that his house was haunted, of all things? Husbands—or at least *her* husband—were not nearly as easily spooked as they were in the pages of Gothic novels, and it was not as though a woman in a white nightgown looked precisely like a ghost, anyway. (She assumed; she had never been personally acquainted with a ghost and could not say for certain.)

Before she could reply—or wait to see if he'd say something further—there came a loud *thump*, remarkably similar to the sound from the wardrobe overturning above Penvale's bedroom a couple of months earlier.

They both glanced at the ceiling, then sprang to their feet.

"How strange," Penvale murmured, and it *was* strange, since Jane had not arranged it.

This had happened before, when they'd heard the baby's wails; at the time, her inquiries among the staff had led nowhere, and she'd put the matter out of her mind, but this was taking things too far. She was—obviously—not opposed to staging a haunting, but she did like to be *aware* of when the ghost was going to put in an appearance.

Without a word, she brushed past Penvale to the doorway, then up the side staircase next to the library. She emerged on the third floor, which was largely unused; the portrait gallery occupied one wing, and a number of well-appointed guest rooms made up much of the rest of the floor, the furniture covered by sheets, waiting to be aired out in advance of their house party.

Jane paused as Penvale ascended the steps, coming to a halt next to her. They stood in silence in the hallway, listening for any sound of the mysterious noises that had summoned them, and then—

Thump.

Penvale jerked his head to the left. "That way," he murmured, striking off down the hall, and Jane trailed behind him. He came to a halt before a door, but before he could open it, another loud *thump* sounded; evidently, that was enough to spur him to action, for he reached out to seize the doorknob and yanked the door open.

Within, the room was dimly lit, the curtains drawn, the furniture appearing as strange lumps concealed under fabric, the overall impression one of a space that was somewhat forgotten.

Another *thump*—not as loud this time.

"Did you hear that?" Jane asked.

"I did," he said, turning to scan the furniture, the shadows—nothing that, on the surface, looked out of the ordinary.

"I think it came from the wardrobe," Jane said, nodding in the direction of the wardrobe in question, pushed into a corner.

"The wardrobe," Penvale repeated, regarding it skeptically. "I suppose I should check inside." He did not sound terribly enthused about the prospect, and Jane could not blame him; even for the least superstitious of men, there was something decidedly unpleasant about the thought of peering into a dark wardrobe with no notion of what he might find inside.

By the time Penvale made it a few feet in the direction of said wardrobe, however, there was another ominous *thump*—one that had come from the opposite wall. Penvale paused. "That did not come from the wardrobe." He turned to Jane, and all at once, Jane didn't know what to say. Because he was right; it *hadn't* come from the wardrobe. It had come from the portion of wall that she knew hid a staircase, and where, she assumed, a member of staff was hiding at this very moment, intent on causing some sort of mischief.

"No?" she said weakly.

"No," he said, walking slowly toward her. Their gazes caught and held in the dim light, the silence between them full of the questions and accusations that Jane knew must be simmering within him, ready to burst out—

And then, suddenly, another earsplitting scream.

As if on cue, her candle's flame was extinguished.

"Blast," she muttered. The sound had jolted her, causing the candle to flicker—a perfectly rational accident, albeit one that felt a touch melodramatic in the moment.

"For Christ's sake," Penvale said at once, and with a sharp motion, he reached out to seize the candle from Jane's hand. "We're going, all right?" he announced to the room at large as he ushered Jane through the door. They made their way downstairs—at the second-floor landing, Jane paused as if to return to the library, but Penvale urged her onward, and before she quite realized what was happening, Crowe was opening the front door for them, and Jane found herself blinking in the warm spring sunshine.

Penvale was not done walking. Instead, he took Jane's hand and tugged her along as he made his way around the house and toward the cliffs overlooking the sea. It was only when he began picking his way down the slope that led to the cliff path that Jane drew him to a halt.

"Wait a moment," she said, reaching up to push a lock of hair from her eyes that the wind had pulled loose from her coiffure. "Where are we going?"

Penvale turned to face her, his expression some mixture of impatience and frustration and devilish amusement all at once. "To the cove."

"The cove," Jane repeated. "For what purpose?"

He reached out and took her hand again. "To do what I always do when I need to think. I'm going swimming."

"You cannot think I'm going to get in that water," Jane said for at least the third time since they'd left the house. Penvale, busy removing his boots and shrugging out of his waistcoat, did not respond immediately.

He turned to face her, his hands going to the placket on his buckskins. "I didn't say you had to," he said, opening the placket and beginning to tug his breeches down. He saw Jane's eyes drop to his hands, and then flick back up to his face, where they stuck so resolutely that he thought she must be exercising a considerable amount of will to keep them there.

He kicked aside his breeches, standing before her in his smalls. Despite the unseasonably warm weather, the wind was cool, and gooseflesh rose on his arms. "And I understand if you're too frightened . . ."

He trailed off deliberately, and something in her eyes flashed.

"Don't try to bait me," she snapped. "Do you think I'm a child who would fall for such tricks?"

He paused to consider. "Hmm. What an interesting question." He began backing slowly away from her toward the water. "It certainly would be *childish* to allow someone to taunt you into doing something you didn't want to do. Just like it would be *childish* to creep out of one's bed at night and put on a nightgown and impersonate a ghost, for example. Or to arrange for one's husband's sleep to be interrupted for several nights running, thanks to a never-ending stream of wailing." He looked her straight in the eye. "Another purely hypothetical example, naturally." His feet touched damp sand, and he felt the rush of the surf against his toes. "I can understand why you wouldn't want to do anything *childish*, Jane." He held her gaze for one final moment, and then he turned and flung himself into the waves.

Behind him, he heard a muffled exclamation, the words snatched away on the wind before he could make sense of them. His immediate concern was the breath-stealing, numbing cold of the sea; he ducked his head beneath the water, diving under an oncoming wave, and when he emerged, shaking his head like a dog, he turned to see Jane struggling out of her dress. She managed it after a few seconds and flung it down, and his heart stuttered in his chest at the sight of her in her chemise, no corset in sight, backlit by the afternoon sun, every dip and curve silhouetted through the fine cotton. Her hair was coming loose, curls tugged in every direction by the wind, and her eyes were fixed on him as she strode toward the surf, irritation and frustration and determination written clearly in every line of her face.

Had he ever thought her face stern, or harsh, or anything other than beautiful?

It was beautiful to him in that moment. He could not imagine thinking it otherwise ever again.

She broke his gaze only when she dove into the waves.

Predictably, she came up swearing.

"Jesus Christ!" Her teeth were chattering, and by the time he made his way to her side, she was shivering violently as she found her footing in the shallow water, looking somewhat like a drowned rat and glaring at him more ferociously than she had at any previous point in their acquaintance. "I will never forgive you for this," she said bitterly.

"It's not so bad once you get used to it," he said, treading water before her; this was, in fact, a lie—the English sea was never balmy, and in late April, it was positively glacial. Penvale himself was beginning to shiver. Her scowl intensified, and she shook her head to try to get her wet hair out of her eyes; Penvale reached out and brushed it away for her.

"Did you wish to say something to me, *husband?*" He wondered if anyone had ever uttered that particular word with such hostility.

He gazed at her for a long moment; salt water clung to her eyelashes. "Did you?" he asked at last. "What are you doing, Jane?"

"I haven't the faintest idea what you mean," she said, but she was looking furtive, and there was no real conviction in the words. She fixed him with a wheedling expression that Penvale found disconcerting. "But if, perhaps, you are feeling unsettled by recent events and wish to call off the house party—"

Penvale's jaw dropped. "Is that what this is about?" She paused as if weighing her words carefully, which was all the acknowledgment that Penvale needed. "Jane, for Christ's sake, did it ever occur to you to just talk to me?"

"Oh, yes, and you'd have immediately changed all of your plans just because I was *nervous?*" Her voice was so sarcastic that Penvale felt an entirely uncharacteristic rush of anger course through him, hot and fierce.

"Yes, damn it—it's your house, too, you know—I don't want you to be utterly miserable! I already reduced the numbers so that you wouldn't have to converse with as many people, but if—"

"You did what?"

He realized only belatedly what he'd said, the words having poured out of him in a rush. He sighed. "I . . . I didn't extend a few of the invitations," he said, barely loud enough to be heard over the waves. "I didn't invite Belfry's siblings or Sophie's—only my closest friends. I thought you would be more comfortable with a smaller crowd."

She opened her mouth to reply and inhaled a mouthful of seawater, which sent her into another fit of coughing that lasted several seconds. Penvale reached over to none too gently thump her on the back.

"I don't suppose you were ever going to tell me this?" she demanded once she had recovered.

"I was," he insisted. "I already let Crowe and Mrs. Ash know, so they could plan accordingly. I was going to inform you eventually—I just—" Here, he broke off, because he could not explain, precisely, why he'd delayed telling Jane, other than the fact that it felt dangerously like revealing something about *himself*, and what he felt for her, that he didn't yet fully understand.

She shook her head and said, half frustrated, half amused, "Why will you never be as insufferable as I expect you to be?"

"How is it that *you're* the one annoyed right now?" he asked, finding himself perilously close to laughter, of all things. "In the nearly three months I've been in Cornwall, I've had to endure a hostile wife, a suspicious staff, and a *house that appears to be haunted!* What do you have to complain about?"

"Perhaps the fact that you think the middle of the freezing sea is a reasonable location to have an argument," she shot back as he paddled close enough that her face occupied his entire field of vision. Her eyes looked bluer out here, beneath the wide blue sky and surrounded by the sea.

"I wouldn't have dragged you out here in the first place if you hadn't decided to impersonate a ghost!"

The words were out before he'd quite decided to utter them, and they landed heavily, like stones sinking into the water. A moment of silence stretched taut between them, their eyes locked in an unblinking stare, and then, without warning, a large wave surged behind Penvale and shoved them both beneath the surface.

It was powerful enough to spin Penvale around, momentarily disorienting him; he cracked his eyes open, the salt water making them sting, and another wave crashed into him, dragging him until he felt sand beneath his knees. He emerged with a deep gasp, turning his head first to the left, then the right, looking for Jane. He felt something brush his leg, reached down, and closed his hand around sodden fabric, bringing Jane coughing to the surface.

One final smaller wave pushed them fully onto the shore, and Penvale collapsed onto his knees on the sand, one arm tight around Jane's waist, the surf crashing around them. Next to him, Jane flopped onto her back, trying to catch her breath; her chemise had gone sheer in the water, and his gaze caught on her breasts and lingered there. A moment later, a seashell flew half-heartedly past his ear.

"You could at least pretend not to be leering," she said, still a bit breathless, and his eyes flew up to hers, surprised; she smiled at him a bit tentatively, and it felt like a peace offering.

"I'd have to be a monk not to be leering at you right now, Jane," he said, without the teasing note he'd intended, and her smile widened.

She took a deep breath; he virtuously kept his gaze fixed on her face as she did so, for which he thought he likely deserved a sainthood. "Should we ... discuss it? The haunting, I mean?" she asked.

All at once, he felt tired—after an afternoon spent outdoors; after a bloody irritating bout of ghost-hunting; after an unexpected swim, and an unexpected dunking, and an unexpected argument.

He reached out and slowly cupped her cheek.

Her skin was cool against his hand, and her eyes were wide.

"Shall we call a truce?" he asked softly.

She swallowed. Nodded. And turned her head and placed a kiss, whisper-soft and fleeting, in his palm.

"So long as you'll allow me to take a bath," she said, and there was a smile in her voice and her eyes.

"Fair enough," he said, and immediately, she was scrambling to her feet, cursing when a particularly stiff breeze hit her, reaching down to scoop up her dress and clumsily struggle back into it.

Penvale rose to his feet more slowly and closed his hand around his palm where the feeling of her lips lingered.

Jane glanced over his shoulder at him as she pulled her wet hair free from her dress. "Thank you," she said simply. "For the house party."

He attempted a casual grin, though he wasn't certain he carried it off; nothing about this conversation had felt very casual. "It was nothing."

Not inviting a few friends to visit *was* nothing to him, not compared to Jane, and her happiness, and her comfort. He suspected that she could have asked him to cancel the entire damned house party and he'd have done so happily, and this thought felt so surprising and profound to him that he stood rooted to the spot for a moment, mindless of the cool wind causing gooseflesh to break out on his damp skin.

"Race you to the house!" Jane called, her teeth chattering again, and she was off, leaving Penvale to fumble for his breeches.

As he followed her, he recalled his conversation with his friends on the night before his wedding, his blithe assurance that marriage would change nothing about his life, about him.

Now, chasing his mercurial, maddening wife up the cliff path, the wind at his back, he experienced a fierce rush of joy at the sight of her tangled hair and the sound of her breathless laugh carrying on the wind, and he knew without a doubt that he had been very, very wrong.

Chapter Nineteen

Somehow, it was nearing the end of April, and their houseguests were due to arrive in little more than a week. And Jane . . .

Jane was nervous. But she was determined not to let her nerves show—not when Penvale had tried so hard to make her comfortable.

Per her agreement with Penvale—if it could be called that—Jane had retired her ghostly performances at night, and Penvale had made no more mention that he knew her to be the culprit. Mrs. Ash had been perplexed when Jane had informed her that the haunting was to come to an immediate halt, and that said halt was to last for the duration of the house party, but Jane had informed her vaguely that she needed time to assess whether their aims were on course, and the housekeeper had accepted this.

In the meantime, Penvale had busied himself in his study with his steward at all hours of the day, sometimes late into the night. Jane had continued gathering books for the village library—she went into St. Anne's twice a week now. She'd never set a firm schedule, but she'd begun bringing a basket on Tuesdays and Fridays, and the villagers had come to expect her visits. Now, when she was spotted with her basket, it was no time at all before someone was inviting her in to take a seat and perhaps have a cup of tea, what about a biscuit?, and before Jane knew it, she had seen her way into the parlors of half the cottages in the village.

And it was all rather . . . nice.

Jane could scarcely believe it when she realized that she was enjoying herself. *She*, Jane Spencer, actually making polite conversation, smiling—well, perhaps not always *smiling*, but at the very least not scowling. She'd spent so much time dreading these sorts of interactions that she'd never realized they could be rather enjoyable. Any conversation could be enjoyable, she found, when she was discussing books.

And so she kept busy with this pet project of hers, and Penvale kept himself busy with the estate, and they passed their days at a polite distance, and Jane would have begun to wonder if she had *imagined* their kiss, and their argument, and everything that had passed between them, if not for a certain tension that seemed to spread between them whenever they were in the same room. Jane did not know how to describe it as anything other than an awareness—she had never felt so acutely conscious of the exact distance of another person's body from her own. And she knew that he felt it, too—it was evident in every line of his body whenever she passed slightly too close to him in the hallway or brushed against his seat in passing.

She found herself watching Penvale carefully whenever they did occupy the same space—she wished she could crack his head open and read its contents like a book. It was far easier to understand the thoughts and motivations of characters in her novels when they were all laid out plainly on the page. An actual husband composed of flesh and blood and an at times maddeningly inscrutable face was another matter entirely.

And Jane *did* wish to understand him. It was rather lowering, after years of relying on no one but herself, to realize how much someone else intrigued her.

But now she had a more pressing concern: In a few days' time, she would be expected to play hostess to Penvale's set of polished London friends. Rather than contemplate this terrifying fact until she curled up on her side in despair, she was passing her afternoon safely out of the way of the servants' preparations by quietly reading in her morning room, one hand holding up her book, the other maintaining a steady supply of ginger biscuits to her mouth. It was as she was reaching for her fourth—fifth? sixth?—biscuit that she happened to glance up and spot it: the largest spider she'd ever seen in her entire life, sitting approximately three inches away from the biscuit she was reaching for.

Jane dropped her book and her biscuit and let out a screech.

She had become somewhat practiced at various noises of late; moans, wails, even screams were all within her repertoire. But *this* noise was something else entirely.

The sound of her heartbeat pounding in her chest drowned out everything else, which was why she did not hear the telltale sound of running footsteps and was therefore badly startled once again when the door to the room banged open with a crash.

Acting on some long-dormant instinct she hadn't known she possessed, Jane seized her book, leaped to her feet, whirled around, flung it at her attacker—

And hit Penvale squarely in the forehead.

"Jesus Christ," she breathed out in relief, lifting her hand to her chest, where her heart was still racing.

"Jesus Christ!" he howled, rubbing the red mark on his forehead that the book had left. Jane leaned forward—good heavens, was a lump already forming?

"I think that might leave a bruise," she said.

"I should bloody well think so," he said indignantly.

"How was I supposed to know it was you?" she asked defensively. "You practically tore the door off its hinges—"

"Because I was in rather a hurry, you see," he said, stalking toward her. "Which seemed a reasonable reaction to the scream I heard. It sounded like you were being murdered."

Jane was beginning to feel a bit sheepish. "Well. Right. That was very considerate of you."

Penvale paused, regarding her with great suspicion in the wake of this uncharacteristically conciliatory statement.

Jane nodded at the spider, which had begun making its way in a leisurely fashion across the ottoman atop which the biscuit plate was perched. "It just startled me, is all."

Penvale's eyes followed the direction of her nod, and he pressed his lips together as if trying not to smile. "Screaming about a spider, Jane? When you've lived among ghosts and bloody christening gowns without batting an eyelash?"

"You sound almost nostalgic. Are you missing the ghost already?" she asked him.

"Funnily enough, I've found I like getting a full night's sleep," he said, leaning closer to her as he spoke, using all his height to tower over her in a way that should have been irritating but which Jane found distressingly attractive. She took a couple of steps backward, attempting to put some much needed space between them. She found herself staring at his throat and the top of his chest, and it was all, frankly, quite distracting. (Were *throats* alluring now?)

"Since you're feeling well rested, perhaps you'd like to kill the spider?" she suggested innocently.

His gaze didn't leave hers. "I find I'd rather use my newfound energy for other pursuits." He continued to step toward her, and she continued to back up until she felt the press of the wall. He reached an arm up to brace on the wall above her head and proceeded to *lean.*

Leaning! A truly dirty trick. Everyone knew that gentlemen were particularly alluring when they were *leaning.*

"Though, if it's going to terrify you to the point of screaming, perhaps I ought to dispose of it for you." He ducked his head; this close, she could see faint purple shadows under his eyes, despite his claim of being well rested. Had he, too, she wondered, lost sleep over the past few nights, recalling the heat of his gaze on her breasts through her translucent chemise? Or the warmth of his palm against her lips? She felt her heart kick up a rapid pace in her chest.

"Or," he said slowly, his head lowering as he spoke, "perhaps I *shouldn't* do that. I think I'd like to hear you scream." His breath was warm against her cheek.

At which Jane—who, while still mildly irritated and a number of other emotions, was, after all, only human—reached up and pulled his mouth down to hers.

It was like setting a flame to kindling. No sooner had her lips touched his than he was kissing her back furiously, lips and tongues and teeth—it was not a well-choreographed kiss, nor a terribly polite one. It was, quite simply, a kiss that made Jane feel as though there were a fire racing beneath her skin, and she wanted nothing more than for it to consume her.

One of his hands came to cup her jaw, his thumb resting at the spot in her throat where her pulse was pounding, and Jane pulled back, took a deep, shuddering breath, then kissed him again, both of her arms twining around his neck. His other hand came to her waist, pinning her to the wall with its force, then with the weight of his body as he pressed it against hers. She reached a leg out to wrap around his, pulling him even tighter against her, eliciting a satisfying groan from him in response.

He drew back, and she opened her eyes to see him gazing down at her through heavy-lidded eyes, color high in his cheeks.

"Do you know the date, Jane?" he asked, his breathing slightly ragged.

"I— What?" she asked stupidly.

"The date," he repeated slowly, leaning in to take her mouth in a lingering kiss. Eventually, he pulled away. "It seems to me that it's been about three months since we wed—and I do believe we're meant to be revisiting our discussion on consummation."

Jane nearly laughed; she bit the inside of her cheek to stop herself, and she could see a glint of triumph in his eyes, as if that had been his aim all along.

"Did you wish to call in a solicitor to help us sign a bit of paperwork, or can we simply get on with things?" She rolled her hips against his in an instinctive motion, and he bit off another groan.

"I don't think that will be necessary," he said, lowering his mouth to her neck; she closed her eyes again, tilting her head back against the wall to give him better access. She felt the scrape of teeth against sensitive skin, and she shuddered, then those same teeth tugging at the neckline of her gown, and the rush of cool air over her breast, soon replaced by the wet warmth of his mouth. She arched her back against the wall, her hands sliding into the short hair at the nape of his neck to keep him firmly in place, and she gasped out a wordless cry.

Penvale raised his head. "Did you hear that? It almost sounded like a ghost," he said thoughtfully.

"So help me—"

"I'll have to conduct further investigations," he concluded, and lowered his head to her other breast, and all Jane was conscious of was warmth and suction and the feeling of his hands sliding up her legs, tugging her skirts up as they moved, the cool air of the room hitting the bare skin of her thighs above where her stockings ended, and then he had got a firm grasp under her thighs and lifted her so that she was braced more firmly against the wall, her legs wrapped wantonly around his hips. Then his mouth was on hers again, just as his hand was suddenly between her legs where she was warm and slick and wanting, his fingers striking up a rhythm that had Jane's hips lifting, seemingly of their own accord, moving against him and seeking more, *more*, even as his mouth took hers in another bruising kiss—one that Jane broke on a gasp, then a cry, her head banging back against the wall and her eyes opening to stare unseeingly at the ceiling as sparks raced down her spine and she felt as though she was at the precipice of something, and then with one careful application of his thumb at the spot where all the nerves in her body seemed to be concentrated—

It was like falling from some great height, and before she could even properly return to herself, she could feel his hand on his trousers, and then his voice was in her ear, rough-edged in a way she had never heard it—

"Is this all right?"

And despite the fact that, at that moment, she could barely

remember her own name, much less summon anything more than a quick nod of consent, something within her went soft at the sound of that uneven quality to his voice, this private version of Penvale that only she got to see. Nothing about their marriage had been traditional thus far, and yet, in that moment, she felt the intimacy of the institution, of what they were doing, of all that they shared.

And then he was pushing into her, and now it was Jane who was kissing him, stealing the groan from his lips, and if she'd ever had cause to wonder about marital relations, about wedding nights and the loss of one's virtue and perhaps the passion described in her books, nothing she imagined would have matched the rawness of this—of being pinned to a wall as he thrust within her, her arms and legs wrapped tight around him, of his tongue in her mouth until it wasn't, until his breath was on her bare skin as he buried his face in her neck while he shuddered and then went still.

Slowly, Jane allowed her legs to unwind from his hips, and her feet slid to the ground; she reached out to grasp the wall for support as she once more bore her own weight on legs that were not quite steady—

And then—proving, perhaps once and for all, that marital relations conducted anywhere other than the decent, virtuous confines of a bed are truly dangerous—the wall chose that moment to remind Jane that it was not, in fact, a wall but, rather, a cleverly concealed door with a cleverly concealed latch behind a picture frame that Jane had not so cleverly managed to press by mistake, and it clicked silently inward, sending Jane and Penvale tumbling after it.

Chapter Twenty

It had been longer than Penvale cared to admit since he'd last bed-
ded a woman, and it had been considerably longer than that since he'd
had anything approaching the experience he and Jane had just shared,
so it was perhaps to be forgiven that his brain—along with all his other
faculties and reflexes—was operating at a slower speed than usual.
Meaning that when the wall behind Jane saw fit to suddenly turn into
a door and send him tumbling to the floor, Penvale did not twist his
body in a fit of noble contortions and take the brunt of the fall, thus
preserving his sweet, just-deflowered wife from any pain and suffering.

Instead, he uttered a curse that was no doubt entirely inappropriate for the aforementioned wife's ears, and then proceeded to fall
directly on top of her.

"Oof," Jane said.

"Oof," Penvale said.

Jane poked him in the side. "If you do not remove yourself in the
next three seconds—"

Penvale sprang lightly to his feet, then reached a hand down to
Jane, which she reluctantly accepted. "Are you all right?" he asked,
hastily tucking himself back into his trousers, as this did not seem like
a moment in which he wished to be partially unclothed.

Jane paused in her attempts to adjust her bodice to something resembling decency. "It's all a bit . . . sticky," she said, wrinkling her nose and gesturing vaguely at her legs.

Penvale gave her an incredulous look. "I meant, did I injure you when I *fell on top of you?*"

"Oh." Jane waved a dismissive hand. "I'm fine. The stickiness is my primary complaint."

Penvale, meanwhile, was a jumble of sensations—his elbows in particular, which had borne the brunt of the fall, were beginning to make their grievances known—but his primary feeling was . . .

Utter confusion.

"Where are we?" he asked, craning his neck to peer at their surroundings. It seemed to be a narrow corridor, poorly lit; the only light was that which spilled around the doorway leading back into the morning room. Penvale could make out stone walls; he squinted and spotted a shadowy set of stairs. It wasn't a passage, he realized; it was a *landing*.

"Er," Jane said, and there was a note of such unmistakable, sheepish guilt in her voice that he immediately wheeled around to face her once more. "We're in a stairwell."

"I can see that, thank you. What stairwell is this, precisely? I find myself unfamiliar with it."

She sighed, but—owing to the barely leashed note of frustration in his voice—did not attempt to prevaricate further. "The secret one."

"The secret stairwell," he repeated, taking a step toward her.

She lifted her chin. "Yes."

"And how many secret stairwells does Trethwick Abbey contain?" he asked, scarcely aware of what he was saying, his mind racing as a number of things suddenly became quite clear. A disappearing ghost, indeed.

"Well," Jane said slowly, "there's just the two—one in this corner of the house and one in the opposite corner, where . . ." She trailed off.

He came to a halt before her. "Yes?"

"Where your bedroom is," she said guiltily.

"Ah." He reached out a hand to touch her chin, tipping her face up so that her eyes met his. "How very, very convenient."

She inhaled a bit unsteadily. "It was, rather."

He waited for the anger, the frustration, to return—at the trouble she had caused him, at the lengths she had gone to in order to frighten him from his own home. He waited . . . and yet it did not come. He opened his mouth to speak and then paused, weighing his words. Something had shifted between them, without either of them acknowledging this outright, and their relationship, such as it was, felt somehow more . . . fragile. It was as though he'd been carrying something carelessly that he now realized was actually made of glass.

And he wasn't willing to risk shattering it.

He looked at her for another long moment, his eyes taking in the tendrils of hair around her face that were in disarray from his fingers, the color still present in her cheeks—color that *he* had put there.

"Was it me?" he asked simply. Her brow furrowed slightly. "Was it something I did?"

Understanding crept in.

"No," she said, so immediately, so *vehemently*, that he found himself believing her in spite of it all. "It was just . . ." She blew out a frustrated breath. "It was just, you grow tired of having men decide the course of your life, you see. And so, if you can think of a way to, well . . . to rid yourself of the men making the decisions, and live life for yourself . . ." Her face twisted into something approaching a grimace, half apologetic, half defiant. "You have to try."

"I see," he said evenly—and he *did* see, to some extent. He'd never understand, obviously, what it was to live as a woman, to have so little say over one's own future. But had he not spent the majority of his life trying to regain control over the circumstances—the loss of his parents, of this house—that had dictated his fate?

"And are you still, then?" he asked, striving to keep his voice neutral, not to pressure her in any way. "Trying?"

It was her turn to regard him for a long moment, the silence stretching tight between them, like a rubber band about to snap. "I don't think so," she said quietly, offering him her hand. He reached out and took it and felt her pulse against his palm.

"Will you show me these staircases, then?" he asked.

And so she did.

"I can't believe I never discovered this as a boy," he said, ducking his head as he came to the bottom of the narrow, steep stairs; by this point, they should have been behind a wall of his study, which was directly below Jane's morning room. Another piece of the puzzle solved. "I'm honestly feeling a bit ashamed."

"You were only ten when you left," Jane reminded him. "I'm sure, given more time, you would have found them—I don't suppose you spent much time in your father's study or crawling about your parents' bedroom."

"How did *you* find them, then?" he asked.

"The first winter I lived here was a particularly damp one," she said with a shrug. "My guardian was away for a few weeks at one point, and I was left to my own devices with an entire empty house to explore. I was perusing the bookshelves in the study, checking to see if there was anything worth reading, when I noticed a crack and a latch hidden behind the books. Once I'd found that one, I made a more careful examination of the rest of the house, to see if there was another."

She spoke casually, but Penvale could envision what a long, lonely winter that would have been for a girl who had only recently lost her father, in a strange place, with no one her own age to speak to, abandoned by her guardian. He remembered, with unfortunate clarity, the winter after his parents had died, in the home of his vague, distant aunt and uncle. And at least he'd had a sister.

He voiced none of this, however, merely looked at her and said, "I see." She lifted her chin, almost defiant, and he could tell that she knew he really *could* see—that he understood the particular heartache of feeling alone in the world.

He turned to face the dark wooden door before him, still conscious of her palm in his. He'd never thought himself the sort of man to become flustered over the weight of a woman's hand, but something powerful seemed to crackle between them—now that he'd finally consummated the marriage (and what a bloodless, inadequate word to describe that act), all he could think about was pressing her up against the closest wall he could find and doing it all over again.

Belatedly, he wondered if deflowering one's wife against a wall was perhaps not quite how it was done in polite circles. No doubt he should have laid Jane down upon a bed covered in rose petals and solicitously inquired as to her comfort and enjoyment at every turn. But the truth was, Penvale didn't particularly like the smell of roses, and Jane herself had not seemed to have any complaints about the arrangement.

He frowned. Maybe he ought to ask her, just to be certain. It seemed like the gentlemanly thing to do, even if it was a bit belated.

"Jane," he said slowly, his gaze fixed on the door; before setting off, Jane had ducked back into the morning room to seize a lamp, which now lit their way, but it was still very dark in here, and Penvale wasn't able to make out much beyond the shallow pool of light that the lamp provided. "Are you . . . all right?"

"What do you mean?" Jane's voice was a bit cautious, guarded, and—acting on some instinct that he didn't entirely understand but which he was oddly certain was the correct one—Penvale carefully did not look at her as he spoke.

"I mean—earlier. What we did in your morning room. Was it . . . all right?"

"Did I not make that clear enough?" Jane sounded vaguely annoyed, because of course she did. Before Penvale could hasten to reassure her, she added, "Am I expected to wander around in a daze afterward, bumping into furniture with a dreamy faraway look in my eye, so that you are assured of your manly prowess?"

"No," Penvale said, dangerously close to laughter. He hadn't intended to irritate her, for once, and yet he could not help but enjoy the result all the same. "I merely meant to ensure that you weren't uncomfortable, considering we—" Here, he broke off. Paused to consider the polite way to phrase such a thing. Then, unable to think of one, he finished: "—tupped against a wall."

He glanced sideways in time to see Jane arch a cool brow. "Is there something wrong with that?"

"No," Penvale said, quite fervently. "It just occurs to me that it perhaps wasn't the most appropriate spot, since it was your first time."

Jane placed a firm hand on his arm. He turned to her in the flickering lamplight and saw that she looked impatient. Her brow was faintly furrowed, a crease appearing between her eyes, and he resisted the temptation to reach out with his thumb and smooth away that crease.

"I've just told you that I enjoyed it," she said, a hand on her hips.

"You didn't, actually," Penvale felt compelled to point out. "Not in so many words, at least."

Jane waved an impatient hand. "Fine. I liked it. I can see what all the fuss in the books was about."

Penvale paused. "You truly read books about *that?*" He recalled that she had mentioned as much that day in the library, when they'd kissed in the armchair, but he had not stopped to fully consider all the implications.

"Penvale." Jane's voice had slid into outright exasperation. "Do you see how much time I spend reading? Don't you think I would find something else to do if the books weren't about something *interesting?*"

"I . . . I suppose so." He was familiar enough with the salacious volumes that made their way around the bedchambers of Eton and Oxford, but he hadn't thought to wonder whether ladies were reading these, too. Though, considering the ladies he was closely acquainted with—none of whom were precisely shrinking violets—he supposed he shouldn't be surprised.

But still—where the devil had she acquired such a thing? It wasn't as though there were purveyors of pornographic texts out in the middle of the Cornish countryside. He said as much aloud, and his interest was piqued further when Jane looked a bit furtive.

"Well," she said; in the dim light, Penvale couldn't quite tell, but he thought her color was a bit high. "It turns out that the library here at Trethwick Abbey is . . . extensive."

Penvale regarded her with renewed interest. "There are illicit books in the library?"

Jane rolled her eyes eloquently. "Oh, of course *this* will be what convinces you to spend more time in the library. But yes . . . someone, at some point, amassed quite a collection. It was, naturally, hidden rather

cleverly behind a row of horribly dull books on bridge-building—"
Here, she cast him a narrow look. "The sort of thing *you* would find
fascinating, no doubt, but which any other sane person would skip
right past. I was making a careful inspection of the entire collection
last winter, as I hadn't much else to do, and I discovered them. And ..."
Here, she trailed off; Penvale gave her what he hoped was an encour-
aging look, but that caused her to gaze at him suspiciously. After a
moment, she continued.

"Well, there are certain volumes that I am fond of, by an authoress
who identifies herself only as 'A Lady of Ill Repute.' They've proved
most illuminating." Her voice took on a distinctly appreciative tone,
and she shook her head as if to clear it. "The point is, I liked what
we did. I don't know much about the act, barring what I've read, but
I don't believe there are any rules regarding where, specifically, such
activities must take place. So I don't understand why you've gone all
prim and scandalized just because we made use of the wall that was
so readily available."

Penvale was near laughter. He wondered what marriage would
have been like if he'd married someone else—some sweet, blushing
bride who would come quietly to the marital bed in a nightgown of
pristine white lace, who would lie beneath him, performing her wifely
duty, and in short order proceed to produce a few children as souvenirs
of these activities.

The vision held no appeal for him whatsoever—not when compared with the very real memory of Jane's gasps in his ear as his hand
worked between her legs, her arm in a tight grip around his neck. He
surreptitiously adjusted his breeches and sternly willed that memory
away, as it was not terribly helpful at the moment.

"I was going to say that I thought it might have been more

appropriate to do it in a bed for the first time—for *your* first time," he said. "So I might have been assured of your comfort. It's often not very enjoyable for ladies at first, I understand."

"We seem to have avoided that difficulty, so you may cease your fretting," Jane said, making Penvale feel more like an anxious maiden aunt than he would have thought possible. "But if it will soothe you, we can try a bed next time. I suppose a change of scenery might keep things interesting."

And with that, she turned and took two steps toward the door before reaching out and turning a small bronze doorknob, pushing the door firmly forward.

Which was how, moments later, Penvale found himself standing in his very own study.

"I can't believe I didn't know this staircase was here," he said, feeling vaguely indignant.

"If you had spectacles, perhaps you might have," Jane said coolly, brushing off her skirts in businesslike fashion.

Penvale ignored this, turning in a slow circle. The entrance from the passage was just wide enough for a person of average build, though high enough that Penvale did not have to duck—and it was part of the bookshelves themselves, he saw. It was no wonder he'd never discovered this entrance as a boy; he certainly would have been punished if he'd been found crawling around the bookcases. His father had always impressed upon him the importance of the work that took place within this room—he'd been very firm on the matter, Penvale recalled. He'd made Penvale understand, from a young age, that the care and keeping of Trethwick Abbey and all its surrounding lands was a heavy responsibility, and one that should not be taken lightly.

Now that responsibility was his—and he experienced a moment

of fierce longing that his father had lived longer, had better prepared him to take it on. He had spent the past decade attempting to fill the gaps in his knowledge—had read books about estate management and innovations in agriculture. And he'd spent the past months carefully reviewing the estate's finances, determined not to be the viscount who mired future generations in debt.

And yet, he thought, none of that replaced the knowledge his father might have imparted of how to bear the burden of the title, of ownership of this house and land, the weight of responsibility that fell upon his shoulders.

No book could teach him that.

He realized that Jane was watching him carefully. "Is something wrong?" she asked.

"Nothing," he said shortly.

"Penvale?" she asked, turning to face him more fully, something in his voice clearly alerting her to some of the mental turmoil he was experiencing. She took a few careful steps toward him, and he nearly laughed at the sight—Jane, who was so rarely tentative, who hid her discomfort behind a curt demeanor and scowls, was now walking toward him slowly, a worried frown creasing her forehead.

She drew to a halt before him and reached a hand out to take his. He let her.

And then, after a moment during which she gazed steadily at him, her eyes meeting his without any hesitation—so different from the creature Penvale had encountered in his drawing room in London a few months earlier—he spoke.

"It's . . . difficult for me, I suppose. Being here sometimes." Jane frowned but did not speak, allowing him the time he needed to say what was on his mind. "It reminds me of my mother and father—it makes me miss them." His voice broke at this point, and he fell silent, the only sound in the room his own ragged breathing. "And I'm here, back in this house, where I've always thought I belonged, and . . ." The words drying up, he trailed off, not knowing how to express the ache so deep within him.

"And it still didn't bring them back," Jane said softly.

He shook his head. "I knew it wouldn't bring them back," he said. "But I don't think I realized how angry it would make me, being here without them. Realizing that my father died before he could teach me how to do this properly."

"How to run the estate?" Her frown deepened. "The tenants seem very fond of you, and I expect some of the ladies in the village to start composing poetry in your honor at any moment." This was uttered in tones of great skepticism, as though Jane personally questioned the wisdom of anyone who would think him worthy of such an honor, and he couldn't help but smile at the thought. It was so very *Jane*. And, at some point, so many of the things he'd once disliked about her had become things that made him smile instead.

"Not the estate, specifically." He shrugged helplessly. "It's just that there's no one to tell me how to be the viscount. I've held this title since I was ten years old, but I've never felt as though I really had to *be* Viscount Penvale until now."

"I think you're doing just fine," she said. She didn't say anything else, but she didn't need to. Coming from her, this was effusive praise, and it warmed him as no flowery words from anyone else could have.

He squeezed her hand, and her grip tightened on his in turn.

It was an odd moment as they stood there in the afternoon light of Penvale's study, the room silent around them, the bookcase still ajar, showing the entrance to the staircase. And he had the strangest thought—that when, on occasion over the past few months, he'd worried Trethwick Abbey was not enough to sustain him, that he needed some new goal, new purpose to give his life shape . . . he'd never considered this.

That the weight of Jane's hand in his—and all it signified—could perhaps serve that purpose.

He did not say this aloud—not yet.

Instead, he held her hand and allowed himself, in that moment, to feel content.

Chapter Twenty-One

May in England! The month of blossoming flowers, of sunny skies and fat white clouds and warm breezes. It was glorious! It was beautiful!

It was making Jane feel mildly ill.

It was not the weather itself that caused this feeling—even the most crotchety of souls could remain unmoved by the spectacular show that nature was putting on, and Jane was alarmed to discover that she seemed to be growing less crotchety by the day—but instead the event of which it was a harbinger. For the warm weather and the bright sun overhead were not a herald of only glorious springtime and a happy summer to come.

No, they were also a herald of guests.

Despite the relatively small number of invitations that had been sent, the arrival of each letter of acceptance as April trickled by had caused a sinking feeling in her stomach, even as she plastered a smile on her face to inform Penvale each time another friend wrote to express eager anticipation, et cetera. To Penvale's credit, he didn't seem fooled by her attempts at good cheer—on more than one occasion, he seemed mildly disturbed by it, thus informing Jane that her feigned smile was not quite credible. However, he seemed to understand that she was *trying,* so he didn't tease her too much about her ludicrous efforts to appear cheerful for a looming event that she found terrifying.

"It's only eight guests," he said one evening over dinner in the last week of April, for at least the third time that week. "It barely counts as a house party."

"To *you,*" Jane said darkly, though she knew, logically, that he was correct, that this was not a terribly burdensome gathering to host.

He regarded her for a moment, his finger running idly around the rim of his wineglass. "If you want to call it off, I will write to them tomorrow. I'll send a rider on a fast horse, to make certain the notes reach them in time." Despite how appallingly rude this would be—and how utterly contrary to his own wishes Jane knew it to be—she did not doubt his sincerity.

And here, she hesitated—for was this not what she had been attempting over the past few weeks? Had this not been the entire point of donning that nightgown and leading her husband on a chase around the halls? The reduced guest list had gone some way to soothing her nerves, but she undoubtedly would be more comfortable if they were not hosting any guests at all.

But Penvale would not be more comfortable, she realized. Penvale missed his friends—she knew he was looking forward to seeing them. And at some point, this knowledge had come to matter to her.

Her eyes caught his and held. "No. That won't be necessary."

Soon enough, it was the first of May, and their guests were upon them—carriage after carriage arriving from London, polished to a shine, impressive teams of horses tossing their glossy heads as they pulled up before the manor. First to arrive were Lord James Audley and Lady James—Violet, Diana's friend. Then it was Lord Julian

Belfry and his wife, Emily, who was looking to be in exceptionally good humor, and whose welfare her husband appeared puzzlingly obsessed with.

"We'll just be going upstairs so that Emily might lie down," Lord Julian announced almost as soon they arrived.

"I do not need to lie down," Emily assured Jane as she resisted her husband's attempts to propel her toward the staircase, her grip firm on a basket in one hand from which a small, furry, black-and-white bewhiskered face was evident.

"And perhaps a cold compress? She appears flushed."

"It was warm in the carriage," Emily confided in the moment before Lord Julian secured a firm grip about her waist; Jane would not have been surprised to see him sweep his wife entirely off her feet and carry her upstairs. Emily clearly had similar concerns, for she gave a bemused wave to Jane and Penvale before allowing herself to be whisked away. "And if you could send a dish of milk up for Cecil—!" she called over one shoulder, gesturing at the basket, from which a series of increasingly audible meows was emanating.

Jane glanced at Penvale, who grinned at her, their shared amusement and confusion somehow conveyed without speaking, and in that instant, she felt more married than she had at any point in the preceding four months, up to and including the moment she'd lost her virginity against a wall in her morning room.

And it was . . . nice.

She didn't have time to reflect upon this, because there were guests to get settled in their rooms, polite conversation to make, all the niceties of society to observe. None of these things put Jane at ease, and then, even more alarming, was the arrival of Diana and Lord Willingham, the former alighting from her carriage like a queen surveying her territory. Her imperious expression faded as she gazed up at the house, replaced by a slight frown, a look of uncertainty in her eyes, that was not at all in keeping with the woman Jane had met.

"All right, my magnificent sapphire?" asked her husband, stepping down from the carriage behind her and not sidestepping fast enough to avoid a sharp elbow to the stomach. "Oof," he said good-naturedly, but he winked at Jane as he said it, and she was quite certain that he was annoying Diana on purpose. She liked him all the better for it.

"Lady Penvale," he said, bowing over Jane's hand quite gallantly.

"Jane," she said; hearing it come out a bit stiffly, she added, "If we are family now, you should call me Jane."

He smiled at her, a dazzling smile that she imagined must have set every female heart within a ten-mile radius aflutter before he was wed; perhaps it still did. "Then you must call me Jeremy," he said. "Everyone else does."

"All right," she said cautiously, still unaccustomed to friendly overtures, but he didn't seem put off by her hesitant tone.

"Jane," Diana said, nodding at her like a soldier recognizing a worthy opponent.

Jane gave her a cool nod in return. "Diana."

"This is friendly!" Jeremy said brightly, and Diana rolled her eyes.

"Where is that idiotic brother of mine?" she asked Jane, who was surprised to feel a strange rush of protective irritation on the part of Penvale.

"He's getting everyone else settled," she said a bit sharply. "Since you took your time getting here."

Diana lifted a single eyebrow, while Jeremy grinned; they were not, in fact, that much later than anyone else—they were not even the last to arrive—and Jane knew this perfectly well, and she guessed they did, too. Diana opened her mouth to reply, but before she could do so, Jane felt the weight of a hand on her shoulder and knew without turning that it was her husband. He gave her shoulder a quick squeeze.

"Diana, Jeremy," he said, not removing his hand even as he drew up next to her, reaching out with his free hand to clap Jeremy on the back, then to ruffle Diana's hair, which earned him a sharp punch on the arm from his sister.

Diana made a great show of inspecting the state of her brother's shoes. "You haven't become so rusticated that you've taken to mucking about with the pigs, I see."

Glancing at Penvale, Jane saw him flash a grin at his sister—his grins were a glorious sight, she thought, watching his face light up— and she looked back at Jeremy and Diana in time to see them both look rather surprised at whatever they saw in Penvale's expression.

"It's good to see you, too, Diana," he said dryly, then added more gently, "Do you . . . want to look around?"

Diana's eyes flicked back up toward the soaring turrets and imposing stone walls of the house before her. That hesitant look crept across her face once again; Jeremy clearly saw it, too, because he nudged her gently. "Why don't you and Penvale go on a walk together? Jane can show me inside."

Diana nodded after a moment, her mouth a firm line as she pressed her lips together, and Penvale gave Jane's shoulder one last squeeze before he reached out to curve his arm around Diana's shoulders. Jane watched as Diana immediately shrugged him off, but then inclined her head so that it rested against his shoulder briefly before they set off slowly along the drive.

"It's so *green*," Diana said for at least the third time. The first two times, Penvale had good-naturedly agreed, since it had been more than three months since he'd seen her—the longest time they'd been apart since his school days—and he didn't wish to immediately commence a quarrel, but by the third time, his patience had worn thin.

"Diana, it's bloody Cornwall, obviously, it's green," he said as they rounded the corner of the house and set off in the direction of the cliff path. "It's nothing but moors and rolling hills and sheep and the damned ocean, what did you expect?"

"Have you considered a future of gainful employment in which you give tours of the estate?" Diana asked waspishly. "Sheep, hills, very helpful, thank you so much for that illuminating description."

"Do you know," he said thoughtfully, "there have been moments when I've come perilously close to missing you whilst I've been here? I'm so glad you've come to visit to cure me of such uncharacteristic bouts of sentimentality."

"Do *you* know I was worried that wife of yours was going to murder you and leave your body on a moor for the sheep to eat—"

"I do not believe sheep are carnivorous."

"—but now that I've been reminded of how irritating I find you, I think that *I* might murder you and feed you to the sheep myself."

"A nice diet of grass is more to their liking."

"Of course, you know that now!" she said. "You've become countrified. We're never going to see you in town again! You're going to be whiling away your years wandering around the cliffs until a gust of wind catches you and you're swept into the sea and we never recover your body."

"You seem oddly preoccupied with my death," Penvale said, steering her past a muddy puddle, the prospect of mud on her dress sufficiently distracting to prevent her from further catastrophizing about the likely bleak future that awaited him here.

"Someone has to be," Diana informed him, once she was clear of that harrowing danger.

"Then allow me to reassure you that I'm fairly certain Jane does not intend to murder me." He delivered the words in what he thought was an offhand manner, but Diana's head swiveled to look at him so fast, he was surprised she didn't have whiplash.

"*Are* you?"

"For God's sake."

"And what, precisely, makes you so certain of that, dearest brother?"

"We've become . . . friendly," he hedged, which was about as successful an evasion as he might have expected.

"I'll bet you have," Diana said, letting out a decidedly witchy cackle. After a moment, however, her frown returned, and she regarded him with considerable scrutiny. "Are you . . . happy here, then?" she asked, her tone more serious than Penvale was accustomed to hearing. He considered.

It pleased him that he'd accomplished what he'd set out to do, had once more claimed ownership of the house and the land that was his birthright. It was satisfying to work with the tenants, mending their cottages, discussing the intricate details of their crops, potential improvements to the land, to learn about their lives, to earn their trust. It was a nice change of pace, after years in town, to spend months on end breathing in the clean air of the countryside, to look out his window each morning and see hills and the sea, rather than a small patch of green in St. James's Square, and then nothing but other buildings as far as the eye could see.

But was he truly *happy*?

He wasn't certain what that even meant; happiness had never been a particular goal of his. It was only after watching his friends marry and settle down to domestic bliss that it had occurred to him that happiness might be achieved. Might be something he was missing.

And it was only in the past couple of weeks that he'd realized he might like such a thing—and that it might be within his reach with the woman he'd married.

"I think . . . I could be," he said, which was nothing more or less than the truth.

"Well," Diana said indignantly, "that's not good enough. You're *my* brother. If you want to be happy here, with Jane, surrounded by all these"—she cast a dubious eye at their surroundings—"*sheep*, then we need to see to it that you are!" She said this with such determination that Penvale would not have been surprised to see her dash away only to reappear with an army at her back, if she thought it would help.

Penvale, for his part, was feeling rather touched, but he didn't want to risk his own physical safety by informing Diana of this fact. "I appreciate it," he said. "But this is my marriage—I need to work it out for myself. Something that I know may be difficult for you and the rest of our friends to comprehend," he added dryly.

"Jane is the trouble, then?" she pressed. "Because if she is making you miserable, then I assure you, I will have little difficulty in being rid of the minx."

"Jane is *not* the trouble," he said sharply. "In fact, Jane is the best part of living here." He broke off, surprised by the words that had come out of his own mouth—words that he had not intended to speak.

Words that he realized he *meant*.

"I know you don't like her," he said more calmly. "But *I* like her quite a bit, and that's the only thing that matters to me."

Diana came to a halt, the wind whipping at her hair as she stared at him. "Penvale," she said slowly, "are you in *love*?"

Penvale sighed, raking a hand through his hair. "I don't know," he said, because it was the only answer he could give in that moment. The only answer that didn't require far too much examination of his own heart, a practice with which he had little experience.

"All right," Diana said, taking this admirably in stride. "I apologize for insulting her. I don't dislike her, as it happens; she wouldn't have been my first choice for you—"

"You'd rather have someone you could bully?" he asked, unable to resist provoking her.

Diana ignored this. "But she is certainly spirited, which I approve of, so you needn't worry I'll attempt to poison her."

"I had not previously been worried about that, but now you've made me wonder if I should be."

Diana rolled her eyes and turned to glance over her shoulder; they'd walked a ways down the path, but the manor loomed large behind them. "Shall we return to the house?"

"I— Why?" he asked suspiciously.

"Because," she said, a speculative gleam coming to her eye, one that Penvale knew from past experience to be very wary of, "if I'm going to work out whether *she* loves *you*, I'll need to observe the two of you together."

"But I didn't ask—"

"I know. That's never stopped me before," she said serenely, which was true.

"You're not to say anything to her," he warned.

"Calm down, you're making a terrible fuss," she said, tugging on his arm. She held up her hand to block the sunlight as she squinted ahead. "Is that West's carriage pulling up? Oh, yes, I can see the crest."

Penvale stared in the direction she was pointing. "How can you possibly see his crest from this distance?" he asked incredulously; all he saw was a somewhat blurry carriage-shaped thing making rapid progress down the drive.

Diana gave him a strange look. "Do you need spectacles?"

Penvale heaved a sigh. "You are not, as it happens, the first person to ask me that question recently," he said, and then took her by the elbow as he headed to greet their guest.

Chapter Twenty-Two

Jane was certain she was being watched.

Oh, not in a frightening way—or at least not in a way that made her fear for her safety. Not even in the uneasy way that she felt when she was in a roomful of strangers and was expected to speak, everyone's eyes on her.

No, what she was feeling now was merely a strange, overpowering suspicion that Diana was watching her, though she was giving every appearance of *not* doing anything of the sort. Every time Jane glanced at her, she was flirting with her husband, laughing with her friends, teasing her brother. And yet Jane was nonetheless certain that, when she was not looking, Diana's gaze was burning into her back.

Jane might not be terribly socially skilled, but even she knew that to stand up and dramatically denounce one of her guests for *staring at her!* would not be at all the thing, so she did her best to put the suspicion out of her mind. It was exhausting enough playing hostess without accusing her sister-in-law of—well, of looking at her.

"Is something wrong, Lady Penvale?" inquired Lady Fitzwilliam Bridewell at this juncture, drawing Jane out of her thoughts. It was after dinner, and they'd adjourned to the library—there had been talk of a game of charades, but the crowd had naturally split into a few small groups, all in eager conversation. The sound of laughter and clinking glasses filled the room, and a fire crackled merrily in the grate.

It was lovely, Jane thought. If only she could relax enough to enjoy it.

She blinked at Lady Fitzwilliam—Sophie, as she'd been given leave to call her. Sophie had been the last to arrive that afternoon, alighting from her carriage with a weary smile, accompanied by her maid.

Jane shook her head. "I'm sorry," she said. "I'm not terribly good in crowds—I'm much more comfortable observing these sorts of things rather than actually participating in them."

Sophie smiled. She had a beautiful smile, and Jane happened to glance over just as the Marquess of Weston's casual perusal of the room landed on Sophie; he looked like a man who'd been struck in the chest with a forceful blow. Jane stared at him: Penvale had mentioned some matchmaking scheme on the part of his sister and her friends regarding West and Sophie, and some sort of tragic history between the two, but this single expression on West's face told Jane more than anything else how deep that feeling ran.

"I think you're doing just fine," Sophie said.

"You lie very convincingly," Jane told her, and Sophie let out a peal of delighted laughter.

"Thank you, I suppose," Sophie said. "But I truly do think you're doing quite well, all things considered. It can't be easy, being thrust into this group, not knowing anyone, when they're all so . . . attached." A slightly wistful note in her voice made Jane take notice.

"Have you not been friends with them long?" Jane asked curiously, so genuinely interested to know the answer that she didn't even waste time congratulating herself on managing to phrase a question in a somewhat normal fashion. Sophie seemed entirely at ease—Jane had seen her making merry conversation with Violet and Emily earlier, and she had said something to Penvale upon her arrival that had made him laugh out loud.

"I've known West and Audley for years," Sophie said lightly, her tone not inviting any further questions regarding that particular history, "but I only became better acquainted with Violet and her friends last summer. They're all lovely, of course," she added, and there was genuine warmth in her voice, "but they *have* known each other for an awfully long time."

"I've never—" Jane began, and then fell silent, willing the words to come. Speaking her feelings had never come easily to her. "I've never had friends the way Penvale does. To hear him speak of them—they sound like family to him." She cast her eyes down at her lap as she spoke, unable to face whatever pity she might see in Sophie's gaze. "I don't wish to force myself into a place where I'm not wanted when it seems he already has everything he needs."

Or, rather, every*one* he needed. Jane did not voice this thought, however.

Sophie did not reply for a long moment—long enough that Jane risked lifting her eyes to take a quick peek. Instead of whatever she feared she might see on the other woman's face, she saw nothing more than a thoughtful expression; she had the impression that Sophie was choosing her words carefully.

"I do not think you have spent enough time with Penvale around his friends to see some of what I have seen," Sophie said at last. "I do not presume to know him remotely as well as you do—he and I have never been particularly intimate, and I am not one he would share confidences with. But I have spent enough time at the edges of this group to observe them at some length, whether or not they realized I was doing so. And I can tell you right away that Penvale has always existed . . . Hmm." She gave a frustrated sigh, as though the words were not coming as easily to her as she might wish, and Jane experienced a moment of empathy—this, after all, had been her own experience for much of her life.

"He's always present—he loves his friends dearly, and he loves his sister, too, despite how often they attempt to provoke each other." Sophie's mouth curved up slightly, and Jane gave her a small smile of her own. "And they undoubtedly love him, too."

Jane wondered what it was like to speak of love so confidently, so assured of its existence. Love had never felt like that to her. To her, it was a rare, precious commodity—one that she had convinced herself she didn't care about. Only now was she coming to realize how obvious its absence was in her life.

"But," Sophie continued, "I can't help thinking that he's always held himself somewhat . . . apart."

"Because he was not married?" Jane asked, though she realized immediately that this couldn't be it; after all, until the previous autumn, there had been only one married couple among Penvale's set.

"Because he cared about this house more than he cared about anything else," Sophie corrected. "It makes for a lonely existence, I suspect."

Jane glanced across the room at her husband, who was lounging on a settee next to Emily and Lord Julian with that peculiar lazy grace of his. He looked relaxed and happy; he'd discarded his jacket at some point, and Jane's gaze lingered on the breadth of his shoulders. At that moment, he laughed at something Lord Julian had said, his entire face lighting up. He did not look like a man who had much experience with loneliness—even a month earlier, Jane might have been fooled. But she had come to know him better now, and she realized, with a faint rush of surprise, that she knew a side of him that his friends did not. And she knew that Sophie was correct.

She glanced back at Sophie. "You're very observant," she said carefully.

Sophie gave her a rueful smile. "I've been widowed for a few years now. You find yourself spending a lot of time . . . watching." Her voice held a melancholy note. Jane felt a rush of sympathy; she had never been widowed, but she knew all too well the feeling of hiding herself away from the world, reading of it in the pages of her books rather than experiencing it for herself.

But that had changed, she thought. Because of Penvale, and marriage, and all the complicated feelings that had arisen between them, her life had taken a new, nearly unrecognizable shape. And she was *glad* of it.

Sophie was still gazing at her with a faint smile, and Jane could not help but think that Diana, perhaps, was not the person she ought to worry about watching her after all.

On the fourth day of the house party, the weather was particularly fine, and they determined that they would all enjoy a picnic and some lawn games.

Jane, being a sensible creature, was naturally horrified by this prospect.

"*Lawn games?*" she demanded, bursting into Penvale's dressing room. It was just after breakfast, and everyone had retreated to change into clothing more appropriate for sporting. Jane stopped in her tracks upon discovering Penvale in the process of yanking a shirt over his head. "Have you started swimming again?" she asked, noticing a hint of sunburn on his shoulders.

Penvale turned to face her, handing his discarded shirt to Snood, who maintained a carefully neutral expression, as if indignant wives with questions about athletic activities burst into his employer's dressing room on a daily basis.

"I have," Penvale said distractedly, reaching for the fresh shirt Snood provided and pulling it on. She saw that he'd already changed into the buckskin breeches he usually wore for riding. "What has you upset now?"

What did have her upset? It was difficult to recall, following the sight of a shirtless husband in tight breeches.

"Lawn games!" she said after a distressingly long moment. "I can't play lawn games!"

Penvale paused in the act of buttoning his waistcoat. "Jane, children can play lawn games."

"Children can swim, too, as you so helpfully pointed out. I don't know why you're so fixated on what fearless, noisy small persons can do, as if that has any bearing on my own abilities."

Penvale flashed a grin at her. "Is that a request for me to continue our swimming lessons?"

"I did enjoy the view," she said boldly, "but no."

Penvale glanced at his valet. "Snood, I can handle the rest myself." Snood bowed and made a hasty, discreet retreat. When they were alone, Penvale walked slowly toward Jane. She was conscious of the fact that they hadn't spent much time alone together since his friends had arrived—in the wake of their interlude in her morning room, Penvale had taken to tapping on her bedchamber door most evenings (and Jane, naturally, had greeted him most enthusiastically), but once the house party had commenced, they'd been staying up later with their company, often retiring to bed at different times.

He reached out a hand to draw her closer to him. "What's this about, then?"

Jane opened her mouth to shoot back a sharp reply, but he ducked his head to kiss her before she could say anything. Her arms twined around his neck of their own volition. By the time he pulled back, she was blinking dazedly. "Were you about to say something?" he inquired solicitously.

Jane mustered the wherewithal to glare at him; perversely, this made him smile.

She loved his smiles.

After a moment, her scowl faded, and she did something that, a few months earlier, she never would have considered: She answered him honestly. "I'm going to make a fool of myself," she said softly, her hands still resting on his shoulders.

"You won't." He ducked his head to press a kiss to her forehead. "You've been doing splendidly so far."

"Ha."

"I'm serious," he said, and when she met his eyes, she saw that he was. "You and Diana have yet to spill any blood—"

"'Yet' being the operative word," Jane muttered.

"—and everyone is having a splendid time." He paused, mock-thoughtful. "Perhaps you have grown so accustomed to living in a haunted house that you can't recall what it feels like when things are proceeding normally and everyone is enjoying themselves?"

Jane smacked him on the shoulder. "Penvale," she said a touch uncertainly, "about the ghost—"

And what she would have said next—if she could have managed to put all of her complicated feelings for him into words, if she could have somehow explained that the prospect of living in this house without him in it, the thing she once thought she'd wanted above all else, was suddenly wildly unappealing to her—she'd never know. Because at that very moment, they were interrupted by a faint pounding on Penvale's bedroom door, audible even through the open doorway in the dressing room.

"Penvale!" came Diana's voice. "Are you ready? I want to thrash Jeremy at cricket!"

Penvale grinned down at Jane. "Shall we?"

As it turned out, Penvale reflected, Jane's fears might not have been entirely unfounded.

"For God's sake," she muttered, stalking back toward him after another unsuccessful round at bat.

"At least you didn't manage to hit yourself that time," he said encouragingly, earning a glare. He thought he was beginning to appreciate her scowls to a degree that was possibly perverse.

"I give up," she said, flopping down next to him on one of the blankets that had been laid out on the grass. Their even numbers had led to two teams of five, with West, Violet, and Diana on their team. Penvale glanced up in time to see Sophie bowling with a look of intense concentration, and West so distracted at bat that he seemed in very real danger of getting hit in the face by the ball.

"West!" Diana yelled from where she stood a few feet away, her arms crossed over her chest. "Focus! We need you to make up for the fact that Jane's utterly hopeless."

"I can't even work myself up to being offended," Jane said, lying down and flinging an arm across her face to shield her eyes from the sun.

"Jane!" Diana barked. "You should be practicing!"

Penvale shot his sister an exasperated look, but before he could tell her to shove off, Jane raised herself onto an elbow and fixed Diana with a hostile glare. "It's a friendly game of cricket. It doesn't matter whether I'm any good or not."

"Winning always matters," Diana said in superior tones.

"Of course she thinks that," Jane muttered, and Penvale burst out laughing, earning himself a share of Jane's glare as well. She punched him in the arm.

At that moment, there was a sympathetic groan from all the other gentlemen present, and Penvale turned in time to see West doubled over, his face white, Sophie evidently having hit him with the cricket ball in a rather delicate location. Sophie, for her part, had her hands clapped to her mouth with what Penvale initially mistook for horror but which, a moment later, was revealed to be hysterical laughter.

Diana threw her hands in the air in exasperation as the game broke up.

"I never would have thought Sophie had such an arm on her," Emily said, accepting Belfry's hand as she lowered herself to the ground; a few feet away, Diana and Jeremy were arguing loudly about whether Jeremy's team could claim victory based on their lead when the game came to a halt.

"To be fair, I don't think West really had his mind on the game," Belfry said, crouching beside Emily.

"No," Emily said, very cheerful. "I don't think he did, either."

"Penvale did not exaggerate how much his friends liked to meddle," Jane said.

Emily laughed, while Belfry looked mildly offended. "Don't lump me in with the rest of them," he said.

"Too late," Emily said, poking him affectionately in the side, and he gave her a smile that Penvale had only ever seen him direct at his wife—one that he never would have guessed Belfry possessed in his inventory of facial expressions.

At this point, the rest of the party rejoined them. West had apparently recovered sufficiently to walk once more, with Sophie hovering next to him offering a litany of apologies that would have been a bit more convincing had she not continued to break into fits of giggles. Violet and Audley trailed behind them, while Jeremy and Diana appeared to have resolved their argument without bloodshed, which Penvale always found to be a relief.

Mrs. Robin, the cook, had prepared an array of food for their picnic—sandwiches, cold meats, cheeses, an entire cake, a few bottles of wine—and they fell upon this now, and Penvale allowed himself to bask in the pleasure of being surrounded by his friends in the spring sunshine outside Trethwick Abbey with Jane by his side. It felt . . . right, somehow, everything about the scene, and all at once he had the oddest thought: *This* was what he'd truly wanted when he wished to buy the house. The feeling right now in his chest, the smile tugging at the corners of his lips unbidden, for no real reason other than that it was warm and there was good food and good wine and good company, and a single curl of Jane's dark hair was clinging to the nape of her neck and he couldn't bring himself to tear his gaze away—

This feeling that had only a little to do with the house itself and an awful lot to do with everything else.

He was so distracted by his own thoughts that he didn't catch whatever had just been said; he became aware that something was amiss only when Jane went very, very still next to him. She had a piece of cake in hand, raised slightly as if she were about to lift it to her mouth, and this was what made Penvale initially take notice; Jane was often still, but never when there was food to be consumed. It was one of the countless small things he'd come to know about her.

That he'd come to . . . like about her.

That word—"like"—suddenly didn't feel quite strong enough.

" . . . strangest noises," Violet was saying when he rejoined the conversation.

"I heard them, too!" Emily said. "A sort of eerie wail?"

Penvale carefully avoided looking at Jane. "As it happens, we've been experiencing some strange happenings around the house of late. Noises of the sort you mention—moved objects—that sort of thing."

"Penvale." Jeremy leaned forward; he was sitting next to Diana, a glass of wine in hand. "Do you mean to tell us that Trethwick Abbey is haunted?"

"Apparently." Penvale took a sip of his own wine. "It's most mysterious." He could feel Jane's eyes on him as he spoke, but he continued to avoid so much as a glance at her, lest it give away more than he wished.

"Haunted," Diana said, a skeptical note in her voice. "Funny you didn't mention this in any of your correspondence—or you, Jane."

Jane set down her cake. "We wouldn't have wanted to frighten away our guests," she said, her tone indicating quite the opposite.

"Yes," Diana said, smiling sweetly at her. "I can see how much you enjoy having us here."

"Diana." Penvale threw a sharp look at his sister.

"It's all rather like something out of a novel, don't you think?" Violet asked eagerly. "Penvale moves into a lonely house on a Cornish hillside . . . the telltale cries of a ghost are heard every night . . . the estate is shrouded in an ever-present mist . . ."

"An ever-present mist, yes," Audley murmured, casting a dubious glance at the cloudless sky.

"Someone must be having a laugh at your expense, then, old chap," Jeremy said, and Penvale experienced a pang of uneasiness. He felt very eager for his friends not to spend too much time considering who, logically, might be behind these events.

"Perhaps," he said neutrally. "More wine?" He brandished the bottle with enough exuberance that Audley, Diana, and Jeremy all gave him odd looks.

"If it happens again, perhaps we can investigate!" Violet said brightly. Penvale supposed he shouldn't be surprised—Violet was one of the most curious women he'd ever met, and she shared Jane's affection for novels. No doubt the promise of a bit of Gothic atmosphere was more than she could resist.

"Penvale and I have looked into it," Jane said, more sharply than Penvale guessed she intended. "I don't know why anyone else would be likely to discover something when we haven't."

A short silence fell after these words, and Penvale turned in time to see a fleeting expression of regret cross her face. He looked at her long enough for her to meet his eyes, and then he deliberately turned back to the group and said, "Jane's right. And I expect you're correct, Jeremy, and it's just one of the servants having a laugh. Nothing worth fretting too much about."

"Violet," Sophie said from where she was seated next to Emily, "wherever did you purchase that bonnet?"

Penvale was nearly certain this was an intentional change of subject, given that he had never known Sophie to be much of a bonnet enthusiast, and he cast her a grateful glance; as conversation commenced once more around him, he risked another peek at Jane, who was staring down at the cake in her hand with concentration.

Penvale reached out to take her empty hand and couldn't ignore the warmth in his chest when she laced her fingers tightly with his. He was uneasy with the knowledge that she'd broken their truce; he wanted her to like his friends, damn it, and he wanted them to like her, and he was frightened by the degree to which these things had come to matter to him. And the possibility that lurked at the edges of his mind, that refused to go away despite the fact that he willed it firmly to do so—that it wasn't just his friends' presence here, but *his* as well, that had inspired this resurrection of the ghost . . . well, the thought frightened him in a way that he didn't fully wish to examine. Because he thought he'd banished that fear—thought he and Jane had come to an understanding, of sorts. Thought that he might even . . .

Even to himself, he could not give voice to the words.

But even as this turmoil gripped him, he was drawn back to his surroundings by the feeling of Jane's fingers squeezing his own. The sun was shining, and her hand was in his, and she even gave him the faintest, most fleeting of sideways smiles when he offered her more cake, and he could not bring himself to ruin the happiness of this afternoon with questions to which he wasn't certain he wanted the answer.

So instead, he wondered.

Chapter Twenty-Three

Several days passed, and as the house party crept into its second week, Jane would not admit it to anyone, but she was almost enjoying herself.

Oh, to be sure: The house was noisy; she'd had to miss her usual trips into the village to deliver more books; Diana was growing more irritating by the day; she'd had more conversations in the past week than she'd ideally like to have in an entire year; and she'd spent so much time outdoors that her complexion would possibly never recover.

And yet, still, she realized one evening as she made ready for bed, she was rather . . . happy.

She liked Penvale's friends, was the problem. There were an awful lot of them, undoubtedly, but the fact that there were so many happily married couples among their number did make things a bit easier, as these couples had a suspicious tendency to vanish for an hour or two at a time, rejoining the group looking unaccountably cheerful for two people who *claimed* to have been merely admiring the gardens, taking a walk along the cliff path, or visiting the horses in the stables. Even among the unmarried of their party, there was sufficient intrigue to keep them occupied: Sophie was occasionally observed sharing a smile or a private word with West, these interactions so avidly watched by Violet, Diana, and Emily that, at one point, Belfry had to intervene.

"*What?*" Emily demanded when he poked her rather obviously in the side. She looked, Jane thought, like someone immersed in a particularly gripping piece of theater who had been interrupted at a key moment.

"Stop staring," Belfry said quietly. "If the three of you aim to ensure that West and Lady Fitzwilliam become so skittish that they're afraid to so much as walk within ten feet of each other, then by all means, continue, but otherwise, I'd encourage you to desist. It's unnerving."

"It would help," Jane put in, leaning toward the group and speaking in an undertone, "if Violet would blink at least occasionally."

Belfry laughed aloud at this, as did Emily and even Violet. Diana cast Jane a speculative glance, as if reassessing whatever her previously held opinion had been, and Jane offered a small smile by way of reply.

The fact was, Penvale's friends had been nothing but kind to Jane; even Diana, in her own way, had made friendly overtures. She had invited Jane on a walk a day earlier, and they had managed a pleasant half-hour turn about the estate gardens without murdering each other, which Jane counted as a promising development in terms of their sisterly relations.

She was in real danger, she realized, of approaching a state alarmingly close to happiness. And, she thought later, she should have known then that it couldn't last.

"When are you coming back to London, then?" Audley asked.

It was late on the last night of the house party. The evening had turned celebratory when Emily and Belfry announced at dinner that they were expecting a baby in the autumn, with many a glass lifted in their honor, but eventually, everyone had begun to make their way to bed, and now only Penvale, Audley, and Jeremy remained in the downstairs drawing room. No sooner had Belfry and Emily departed than the interrogation began. In truth, Penvale was surprised it had taken this long; but then, there had been few opportunities for him to be alone with Audley and Jeremy. He hadn't minded this—Belfry had become a good friend in the months since his marriage to Emily, and West was a capital fellow, but it was only now, left alone with his two oldest friends, that Penvale felt himself properly relax.

For all of three seconds, that is, before they attacked.

"I don't know," he said in response to Audley's query. "Sometime soon, I expect."

He wasn't certain why he was hedging; after all, his plan had always been to return to town for a good portion of the Season, regardless of whether Jane wished to accompany him. Why did he hesitate now?

"You should come back with us," Jeremy said lazily from his spot by the fire; he'd claimed the fattest armchair and was reclining with his legs kicked up onto the tufted ottoman before him, a glass of brandy dangling from one hand. He took a healthy sip. "You can't rusticate here all summer long."

"There is work to be done here, Jeremy," Penvale pointed out, his voice laced with mild irritation. "You might be unfamiliar with the concept."

This was a bit unfair, since Jeremy, despite the image he presented to society, was actually a very careful steward of his own land. His country estate was in Wiltshire, and Penvale knew that Jeremy and Diana had stopped there for several days on their journey to Trethwick Abbey, going considerably out of their way to do so.

Jeremy, however, appeared to take no offense. "Work can wait. What have you been doing all winter, if not working?"

"My uncle didn't leave the estate in precisely the condition I'd like it to be," Penvale said tersely. "I've been making improvements." Seeing his friends' unimpressed faces, he added, before thinking better of it, "Besides, I don't think Jane wishes to go to town."

No sooner were the words out of his mouth than he regretted them, knowing how much they had just revealed. He darted a glance at his friends to find them regarding him with expressions of mingled astonishment and wicked, knowing glee.

Jeremy went so far as to sit up straight in his chair and set his glass down with a faint *clink*. "Of course," he said seriously. "You are married, after all. You wouldn't wish to go anywhere without your wife." He nodded slowly. "It is not at all as if you are a man who, just four months ago, informed us quite earnestly that nothing about your life would change whatsoever when you were wed."

Penvale offered a rude gesture, which did nothing more than make Jeremy abandon any attempt at suppressing his grin.

"Indeed," Audley agreed calmly. "I can't imagine any reason that a man who has been recently married—not at all for love, if I recall correctly—and who has spent several months in close company with his wife and precious few other humans, should suddenly be oh so reluctant to leave said wife." He flicked an invisible speck of dust from his cuff. "There is not the slightest chance that this man may have realized, after getting to know his new bride, that he perhaps likes her considerably more than he initially realized."

"Go to hell," Penvale said without heat.

"But things are ever so much more interesting here," Audley said cheerfully.

"Penvale, have you truly gone and fallen in love with a woman who gave every impression of wishing you dead?" Jeremy asked. "Because if you have, I really question your instinct for self-preservation, old chap."

"Jane does not wish me dead," Penvale said, his voice quiet but intent. "And if you think I'm going to confess anything to you before I've informed her of it, you're out of your mind. I spent the better part of last summer listening to you two try to convince yourselves you weren't in love with Violet and Diana, when any fool could see otherwise, and I don't think it's so much to ask that you let me work out my own marriage, and without insulting Jane in the process."

"Penvale." Jeremy leaned forward, looking honestly astonished. "Have we *offended* you?"

"Of course not," Penvale said instinctively, because, of course, he was not the sort to get offended—not the kind of man whose feelings were ever engaged, who was ever too concerned by what others thought or any of the complicated matters of the heart that had seemed to plague them so much of late.

But then he paused and considered. He thought of watching his friends find love and happiness and not feeling terribly bothered by it—he was happy enough for them because they were his friends; and despite the fact that he occasionally wanted to strangle them, he largely found that their happiness was rather important to his. And he thought of all the years he'd spent shunning any possibility of such connections in his own life.

And then he thought of the past few months, of Jane's company, of her sharp comments, of her insistence that he needed spectacles, of her abject horror that he didn't read novels, of the peculiar quirk to her mouth when she was trying hard to suppress a smile at something he had said. Of her awkward, halting attempts to befriend the villagers. Of the way her voice softened ever so slightly when she addressed the servants. Of the peculiar fierce look that crossed her face when she was staring at the sea, or the distant moors, or occasionally—when she thought he wasn't looking—at Trethwick Abbey, this house that he'd realized she loved just as much as he did.

He knew now that the house meant little to him if she wasn't within it.

"I think we owe you an apology nonetheless," Audley said quietly, after silence had stretched between them for several long moments. His face was utterly serious as he spoke, his steady green gaze fixed upon Penvale's face. "It was never my intent to disparage Jane—because she is your wife, and because I like her in her own right, truth be told. I did not think that such feeling existed between you two, but if you have fallen in love, I'll confess that I'm delighted. I think she suits you perfectly, Penvale." His tone was unusually affectionate, and his words had a ring of truth to them that warmed Penvale through and through.

"I still find her mildly terrifying," Jeremy said, rising to take a few steps toward Penvale, reaching out to clap a hand upon his shoulder. "But since I married your sister, of all people, I think my fondness for terrifying women has been established. Which is to say, if you, too, suffer from this affliction, then I'm more than happy to welcome you to the club."

Penvale opened his mouth to make some sort of reply, but before he could utter a single word, a familiar sound rang out:

A clear, unearthly wail.

Audley and Jeremy jumped; Penvale, feeling all at once exceedingly grim, did not.

There was a beat of silence and then another shriek—sufficiently shrill to raise gooseflesh on his arms—this time coming from quite the opposite side of the house as the first one.

"Christ." Jeremy set down his glass. "If that's the sort of thing you've been hearing since you've been here, I'm impressed you didn't decamp to the nearest inn months ago."

Audley was already on his feet. "Come on, then," he said. "Shall we follow the sound?"

Penvale sat unmoving, as if rooted to the spot, his mind racing. He'd dismissed it the week before, when Violet had mentioned hearing some sort of noise—he'd thought it a member of the staff having a bit of a laugh at the guests' expense, confident that Jane wouldn't reprimand them for this behavior.

But this . . .

It was coordinated. Because now that he knew of the hidden staircases, he knew that it was not possible to travel from one side of the house to the other as quickly as the sound of that wail had—which meant, logically, that there was more than one wailer. It was a planned effort. And if it had been planned . . .

Well, he was perfectly well aware who the person behind it was.

The three made their way to the hall, where they paused, listening intently, but no further sound was forthcoming. Exchanging a glance, they headed for the staircase by unspoken agreement and emerged onto the second-floor landing in time to see Violet poke her head out of the bedroom she and Audley were sharing.

"James!" Her face brightened at the sight of him, the faint wrinkle in her brow smoothing. "I heard the strangest sound."

"As did we," he informed her. Farther down the corridor, a couple of other doors opened, and before too long, the majority of their guests had assembled. Jane was among the last to arrive; she was already dressed for bed, a flannel dressing gown knotted tightly at her waist, but Penvale caught a glimpse of white lace at her neck.

Jane was not wearing one of her appalling nightgowns.

Instead, she was wearing a white lace-edged one.

Just what she would wear, he thought, if she were planning to spend an evening roaming the halls in the role of a ghostly apparition.

She made her way to his side. "Did you hear the noise, too?" she asked. Before he could make any sort of reply, she added swiftly, pitching her voice low so as not to be overheard, "Penvale, I don't know what that was—it wasn't me."

Hope rose in his chest, lightening the weight that had settled upon his shoulders; a moment later, however, when Violet said with some eagerness, "Let's form a search party, then!" and Jane offered nothing but a frown, doubt crept back into Penvale's mind.

Surely, if she were telling him the truth—if she were not behind tonight's events—she would not look so displeased at the idea of searching for the ghost. She looked downright irritated, however, standing at his side with her arms crossed over her chest, not appearing, in that moment, a single bit more welcoming of his friends' presence than she had that very first afternoon in his drawing room in London. He had thought that she was coming to like them, to enjoy herself—was he that bad at reading her, still, after all these months?

The thought struck Penvale that his friends would be leaving tomorrow—as Jane knew perfectly well. What was there to gain, then, from the ghost appearing tonight? There was no need to frighten them now, not when they were already preparing to depart.

Unless . . .

Unless she was eager to send *him* back to London with his friends—in which case tonight would be her last opportunity to scare him away. By, for example, insisting that she didn't know who the ghost was this time. Surely she didn't think him enough of an idiot to believe the house was actually haunted, after months of white nightgowns and hidden staircases and theatrical wailing.

Unless the past fortnight, spent seeing him in the presence of his friends, had convinced her once and for all that she did not want this marriage, that it—*he*—was not worth all of this bother . . . and she was willing to try whatever it took to be rid of him.

And if that were true, then he could not bear to be the cause of her misery any longer.

Before he could say anything else to her, there was the sound of a *thump* overhead, loud enough to cause a brief hush to fall among the assembled group as their eyes were drawn upward. Penvale instead studied Jane, searching her face for signs of artifice in her reaction. He shook his head—he couldn't live like this anymore, wondering every moment whether his wife wished for him to even be in the house. Not when he had come to realize how desperately the answer to that question mattered to him.

Dimly, Penvale registered the sound of a search party being formed, Violet and Jeremy at its helm. The group was divided between those who wished to remain in their bedrooms and those who wished to join the search; Penvale did not join this discussion for a long moment, still gazing at Jane, unable to look away.

Her frown deepened under his scrutiny, and she said, "Don't you want to go help them search?"

"Of course," he said shortly. She did not blink or avert her eyes, merely continued to frown at him with that faintly perplexed expression—and neither did she offer anything by way of explanation or apology.

Penvale didn't need to see any more. "Let's be off, shall we?" he said, turning to rejoin the group. "Let's head upstairs before the ghost has a chance to escape." He spoke the words without any real conviction, now that he knew of the existence of the hidden staircases; whoever was upstairs tipping over furniture was likely already long gone.

"I'll check the staircases," Jane said quietly to him, making as if to turn in the opposite direction, but he stopped her with a firm hand on her arm—the last thing he needed was for his friends to catch sight of a ghostly apparition and somehow realize it was Jane. Even if she were truly trying to rid herself of him once more, he still felt a strange sense of loyalty toward her and could not bear for his friends to think poorly of her. "Why don't you stay with us," he said to her in an undertone. It was not a question.

"But surely, if they're trying to escape—"

"You're the viscountess, Jane," he snapped. "I don't need you crawling through dusty staircases like a child—I need you to act like the mistress of this house." He lowered his voice even further. "I need you to come with me and behave like a woman who has never impersonated a ghost in her life and who is as confused as everyone else."

Her mouth snapped shut, two spots of color appearing high on her cheeks. "Fine," she said, her eyes not quite meeting his. "Lead the way, then."

He regretted speaking so harshly, aware on some level that it was his own hurt and confusion sharpening his tone, but he was in no mood to explain that to her now.

Instead, he led her and his friends on a search for a ghost he knew perfectly well they weren't going to find. He did not reveal the hidden staircase to his friends, so whichever members of staff had been responsible were able to make their way safely back to bed unseen.

When they finally abandoned the search as fruitless and returned to their rooms, Penvale and Jane paused in the hallway outside their bedrooms. Penvale opened his mouth, though he wasn't certain what words he could muster that would possibly improve the situation, but before he could say anything, she offered him a cold "Good night, *my lord*" and vanished into her room, slamming the door behind her.

So Penvale returned to his own room, and undressed, and bathed, all the while turning over the evening's events in his mind. When he dismissed Snood at last, he stared for a long moment at the connecting door in his dressing room leading to Jane's suite of rooms.

Then, turning his back on it, he climbed into bed. And by the time sleep finally found him, some unknowable time later, he knew what he had to do.

Chapter Twenty-Four

Breakfast the next morning was a less than cheerful affair.

For her part, Jane was exhausted; sleep had been long in coming last night after she'd returned to her bedroom. She'd spent their entire search of the third floor torn between hurt and slowly simmering anger.

She felt like a fool. There she'd been, thinking things were going—well, if not perfectly, then at least as well as could be expected. Penvale's friends had seemed reasonably happy; she and Penvale were getting along; she'd even abandoned her usual array of flannel nightgowns for the single lacy, vaguely seductive one she owned in an attempt to entice her husband—not that she'd got the chance in the end.

Instead, his words from the night before echoed through her head: *You're the viscountess, Jane.*

I need you to act like the mistress of this house.

And that was it, wasn't it? At the end of the day, she could play at being the viscountess, at being comfortable with this role she'd stepped into, one far grander than she'd ever expected for herself. But when it came down to it, she wasn't fooling anyone. All it had taken was the presence of his friends for him to realize this fact.

It was these thoughts that had kept her awake, along with

reflections on the evening's strange events. She wanted to know who had been responsible for the wailing, naturally—the staff had been under strict instructions to cease all such activities while the house party was under way—but it was her snappish exchange with Penvale that had cost her the most sleep. She'd eventually fallen asleep in a temper and awoken to find her mood unimproved.

So she sat, heavy-eyed and faintly miserable, moving her pile of eggs around her plate, avoiding any attempts at conversation with her guests.

Until Penvale arrived.

He, too, looked the worse for the previous evening's events; his eyes were faintly red-rimmed, though whether that was from exhaustion or spirits—the drink had been flowing heavily the night before—Jane wasn't certain. And there was a determined set to his mouth that made her uneasy.

"Penvale, you look dreadful," Diana said, diplomatic as ever; next to her, Jeremy rolled his eyes heavenward, even as he leaned forward to steal a piece of toast from her plate.

"Thank you, Diana, terribly kind," Penvale said, then glanced around the table as he came to a halt before the sideboard, picking up a plate and calling over his shoulder, "I'm glad you're all here, though, there's something I wanted to say."

At this, the table fell immediately, eerily silent. Penvale had been the latest riser that morning, so all of their guests were already present—some still in the middle of their meal, others lingering over last cups of tea and coffee. All eyes turned curious gazes upon Penvale, who was busily loading his plate with sufficient food to feed a small army. Jane wondered if he was stalling. She wondered what he was about to say. She wondered why she felt so *appallingly* nervous, her heart kicking up an anxious rhythm in her chest. Sophie, seated next to her, reached over to still Jane's hands; Jane glanced down and realized that she'd been tying the napkin in her lap into a knot that would impress even the most fastidious of valets.

At last Penvale turned back to the table. "I've decided to return to London with the rest of you today," he announced without preamble, his eyes lingering on various of his guests but carefully avoiding Jane. "The incident last night has made me realize that my presence here is no longer tenable—these strange occurrences seem to have picked up with a fervor when I arrived at Trethwick Abbey, and it is my guess that my absence will hasten their cessation. With that in mind—and with the understandably traumatic effect they must undoubtedly be having on everyone who lives here—I feel that my departure is the only responsible course of action."

He spoke these words almost mechanically, Jane thought, as though he were an actor reading from a script he had yet to memorize.

Belfry leaned forward in his seat, lifting a dark, arrogant brow. "Penvale, do you mean to tell us that you are running away from a *ghost?*" His voice was laced with faint incredulity, and Jane did not entirely blame him; it was a decidedly strange announcement.

"Yes," Penvale said, and now he did look at Jane. It was only for a moment, but his eyes met hers as he said, "From a ghost."

From her. She was the ghost.

This knowledge burned within Jane, hot and angry. He knew that no such ghost existed, and yet he claimed to be leaving on its account, which meant—

That the ghost was an excuse. Just as Jane had made use of it to scare away one unwanted man, so, too, was Penvale using it for his own purposes now. And those purposes were—from all Jane could tell—to get as far away from her as possible. From the wife who, in company with his friends, was awkward and bad-tempered. Who could not even host a handful of guests without nerves. Who impersonated ghosts with ease but could never quite manage to play the role of an aristocrat's wife in a manner that was convincing.

You're the viscountess, Jane.

But out here, on this remote hillside, she didn't really have to act like one—and all it had taken, apparently, was the arrival of his friends from town for him to see that she wasn't the right sort of woman for the role.

So he was leaving.

The thought of months—even *years*—spent alone in this creaking old house, on this wild, lonely patch of cliff, once so comforting, suddenly opened up before Jane like an abyss. This was what she had wanted. This was what it had all been for. This should be her moment of triumph, of victory—

Instead, all she felt was bone-deep yearning for something she'd never thought herself capable of needing:

Companionship.

The companionship of one person, in fact.

The one who was currently regarding her from the opposite end of the table, his gaze cool and distant, his words carving her heart neatly out of her chest.

Congratulations, Jane, she thought dully to herself. *You did it.*

And now it was too late to wish it undone.

An hour later, Diana found Jane in the library. Jane had hidden herself here after breakfast, wondering if she might just linger long enough that the others would give up and leave without saying their final farewells, sparing her the ache in her chest every time she glanced in Penvale's direction and he did not meet her eyes.

But she would not be so lucky.

"Surely you've read that already."

Startled by the sound of Diana's voice, Jane glanced up from the book in her hand; she'd been staring at the same page for a quarter of an hour, absorbing not a single word before her, and indeed had to take a surreptitious glance down at the spine to remind herself what it was she was supposed to be reading.

Ah.

Pride and Prejudice.

"Of course I have," she said coldly, which no doubt was precisely the response—and tone—Diana had expected, a suspicion confirmed by a faint grin crossing her sister-in-law's face. Diana was wearing a gown of light blue muslin, a lace collar and sleeves lending the ensemble a bit more respectability than was offered by the low-necked evening gowns she seemed to favor.

"I like to reread books from time to time," Jane added. "I wouldn't expect *you* to understand."

Diana still did not rise to the bait. "I had hoped for a moment alone with you before we leave," she said briskly. "May I join you?" She sat down next to Jane in the window seat without waiting for an answer. Jane pointedly did not withdraw her legs to make more space, but Diana seemed unconcerned by the hostility vibrating off of her.

"I do not pretend to understand your relationship with that idiot brother of mine," she said without preamble.

"He's not an idiot," Jane said, some dormant protective instinct howling to life.

Diana favored her with a smile, which, naturally, made Jane even more suspicious. "You are merely proving my point."

"I'm doing nothing of the sort."

"Would you believe that I did not, in fact, come here to argue with you?" Diana adopted a tone of such determined cheerfulness that Jane began to feel somewhat alarmed. "And yet you make it so difficult. You make everything so difficult."

"Did you have a reason for coming here other than to insult me?" Jane asked.

Diana inhaled sharply. "I'm sorry—that truly isn't why I sought you out. You do have a way of provoking me, you know." She said this half-frustratedly, half-admiringly.

Jane decided to be flattered. "I've noticed. You do make it so tempting to do so." She gave Diana a cautious half-smile to show that she was not trying to start a quarrel.

"The feeling is entirely mutual," Diana assured her. "But I suppose I would be hopelessly bored if Penvale had chosen someone more docile to marry, so really, I should be grateful."

"This is touching," Jane said. "I find myself at risk of needing a handkerchief. What did you *actually* come here to tell me?"

"That, again, I do not know what is going on between you and Penvale—every time I think I have a grasp on it, one of you does something utterly perplexing that sends me into a fit of despair once again—but I am fairly certain my brother is in love with you and is absolutely miserable to be headed back to London."

"Last I checked, no one was forcing him to go." The words came out sharp, but each one of them took considerable effort on Jane's part to utter.

Diana gave her a speaking glance. "And yet anyone who has taken more than three seconds to look at the man can tell he's not happy to be leaving."

"What is it to you, then?" Jane asked, crossing her arms defensively. "You've not come here to tell me that you're actually desperately fond of me and the thought of a London Season without my presence is too much for you to bear."

Diana let out a hoot of laughter. "You may not believe me, but I find myself growing fonder of you by the day," she said, giving Jane an approving sort of look. "But more important is the fact that I've been watching you, and I've been watching my brother, and much as it pains me to admit, I'm quite convinced you two are in love with each other and too stupid to work it out on your own."

Unsurprisingly, Jane thought, Diana could not manage even a single sentence concerning a matter of great import and emotional weight without sliding in an insult to accompany it.

Diana rose to her feet abruptly, evidently weary of the entire conversation, then gazed at Jane for a long moment. "My brother is not very good at sharing the contents of his heart, Jane—it is a trait common to the Bourne family, I suspect. But I should hate if that failing were to make both of you unhappy."

She departed without another word, leaving Jane alone with her thoughts—a state that was not nearly as restful as it had been even a couple of months before.

At one point, a maid poked a timid head into the room, saying that the viscount was making ready to depart and requested her presence downstairs; Jane, still feeling entirely unsettled—by the events of the night before, and Penvale's announcement at the breakfast table, and her conversation with Diana—pleaded a headache and was left in peace.

And by the time she emerged from the library, they had gone, a note from Penvale promising to write from London all that remained in their wake.

In the days that followed, Jane did her best to fling herself into matters that had gone neglected during the past fortnight—she made a few trips into the village, delivering baskets of books, making arrangements to have the shutters painted on the little storefront she had decided to turn into the village library.

She tried to enjoy her present situation, which was, after all, the one she had often longed for: She was mistress of Trethwick Abbey in truth, not merely as a matter of convenience; the master of the house was nowhere to be found, nor did she have any reason to expect his presence any time soon; it was a warm, glorious spring, and there was no lovelier place on earth to be than the Cornish coast in such mild weather; she had all the uninterrupted reading time she could possibly wish for, even. It should have been bliss.

Jane was miserable.

At first she told herself she was merely weary from the excitement of the preceding weeks; then that she was overwhelmed by the tasks she'd left unattended during the house party. Even once she was forced to unhappily concede that it was Penvale's absence causing her misery, she concocted all sorts of stories to explain the sensation: She'd grown used to his presence, and she disliked change; he was helpful to have around in case she encountered a spider; she very much wanted to kiss him again. All these things were true (except the bit about the spider; he had not proved very helpful with that), and yet within a week she had to admit that none of them was the *real* reason she missed Penvale.

She missed him for himself.

It was dreadful.

It was as she was contemplating this matter, about a week after Penvale had left, that Mrs. Ash found her in the morning room. Jane had continued her habit of retreating here after breakfast with a book in hand, but she found herself curiously listless of late, the book more often than not lying unopened on her lap as she gazed out the window at the distant hills. It was a beautiful day, mild enough that Jane was pondering making her way to the library so that she might open the French doors that led onto the terrace, but before she could make any moves in that direction, Mrs. Ash appeared at the doorway.

"Mrs. Ash," Jane said, mustering a smile; she thought that the housekeeper had been watching her more intently than usual of late, though every time she glanced in the woman's direction, she found her looking elsewhere. Still, she felt the weight of a motherly worry whenever she was in Mrs. Ash's presence, which was both oddly comforting and had the effect of making her feel vaguely guilty for being its cause.

"My lady." Mrs. Ash bobbed a curtsey, which still felt strange to Jane, despite it having been nearly four months since her marriage. "I wondered if I might have a word?"

"Certainly." Jane frowned; now that she looked more closely, Mrs. Ash appeared decidedly unhappy, almost distraught. What on earth could be the matter? Now that she no longer had frequent nightly bits of theater to arrange, Jane would have expected her housekeeper to appear well rested and cheerful, but that certainly was not the case this morning. Dark shadows were visible under the other woman's eyes; she was no longer in her prime, but she'd never looked old to Jane. Not until now.

"Mrs. Ash, please sit down," Jane said, rising to take her housekeeper by the elbow and guide her into the seat next to hers. "Something is clearly troubling you—please, tell me what it is and how I may help."

Mrs. Ash stared down at her hands before bursting out, "It's my fault the viscount left!"

Jane blinked. "Mrs. Ash—"

"And now you're upset, and it's all my doing, even though I was only trying to help!" Mrs. Ash was not the hysterical sort—she radiated steady English common sense, even at the most trying of moments—but with these words, her voice took on a pitch that Jane had never heard from her.

"What do you mean?" Jane asked quietly, deciding that at least one of them needed to remain somewhat calm. "You can hardly be blamed for Lord Penvale's departure, not unless—" She broke off abruptly. "Oh."

Oh. Of course. She should have realized it instantly, the moment there was a single visit from their ghost that she had not orchestrated. She'd been too distracted by other matters to give it much thought—she supposed she'd thought it was one of the young errand boys or footmen having a laugh—but the answer should have been obvious.

"You are the reason for the scream during the house party," she said. A statement, not a question; the misery on Mrs. Ash's face was its own confirmation even before she nodded her assent.

"All right," Jane said, taking a deep breath. "Would you care to explain why?"

"I thought I was helping," Mrs. Ash whispered. "We all became rather fond of the new viscount, don't you see? He's nothing at all like his uncle—Crowe says he's just like his father, honorable through and through. He treats the staff well. He takes care of his tenants. He's kind, even if he doesn't look like it at first. We all began to have second thoughts about trying to frighten him away—it just didn't seem quite right, after a while. And I thought sometimes, when he looked at you—well, no matter. I thought that the two of you were growing closer, spending so much time together. So I arranged for a few more appearances from our mysterious ghost, just to force you into each other's company even more. And I daresay it was working," she added, a touch of her old spirit back, and the knowing look she gave Jane had her fighting off a blush.

"But," Mrs. Ash added, her smile fading, "with his friends arriving, I was worried he'd feel the lure of town and want to return with them. Once they were here and I saw how easy he was in their company, I grew even more concerned. So I thought to arrange for one last showing from our ghost, at night, when he'd likely be near you—I thought it would force the two of you back together, remind him why he couldn't simply leave to go back to town with all those friends of his." Here, she heaved a heavy sigh. "And instead, it had the opposite effect. It frightened him away, and he's left you here, all alone and miserable."

Jane sighed, reaching out to pat the housekeeper's arm. "Mrs. Ash, I promise you, Lord Penvale is not remotely frightened of ghosts—and he's known that we were behind the hauntings for a while now. So you did not frighten him away."

Mrs. Ash went very still. "Why did he leave, then, if he knew there wasn't a ghost?"

"I . . . I cannot say with any certainty," Jane said carefully. She hesitated; unburdening herself did not come naturally to her. But if she could not speak honestly with Mrs. Ash, then whom else did she have? "I think he may have realized, with his friends surrounding us once more, that I am not . . ." She trailed off, searching for the right words. "I am not the viscountess he might have wished for. And I think that he may have used the final haunting as an excuse rather than admit that he was dissatisfied with his life here." She paused, then added more softly, "With me."

But even as she spoke these words, something Diana had said came back to her:

My brother is not very good at sharing the contents of his heart, Jane.

This—and the memory of the sharp frown Penvale had given her when she'd insisted that she did not know who the ghost was that final night—brought another possibility to mind.

What if Penvale had not believed her and had thought she was trying to be rid of him once and for all? Would he return to town if he thought she truly wished him gone?

She did not need to think longer than a fraction of a second to know the answer.

Jane groaned and dropped her head into her hands, wishing heartily, in that moment, that she'd never come up with the haunting scheme in the first place.

After a minute, she felt the warmth of Mrs. Ash's hand pressing comfortingly on her shoulder. "There, there, my lady. If he's not actually frightened of a ghost, then he'll be back, I daresay."

Jane looked up helplessly. "I fear he may not be, Mrs. Ash—I think he may have left because he thought it was what I wished." Because giving her what she wanted was worth sacrificing the only thing that *he* had truly wanted. The thought made her throat tighten—it was not at all something she would have expected of the man she'd thought she was marrying, and yet also exactly what she would expect of the man she'd come to know.

The man she'd come to love.

Mrs. Ash's eyes widened, and then she let out a happy sigh. "That does sound like something he would do, the dear man. Given that anyone with eyes can see he's in love with you."

"Mrs. Ash!"

Mrs. Ash shrugged, unrepentant, bearing no resemblance whatsoever, Jane thought darkly, to the woman who had been on the verge of tears a few minutes earlier. "What do you mean to do about it, then? You're not going to fix this by sitting here moping in Cornwall, are you?"

Jane went still—because, when it was put like that, now that she'd made the realization, it did seem rather foolish. "Well," she said a bit uncertainly, "I suppose I could write a letter—"

A hearty snort was Mrs. Ash's reply.

"He *is* all the way in London, in case you haven't noticed," Jane said sharply, growing the slightest bit annoyed. It was very easy for Mrs. Ash to stand there, all smug and knowing, when *she* was the one who had caused this problem in the first place.

"And you are here," Mrs. Ash agreed.

"Precisely." Jane nodded vigorously. "It's not as though I'm about to just race off to London, of all pl—" Here, she broke off. And considered.

"It is certainly not something the old Jane would have done," Mrs. Ash said slyly.

It wasn't. The old Jane hated London. The old Jane never would have risked looking foolish before a man, before all his friends, to share the deepest confession of her heart.

Because that was, Jane knew, what she wished to tell Penvale—that she loved him. And that she desperately wanted him to love her, too.

The old Jane never could have imagined uttering such words—the old Jane never could have dreamed of feeling this way at all.

But Jane was tired of the old Jane. She wanted to be a new Jane instead.

"You're perfectly right," she said, then gave the housekeeper's hand a quick squeeze. "I suppose I'd better start packing."

Chapter Twenty-Five

"It's too early to be on a bloody horse."

It was, in fact, rather early, certainly by town standards—most men in London were still abed—though at Trethwick Abbey, Penvale already would have been finishing his breakfast or saddling his horse for a tour of the estate. Audley, however, had always been a fan of morning rides in the park and had somehow convinced Penvale to join him today.

"You're cheerful this morning," Audley observed.

"You're particularly *annoying* this morning," Penvale shot back.

Audley grinned. Penvale's sense of doom strengthened.

"I can't help but notice, old chap—"

"Are you supposed to be Jeremy now?" Audley had never called him "old chap" in his life.

"—that you seem rather despondent of late," Audley continued as if Penvale hadn't spoken at all. "And as someone with firsthand experience of a man being unhappy in his marriage, I thought it best that I have a word with you."

"*You* thought, hmm?" Penvale was skeptical.

"We," Audley amended, unrepentant.

"I suppose Jeremy had a hand in this."

"Belfry, too. Remarkable what a romantic he's turned into now that he's married."

"I think impending fatherhood has really been the final nail in the coffin," Penvale said thoughtfully. The last time Penvale had been to Belfry and Emily's for dinner, Belfry, not the lady of the house, had insisted on showing him the room they'd decided to turn into a nursery. And Penvale—who had always considered himself disinterested in children, or in anything that spoke of cozy domestic scenes—had felt the strangest pang of jealousy.

"In any case," Audley continued, drawing Penvale out of his thoughts, "out with it now. What has you so damned moody? You've been miserable company since the moment we returned to town."

Likely on the journey back, too, Penvale thought; he'd returned to London with Jeremy and Diana, resisting all their attempts at conversation, staring resolutely out the window instead. He'd tried to read one of Jane's novels that he'd pilfered several days earlier, but his head had started pounding so badly that he'd had to give it up; this had motivated him to bump a particular errand on his list to the very top, and he remembered that he had an appointment that afternoon to collect the results of said errand.

"I've a lot on my mind," he replied absently.

"A lot," Audley repeated; Penvale glanced sideways at him, but Audley's gaze was fixed ahead. "'A lot' wouldn't happen to answer to another name, would she?"

"For God's sake," Penvale muttered.

Audley's mouth twitched. "So you're miserable over Jane," he said. Penvale remained silent but managed to accidentally grip his reins so hard that his horse reared up, and it took a moment to get him to settle. Glancing sideways, he saw that Audley was losing his battle with his twitching mouth.

Taking this for the confirmation that it was, Audley continued, "Why don't you go back to Cornwall, then? Why did you leave in the first place? Don't give me any more nonsense about a bloody ghost."

Penvale sighed and gave up. He'd been avoiding discussion of the matter with his friends ever since they'd returned to town, and he was suddenly exhausted by the effort. "Jane is the ghost."

Audley was silent for a moment. "Ah." There was a wealth of meaning in that single word.

"Indeed."

"And you assume she was the ghost in order to . . . ?"

"Rid herself of the unwanted men in her life." Penvale felt his mouth curving upward in spite of himself. He hadn't taken a moment to pause and consider her plan, once he'd worked it out, nor to appreciate it for its odd cunning and humor.

Another pause. "That is . . ."

"Demented? Unhinged?"

"Rather clever, actually."

"I know." A sideways glance at Audley confirmed that he was grinning, too. Penvale was oddly *proud* of Jane, despite the fact that he'd had nothing at all to do with this plan of hers and was currently suffering as one of its victims. It was just so utterly her, everything about it, that he could not help but be appreciative of the scheme. It was like being offered a glimpse inside her mind, to see how it worked, and at some point, such a thing had come to feel like a rare and precious gift to Penvale.

Oh, God, he really did love her, didn't he?

"So you left because—"

"The ghost returned during the house party," Penvale confirmed. "I thought we'd agreed to call a halt to the haunting." He blew out a frustrated breath. "I thought we were building something between the two of us. A real marriage. But if she doesn't want me there, I'm not going to force my presence upon her."

"It's your house," Audley said, stating the obvious, and Penvale had no doubt that, a few months earlier, he would have thought the same thing. But now he'd lived in that house alongside Jane, he'd seen her speak to the staff, he'd seen the way her gaze softened when she glanced out a window at the sea, he'd seen the loving care she'd taken each time she pulled a book off the shelf in the library, and now he knew the truth.

"It's her house, too, James."

Audley glanced sharply at him—he could likely count on one hand the number of times in the entire duration of their two-decade friendship that Penvale had called him by his first name—and Penvale met his gaze evenly.

"You certainly worked hard enough to win it back," Audley murmured.

"But she's made it hers," Penvale said determinedly, feeling a pang deep in his chest as he spoke the words, as he contemplated a lifetime in which he spent only a few scattered nights each year lulled to sleep by the sound of crashing waves far below. He'd so quickly grown used to it, to being back in the place he'd always felt he belonged best of all, that it was like a physical pain to contemplate it being snatched away again.

But he would suffer it, for Jane.

"I have somewhere else to go," he reminded Audley. "I've Bourne

House in town—I've a whole life here, in fact. Trethwick Abbey is the only place Jane feels truly at home. She was willing to marry a man she didn't know just to stay there. How can I take it from her if that's where she wants to be? And how can I force myself upon her there if she'd rather be alone?"

Audley reined in his horse abruptly, and Penvale followed suit; it was early enough that there were no other riders in sight, and they stood there on the path, regarding each other from their respective horses.

"You love her, then," Audley said.

"I do," Penvale said evenly.

"Violet will be pleased," Audley said, satisfaction in his tone. "She was so certain . . ."

Penvale suppressed a sigh; there were few secrets among his friends, though this was his first time being the source of gossip this intriguing. He was accustomed to the others' romantic exploits, but he always conducted his own affairs with discretion and little fuss. It wasn't worth getting emotional over something that wouldn't last.

He swallowed, the thought of his marriage belonging to that category hitting him like a blow to the chest.

"Can I offer you some advice, Penvale?" Audley asked abruptly, and Penvale gave a helpless, one-shouldered shrug.

"I don't suppose I can stop you."

"Oh, to be sure you can," Audley replied, surprising him. "I know what it's like to be the recipient of a lot of unwanted advice about one's love life, if you will recall." His tone was dry as toast, and Penvale managed a half-hearted grin in reply. "But occasionally, some of that advice was rather intelligent, you know—no doubt my life would be considerably easier now if I'd listened to it a bit sooner." He inclined his head at Penvale, and Penvale realized this was an apology of sorts. He didn't feel that he was owed one—Audley and Violet's reconciliation the previous summer had been a bit trying for all involved, though they had resolved things so happily that one could hardly hold any sort of a grudge over the ordeal—but it pleased him to be offered one nonetheless.

"All right," he said neutrally. "What's your advice, then?"

"Go back to Cornwall," Audley said simply.

Penvale paused for a beat, processing this. "But—"

"I understand why you left," Audley said, holding up a hand to forestall any protest. "And I think your reasons were good. But you're turning yourself into a bloody martyr without even knowing for certain that it's what Jane wants."

"But the ghost—"

"I know." Audley shook his head. "I don't pretend to know what reason there was for that ghost at the house party, and you may be entirely correct in your assumption. But I learned the hard way the danger of assuming things about the woman you're married to, and right now you've just made a decision for both you *and* Jane without even discussing it with her. It's not what you want—and what if it isn't what she wants, either?"

"But what if it is?" Penvale asked quietly.

Audley quirked that maddening half-smile at him once more. "Then at least you'll know for certain." He lifted his reins, kicking his horse back into movement. "And isn't certainty that you're not throwing away what could be a rather wonderful marriage worth a bit of risk?"

Penvale picked up his own reins, his blood racing faster in his veins, Audley's words echoing in his mind. Audley was right. He had made a decision *for* Jane rather than allowing her to make it for herself. She'd spent her entire life having her fortune dictated by men; what he'd just done was no better than any of the previous instances, when you came right down to it.

He had to go see her. He had to go to Cornwall.

He had to be sure.

"You'd better not leave until tomorrow, though," Audley called over his shoulder as an afterthought. "Violet will murder you if you ruin her numbers for dinner tonight."

"I wouldn't dream of it," Penvale lied, having forgotten until this very moment about Violet's dinner party that evening.

Tomorrow, then.

He'd go to Jane tomorrow.

Of all the scenarios Jane might have imagined upon her arrival in London, the reality proved even worse.

"A dinner party," she muttered angrily as the carriage rattled through the streets from St. James's Square toward Curzon Street, where the Audleys lived. "Of course he'd be at a bloody *dinner party.*"

Upon being informed by Smithers of her husband's location, Jane had briefly considered waiting for his return home. But she'd arrived just at the dinner hour, meaning it would likely be a while before she might expect him, and heaven only knew if he had plans afterward. She had ridden in a carriage all the way from Cornwall; she didn't wish to wait any longer.

Which was how she found herself now, standing before the Audleys' front door, her hand raised to knock. "Steady," she murmured to herself. "New Jane. This is the New Jane."

Summoning her courage, she rapped firmly upon the door, which opened a moment later, and an extremely elderly, kind-faced butler ushered her within.

"Lady Penvale," she announced grandly. "I'm here to see my husband."

Propelled by the force of her own bravado, she swept into the house, barely slowing her gait enough to allow the butler to lead her to the dining room, open the door, and—

Oh, and it was worse than she could have imagined. *Why* had she thought this was a good idea? There was a sea of faces before her, all lit by candlelight. She scanned them, registering dimly that she knew all these people, that these were Penvale's closest friends, but in that moment, they seemed like a school of sharks and she the unlucky fish dropped into their midst.

"Jane."

Out of the blurred array of faces, one came into sharp focus. It was Penvale, of course, rising from his chair, the hasty scrape of other chairs indicating that his motion had reminded the other gentlemen present of their manners as they, too, jumped to their feet. Penvale, looking so familiar, so dear, his hair combed neatly back, his face a bit paler than it had been in Cornwall, his eyes—

Not looking *entirely* familiar.

"You got spectacles!" The words came out more accusing than Jane intended, but she felt a laugh burbling up within her as she spoke, and she clapped her hands to her mouth to contain it. He was wearing gold-rimmed spectacles, but behind them was the steady hazel gaze that had become such a comfort to her at some point. That she'd found she didn't want to live without.

"All the better for reading Miss Austen,. I've found." He smiled at her; somewhere, someone else at the table emitted a happy sigh, followed by a faint "Ouch!" as the sigher was presumably elbowed into silence by a companion.

"And for spotting the hidden doors to secret staircases, I would imagine," Jane ventured. The words were an offering, one that he rapidly picked up.

"That, too." A quirk of the mouth. "If I'd listened to you sooner, it might have cleared up a few things immediately." A deliberate pause, a widening smile. "But then I'd have denied myself so much fun in the looking."

"Was it?" Fun, she meant, but she didn't need to elaborate; she could tell from the look in his eyes, the faint crinkles around them as he smiled, that he understood.

"It was." He began to walk toward her from the opposite side of the table; he *would* be seated as far away as possible, just to ensure that no one else missed a word. Jane no longer cared overmuch, however, as she drank in the sight of him approaching. She'd like to watch him walk toward her for the rest of her life, she thought.

"In any case, I was thinking it was most fortunate that I picked up my new spectacles this afternoon, so that I'd be able to read on my carriage journey tomorrow."

"Your— Oh." She frowned. "Where are you going?"

He rounded the head of the table, only a few feet away from her now. "I *was* preparing to leave at first light, you see," he continued. "I thought a bit of sea air might serve me well." He came to a halt before her.

Jane felt her own mouth curving upward in reply. "Did you?"

"I've found cliff paths and flocks of sheep to be particularly scenic in the summertime."

She reached out for his hand. "All times of year, really, I think."

His grip tightened on hers, pulling her toward him. "You've stolen a march on me, though."

"I like to keep a step ahead of you," she said as his free arm sneaked around her waist, pulling her even closer.

"That does seem to be a particular skill of yours." He leaned closer. "Coming here—to town, when I know you hate it—"

"I find it's much lovelier in June than it is in January, you see," she said lightly.

His eyes were warm on hers. "And here, tonight—" His voice dropped now, so quiet that, even if the others could hear him, she knew these words were meant only for her. "I know you don't like things like this."

She lifted a shoulder. He wasn't wrong, not entirely; she could feel the eyes of the room on her, and the thought still made her heart pound in her chest. But she knew that these people were dear to Penvale—that they might become dear to her, too, with a little effort. "I find I'm learning to like all sorts of things I once didn't," she informed him.

His eyes were smiling at her. "Things."

She smiled back. "People."

"I'm so glad to hear it," he said. "Because I was worried it might be deucedly awkward when I showed up on your doorstep next week to tell you that I love you."

Jane's heart skipped a beat at the words. "Do you?" she managed, which she thought was rather impressive, considering that she suddenly felt the strangest urge to weep.

Penvale drew back slightly, though he kept his arm firm about her waist. "I love you so much that I was prepared never to see Trethwick Abbey again, if that was what you wanted. It occurred to me only today that I didn't have the right to decide that for you, though—that perhaps I ought to let you have a say in the matter."

"Yes, you should, you idiot," she said, a bit of the indignation that had sustained her for the—quite long, really—carriage ride from Cornwall resurfacing.

"I thought you were trying to be rid of me!" he protested.

"Well, I wasn't."

He gave her an extremely skeptical look.

"*Then,*" she amended. "I wasn't trying to be rid of you *then,* specifically. It was only before . . . before I knew you."

"You can understand my confusion," he said, his mouth twitching slightly at the corners. "It is terribly difficult to distinguish between the hauntings that were an attempt to rid yourself of my presence, and the ones that were nothing of the sort. I do not have sufficient experience in supernatural matters to understand, apparently."

"If you'd listened to me when I tried to tell you I didn't know where that scream came from—"

"Where *did* it come from, then?" he asked curiously.

"Mrs. Ash," Jane said darkly. "It seems that it was her idea of matchmaking. She thought the hunt for the ghost was bringing us closer together."

Penvale's mouth twitched. "Ah. Well, she wasn't entirely wrong, was she?"

Jane paused to consider. "I suppose not."

"And I suppose I should tell you, Jane, that I'm prepared to listen to ghost babies crying in the secret passages for the rest of my life, if it makes you happy."

"It does not," Jane assured him, even as her heart skipped several beats in her chest. "I found the baby unsettling. It turns out that it was Hastey's cat."

Penvale paused, nonplussed. "A cat," he repeated.

Jane shrugged. "So I have been informed. Apparently, the cat has achieved some fame among the household staff for this particular talent."

"That cat sounded more like a human baby than any *actual* human baby I've ever encountered," he said.

"Perhaps you've simply not heard enough human babies," she suggested. She also had limited experience with the species; if ever there had been a pair of people likely to be tricked into thinking a cat was a baby, she supposed it was them. "Or cats?"

"Perhaps we can see to amending that ignorance on my part, then," he said, lowering his head to hers. There was a whoop from somewhere in the room, but Jane and Penvale ignored it.

"Jeremy, do *shut up*," Diana said affectionately.

Jane drew back after a moment. "I love you," she said breathlessly to Penvale, who was looking adorably flushed and mussed, with his spectacles ever so slightly askew. "But do you think we might go . . . somewhere else?" she asked, jerking her head in the direction of the table full of friends eagerly watching this particularly romantic piece of dinner theater.

Penvale reached up to remove his spectacles, offering Jane his arm. "Shall we go home, then?"

TO SWOON AND TO SPAR

Jane plucked the spectacles from his hand and set them gently back on his nose. "Only if the spectacles stay on," she said, allowing him to sweep her from the room with only a quick wave of farewell to the rest of the party.

"Don't worry," he said as they descended the front steps to the carriage waiting on the street below. "I want to see you perfectly clearly for what I'm planning to do next."

And he did. And if, the next morning, he had to send for another pair of spectacles to replace a casualty of the evening's activities—well, both Penvale and Jane would agree that it was well worth the expense.

Acknowledgments

A million thanks, as ever, to the large number of people who make this dream-come-true job possible for me. This includes:

My agent, Taylor (even though she made me delete the [fake!] baby corpses), and my editor, Kaitlin (even though she confirmed that no, I could not include [fake!] baby corpses in a rom-com). They were both so enthusiastic about this mildly deranged idea for a book from the very beginning, and I'm so grateful.

The lovely and incredibly hardworking people at Atria and Simon & Schuster, including Megan Rudloff, Katelyn Phillips, Elizabeth Hitti, Samantha Hoback, and so many others—from the copyeditor to the art department to the sales team and beyond. I'm so lucky to have such stellar people working on my books.

The whole team at Root Literary (and especially Jasmine, who is privy to some very strange emails).

Booksellers, librarians, and all the readers who are part of the book community on social media who spread the word about my books with such enthusiasm, creativity, and joy.

ACKNOWLEDGMENTS

The many authors who have been so supportive of my work (and who are always available to lend an ear when needed). Manda Collins, Rosie Danan, and Kerry Winfrey were kind enough to offer their precious reading time and kind words for my last book, so an extra hug to them; one as well to Alison Cochrun, Jen DeLuca, Rachel Hawkins, and Sarah Hogle, A+ partners in (virtual book event) crime.

My family, friends, and current and former coworkers, who don't complain (to my face, at least) about having to listen to me discuss fictional characters a lot.

And, finally: Jane Austen, Susan Cooper, and the women who wrote as Carolyn Keene, whose books—which filled so many hours of my childhood and adolescence—are the reason this book exists.

About the Author

Martha Waters is the author of the Regency Vows series, which includes *To Have and to Hoax*, *To Love and to Loathe*, *To Marry and to Meddle*, and *To Swoon and to Spar*. She was born and raised in sunny South Florida and is a graduate of the University of North Carolina at Chapel Hill. She lives in coastal Maine, where she works as a children's librarian by day, and loves sundresses, gin cocktails, and traveling.

DON'T MISS THE OTHER BOOKS IN THE REGENCY VOWS SERIES BY
MARTHA WATERS

"Sure to delight Bridgerton fans."

—USA TODAY

ATRIA
BOOKS